PRAISE FOR ANDREW MAYNE

THE GIRL BENEATH THE SEA

"Distinctive characters and a genuinely thrilling finale . . . Readers will look forward to Sloan's further adventures."

—*Publishers Weekly*

"Mayne writes with a clipped narrative style that gives the story rapid-fire propulsion, and he populates the narrative with a rogue's gallery of engaging characters . . . [A] winning new series with a complicated female protagonist that combines police procedural with adventure story and mixes the styles of Lee Child and Clive Cussler."

—*Library Journal*

"Sloan McPherson is a great, gutsy, and resourceful character."

—Authorlink

"Sloan McPherson is one heck of a woman . The Girl Beneath the Sea is an action-packed mystery that takes you all over Florida in search of answers."

—Long and Short Reviews

"The female lead is a resourceful, powerful woman and we're already looking forward to hearing more about her in the future Underwater Investigation Unit novels."

—Yahoo!

THE NATURALIST

"[A] smoothly written suspense novel from Thriller Award finalist Mayne . . . The action builds to [an] . . . exciting confrontation between Cray and his foe, and scientific detail lends verisimilitude."

—*Publishers Weekly*

"With a strong sense of place and palpable suspense that builds to a violent confrontation and resolution, Mayne's (*Angel Killer*) series debut will satisfy devotees of outdoors mysteries and intriguing characters."

—*Library Journal*

"The Naturalist is a suspenseful, tense, and wholly entertaining story . . . Compliments to Andrew Mayne for the brilliant first entry in a fascinating new series."

—*New York Journal of Books*

"An engrossing mix of science, speculation, and suspense, The Naturalist will suck you in."

—Omnivoracious

"A tour de force of a thriller."

—Gumshoe Review

"Mayne is a natural storyteller, and once you start this one, you may find yourself staying up late to finish it . . . It employs everything that makes good thrillers really good . . . The creep factor is high, and the killer, once revealed, will make your skin crawl."

—Criminal Element

"If you enjoy the TV channel Investigation Discovery or shows like Forensic Files, then Andrew Mayne's The Naturalist is the perfect read for you!"

—The Suspense Is Thrilling Me

BLACK
CORAL

OTHER TITLES BY ANDREW MAYNE

THE UNDERWATER INVESTIGATION UNIT SERIES
The Girl Beneath the Sea

THE NATURALIST SERIES
The Naturalist
Looking Glass
Murder Theory
Dark Pattern

JESSICA BLACKWOOD SERIES
Angel Killer
Fire in the Sky
Name of the Devil
Black Fall

THE CHRONOLOGICAL MAN SERIES
The Monster in the Mist
The Martian Emperor

OTHER FICTION TITLES
Station Breaker
Public Enemy Zero
Hollywood Pharaohs
Knight School
The Grendel's Shadow

NONFICTION
The Cure for Writer's Block
How to Write a Novella in 24 Hours

BLACK CORAL

A THRILLER

ANDREW MAYNE

THOMAS & MERCER

Published by Thomas & Mercer, Seattle

www.apub.com

Amazon, the Amazon logo, and Thomas & Mercer are trademarks of Amazon.com, Inc., or its affiliates.

ISBN-13: 9781542009645
ISBN-10: 1542009642

Cover design by Shasti O'Leary Soudant

Printed in the United States of America

BLACK
CORAL

CHAPTER ONE
BIG BILL

Everyone is looking at me funny.

When I pulled up to the scene of the accident in my truck, all eyes and flashlights were trained on the small lake into which a car had nose-dived after flying off the highway and through a guardrail. Now the police officers, fire rescue crew, and paramedics are staring at me like I'm about to be declared prom queen and have pig blood dripping from me. From the grim look on the face of the Florida Highway Patrol officer walking my way, I'm starting to think public humiliation might be better than what he's going to tell me.

I feel the momentary panic I sometimes experience when I arrive at the scene of an accident and fear that the face under the tarp might be my daughter, Jackie; my boyfriend; or someone else I care about.

But I left Jackie and Run back on the houseboat when the call came in. Of course, I do have my other family members. My nephews are starting to drive, and they possess the McPherson wild-child genes that I'm sure will be causing my brother headaches soon.

"Detective McPherson?" asks Corporal Finick.

"Yes?" I reply as I look around the scene. There's a paramedic truck parked near the edge of the lake. Three police cruisers and a fire truck wait on the roadway near the twisted guardrail. A set of tire tracks ripped into the grass leads to a rocky embankment and the water below.

Thirty feet into the lake, I see the faint glow of a taillight from a submerged car. How the hell did it get that far out?

"Thirty minutes ago, the car went in. One victim was able to swim ashore. There's a second person trapped in the vehicle, presumably dead."

I hurry to the rear of the truck and grab my diving gear. "Presumably?" I echo as he follows me.

"The rescue crew wasn't able to get a closer look."

I spot the orange raft they use for water rescues at the edge of the water. Two men are in it using poles to probe the water. That's odd.

"Has anybody been able to go down there?" I ask.

"You're the diver on call. Where's your backup?"

"We haven't hired them yet." I pull my wet suit over my shorts and top and zip it up. "So you need me to check inside the vehicle and recover the body?"

"Yes. We also need you to get photos and bag the body as quickly as possible."

"Can't you take photos with a camera on a probe?"

"We, uh, dropped the underwater camera next to the vehicle."

"I guess I'll get that too."

I pull my tank onto my back and check my mask. Another man walks over. He's got a red beard and a Florida Fish and Wildlife jacket. I remember his name: Chris Kaur.

"You tell her the situation?" he asks.

"I was about to," replies Finick.

Fish and Wildlife got here fast. Hold on—I look over the mangroves at the far edge of the lake and the lights in the distance. That would be the power station. There's an outflow pipe that runs straight from the station to the lake, connected by a channel at a narrow junction to the north.

"Wait. Is this Pond 65?" I ask.

"Yeah, I was getting to that," says Finick.

I glance back at the men on the raft and realize what they're doing . . .

They're not probing the water for the victim. They're trying to keep the alligators from eating him.

Pond 65 is a popular spot for our local giant reptiles. They enjoy the warm water of the power station's outflow and tend to congregate here.

"It can wait until morning," says Kaur. "We can try to draw away and tranq any that don't cooperate. But I'll need some time."

"Right," replies Finick. "It's just that . . ."

I put the pieces together. "The guy who got out alive says he wasn't the driver, and you think he's lying, making this a homicide investigation."

"Getting the body before . . . before it gets tampered with would be ideal. Bruising can tell us where they were sitting . . . assuming their skin's still intact."

"And not eaten by a gator. Got it. Anything else?"

"Yeah," says Finick. "Again, no pressure. This car and the survivor are also suspected in two hit-and-runs. Both fatal."

"So he's a suspected repeat hit-and-runner and getting his passenger's body out now is what could help you nail him?" I grab my fins and walk to the edge of the water. "No pressure. Got it."

"McPherson," says Kaur, "there's more to it."

"I've swum in alligator-infested waters, boys. They don't bother me; I don't bother them." Although I'm usually not trying to yank two hundred pounds of human meat away from them.

Florida has so many alligators that if you got rid of the humans and only counted them, it'd still have a higher population than many other states. With over a million of them in our waterways, if they were the ferocious man-eaters people thought, then encounters would happen all the time. Instead, attacks are incredibly rare. Gators avoid us as much as possible.

I call out to the men in the boat, "Keep anything with a tail and teeth away from me." I point to their spotlight. "And keep the area lit."

I give my tank a last-minute check.

"Sloan!" Kaur calls out. "Hold up, you idiot."

"What? Time's ticking, Chris. You guys got pointy sticks. We're good. Right?" He shakes his head.

I glance out at the black water illuminated by spotlights and get a buzzing-bee sensation in my stomach. "Don't tell me . . . pythons? Piranha? A grouper on the sex-offender list?"

"Not quite." He glances at Finick for a moment, then back at me. "Three days ago, we tagged Big Bill five hundred feet from here."

"Oh shit." My mouth is suddenly too dry to make a seal with my regulator.

There are alligators, and there's Big Bill. He's to the species what Dwayne "The Rock" Johnson would be to humanity if we were pygmy-size and Johnson were a cannibal.

Fish and Wildlife estimates that Big Bill is one of the largest gators in the wild, weighing in at approximately one thousand pounds. He's also nearly thirteen feet long.

Big Bill runs free because it's his God-given right and he's never hurt a person that we know of. Fish and Wildlife has, on the other hand, found carcasses of other gators and even a manatee they suspect Bill took a chunk out of.

I search the water for any sign of the aquatic T. rex. "Um, any reason to think he's here?" I ask, trying not to sound nervous—and failing.

"Other than the fact that there's a human-size steak in the pond and all this activity's likely to draw his attention? No, none at all," replies Kaur.

While normal alligators keep away from commotion like flashing lights and people splashing in the water, Big Bill is so apex, he doesn't care.

One Fish and Wildlife crew spent a whole day trying to track him in a canoe, only to realize that Bill had been following them the entire time . . . watching.

"We got a bunch of raw chickens delivered from Publix," says Finick. "We can dump them in the far side of the lake, park the raft at the channel entrance, and keep Bill out."

"Unless he's already in here," says Kaur.

"We don't know that. Is your sorry ass the one going in?" asks Finick.

"McPherson's handled worse. Punched sharks and fought off assassins, right?"

Okay, Sloan. Think this through. They can get the body in the morning— after it's been gnawed on and dragged away from the vehicle.

"Your suspect . . . he's a bad guy?" I ask Finick.

"Likely. If we can't nail him on this, he goes free."

"And runs somebody else down," I reply.

"Not without a car," says Kaur, pointing to the taillights.

"You can buy 'em now, I hear," Finick snarls back. He directs his attention to me. "It's up to you. If you can't do it, I understand. We'll keep our guys out there and try to push the alligators away until Kaur and his people can clear the area."

And lose time and evidence.

What's my life worth? How much is my ego motivating me? Do I still feel the need to prove I'm not some white trash girl from a dysfunctional family?

I start to take my air tank off.

"Good call," says Kaur.

"No," I tell him. "I'm free diving. I'm taking it off for speed."

"Oh shit," he murmurs.

"Yeah, I know. I need a body pouch and a rope." I hand him an underwater radio from my bag. "Keep the antenna in the water. If we lose contact, don't panic. Just wait for me to tug three times on the rope."

"How long do we wait for you to come up?"

"Seven minutes, then pull my corpse up."

"Seven minutes?" he replies.

"Yes, seven in this situation. But I like to keep it down to two. Got it?"

He rolls his eyes. I can tell what he's thinking—that I'm an idiot. He's not wrong. But I'm an idiot who still has something to prove.

There's also the fact that if we don't convict the driver, the next time I pull up to a scene like this, it may not be my kid, but it will definitely be someone's child, and I will have failed to prevent it.

I take a few deep breaths, saturating my lungs, then step into the black water.

CHAPTER TWO
FREE DIVE

Diving headfirst into a Florida pond without knowing what's down there is like running barefoot through a junkyard; that's why I never do it. In my years of diving Florida's waterways, I've found everything from department-store mannequins to an entire Airstream trailer in what looked like an empty canal.

Getting into and out of Pond 65 before Big Bill decides to investigate means moving fast and bending some of my own rules about diving. I already broke the never-dive-alone rule, but there's not much I can do about that until my law enforcement unit brings another scuba diver onboard.

Kaur's people are tossing raw chickens into the far end of the pond. A bit of thrashing begins as the gators respond to the sound and start swimming over to picnic. I take a few more steps into the water, and my booties reach the edge of the shelf where the water gets abruptly deep. The outcropping I'm standing on is exactly the kind of formation that can make for an overhang—the kind of place under which a gator like Bill likes to shove his food for long-term storage.

I try not to think about it and take a half-hearted leap, hoping I don't impale myself on a bunch of rusty javelins a high school track team decided to dump into the water.

Hey, it could happen.

The tire tracks and rock embankment the car launched from are to my left. I decided not to head directly from there because there's something funny about the way the car landed in the middle of the lake. It's possible there's a submerged concrete block or barrels of toxic waste that the car skidded across. My gut says stay to the right, so I stay to the right.

I plunge all the way into the water with my hands outstretched. The light mounted to the side of my mask gives me a good two feet of visibility in the murk, which allows me to see almost to my wrists as I put on my fins.

At least I'll see Bill before I swim into his gullet—or what kind of rock I'm about to hit before I smash into it.

I kick hard with my fins, counting my strokes, and head where I remember the car being located. So much of diving happens from memory. You plot a course and keep kicking until you're pretty sure you've reached the spot.

"Sloan? You okay?" asks Finick over the radio.

I'd respond, but I'm holding my breath. Hopefully Kaur will explain that to him.

Given my inability to breathe underwater, now is not the time for a conversation. I get that he's nervous. I'm nervous. Everyone is nervous except for maybe Big Bill.

I kick once more and see the light from the overhead spotlights. The car is nose-first in the muck with the trunk a few feet from the surface. The taillights are still on.

I swim over the car and catch as much as I can with the video camera strapped to the top of the mask. The back window is completely blown out and the reason the car sank. No way there'll be any survivors in this wreck.

I swim to the driver's side and see the open window. The lucky bastard was able to climb out of the car, probably while it was still sinking.

I poke my head inside and check the interior. The airbags are flopping around like flat jellyfish. I push the steering wheel bag aside and feel a moment of relief when I don't see a passenger. Then I get a look from a lower angle.

A young man—late teens, early twenties—floats above the passenger airbag, his back pressed against the roof.

He's dead, and his face looks like it smashed into the windshield—which he's sticking halfway out of.

"Sloan . . . ," comes a garbled voice over the radio. No time or air to respond.

I get a look from the front. The victim's sticking out in a precarious position, his head placed perfectly for chomping.

I linger a few moments longer, getting as many views with the camera as I can, then unfurl the pouch to bag him. This all appears pretty cut-and-dried.

I keep a couple of dive weights in the pouch to make it easy to maneuver as I lay it on the hood of the car and slide the body from the car into the bag's opening.

If you ever want to call attention to yourself, go practice this at a public pool with a diving dummy like I have a hundred times. My daughter calls it "Mommy doing her underwater hit-man thing."

While trying to put the victim into the bag, I'm distracted by a distant metallic sound.

"S—" goes my radio.

Why are they still trying to have a conversation with me?

Suddenly the spotlight jerks.

Damn it. Don't they know I'm working down here?

Dumb girl. They're not trying to get a status update. They're trying to warn you.

A shadow passes overhead, and I realize they're not moving the light. Something is swimming through it.

Something . . . big.

I don't look for him. Instead I go on defense and pull the victim's body in front of me as I back into the car, using it like a hermit crab's shell.

The dark shape glides directly over the top of the car, and I feel it bump the body bag.

Damn. I don't want him getting ahold of that. Although, all things considered, I'd rather he take the dead body than my live one.

Okay. Think fast. Bill is curious. He smells blood. Bill is attracted to motion. I can move; the corpse can't.

Let's change things.

I take the rope attached to my waist and tie it to the body bag. Now let's give it three big tugs . . .

Okay. Nothing.

Let's do it again . . .

Ouch! The body is ripped from my fingers. At first I think Bill grabbed it, but then the rope is pulled taut. My colleagues are pulling it ashore—probably thinking it's me.

As the body flies out of my line of sight, I get ready to leave the car, but my gut says wait a beat.

A couple of heartbeats go by, and my lungs gently remind me that I haven't breathed in a few minutes. I fight my own impatience.

Wait, Sloan. Wait . . .

HOLY CRAP! Bill's toothy snout passes less than a foot in front of me as he chases the body bag.

His form is still passing me. It's like waiting for a train to go by—if that train could eat you.

His massive tail slashes at the water, sending a current so powerful it pushes me back.

Wait a moment.

Now!

I kick off from the seat and circle to the opposite side of the car from where Bill is heading, intending to take the shortest path back to shore.

I move my legs hard and send my body like a torpedo. No time to . . .

Bam!

I see stars.

I almost open my mouth to scream. Almost. I'm dazed.

Where the . . . ?

You're underwater, Sloan. You ran into something.

Remember how you marveled at how the car made it so far into the water? Remember how you decided it must have skidded across something that was at the end of the stone embankment?

This is that something. It's a big something.

Much bigger than a car. It's a van.

You just ran into a van . . . underwater.

From the look of it, this van has been here awhile. It can wait. *You* can't.

Swim!

I push away from the van and swim for shore as fast as possible. The radio crackles again, but I ignore it. I can hear metal banging as my colleagues hit their poles together—either trying to warn me or annoy the heck out of Bill.

I near the shoreline and poke my head out of the water. The sound of the raft's outboard motor roars behind me, and I see a cop on the shore with a shotgun aimed at me . . . correction, aimed *over* me.

It's a horrible weapon to use in this situation, but I don't point that out between gulps of air. I simply keep kicking for land.

When I get a few feet away, men rush over and grab me. They don't even bother helping me to my feet; they just take me by the arms and drag me onto the shore like a large fish . . . and keep dragging me across the slick grass.

We're ten feet in before we finally come to a stop. When I roll over, I see the deputy with his shotgun trained on the water. There's a crack that sounds like a gunshot. But it's not. It's Bill's gigantic tail slapping against the water as he comes toward shore, then veers away at the last moment.

He makes a bigger wake than the raft.

And then everything falls quiet. The lake is calm, and everyone's silent. Bill has gone down to sulk. We all catch our breath.

I take a deep breath, then notice the black shape to my left. It's the body from the wreck. I barely give it another thought as I get to my feet and take off my fins.

I'm still thinking about the sunken van.

My gut saved me several times in the last few minutes. Now it's telling me something else.

This body wasn't the only one in the lake.

CHAPTER THREE
UIU

My boss, George Solar, is sitting next to me in a Florida Department of Law Enforcement conference room in Miami across from Janet Marquez, chief of investigations for the FDLE. While Solar, in his late fifties, is as energetic as anyone I've met aside from my own father, Marquez, ten years his junior, seems tired of her job and doesn't hide her frustration well.

At the moment she's frustrated by us. Not George and me personally, but the existence of our little agency, the Underwater Investigation Unit.

The UIU was formed six months ago, when the governor of Florida needed a quick response to a massive corruption crisis and George stepped in with a solution—deputizing me and pulling himself out of retirement.

Our debut case was a doozy, tying together a massive drug-running operation, public corruption, and renegade intelligence operatives. It's sent several judges to jail, and the repercussions are still being felt around the state.

It would have been a career-making case except that it happened before my new job began and when George's was effectively over.

While the case proved the necessity of the UIU, since then people in other state agencies have begun to ask whether our unit should be a onetime thing. For George, that prospect means being put out to pasture. For me, it effectively equals unemployment. I got fired from my last police job when the powerful people we were chasing put pressure on my superiors.

Even if I were offered my old job, I don't think I could take it, given what happened. I thought members of my police department would take a bullet for me; instead they pushed me under the bus. Or at least that's how it felt.

"I'll be blunt with you," says Janet Marquez, directing her attention at George. "Some people are asking if your unit's even necessary."

"Would these be the same people who had their thumbs up their posteriors while Bonaventure and his pals were bribing judges left and right? If so, I'd love to talk to them." George turns his head dramatically toward the door. "Will they be attending this meeting?"

If Marquez favors a blunt, bureaucratic approach, George is a precision sniper. He doesn't dance around, skirt, or soft-pedal the point.

"My point is that we're considering making a recommendation to the governor that you formally fall under the FDLE." Marquez turns to me. "We could use you here. We need to expand our diving program and could use your help with training."

"McPherson isn't a police diver," says George. "She's an investigator who happens to be really good at scuba diving."

"I see," says Marquez. "And what are you currently investigating?"

"Right now, the UIU is working on a series of burglaries along the Intracoastal Waterway," says George.

"Would this be the New River Bandits? The kids stealing boat motors and fishing tackle?"

"This would be the gang breaking into yachts and stealing millions of dollars' worth of navigation equipment," replies George.

"Jurisdictionally, isn't that coast guard or local police?"

"If they want to put anybody else on the case, they're welcome to it. We also have several other active investigations. Four days ago, we provided an assist to the Highway Patrol with a murder investigation."

"You mean McPherson's body retrieval?" asks Marquez.

"It was more complicated than that," says George.

Actually, his exact words to me when he found out were *harebrained*, *imbecilic*, and *outright stupid*. We have that kind of working relationship.

"That's actually our case now," says Marquez.

George ignores her. "The fact of the matter is that the UIU has expertise that other agencies don't have and, equally important, a mandate to investigate cases other agencies like yours don't have the manpower to look into."

"Like the New River Bandits? If the governor hadn't handed that to you, it would be with us," she says.

Actually, George dropped a whole stack of cases in my lap when I signed up—unsolved ones that could potentially fall within our jurisdiction. So far, we've only looked into a few and haven't turned up any new leads. When the New River Bandits popped up, the governor asked us to take it on, derailing everything else we'd been working on.

"You haven't made it clear to me why you couldn't do that from within the FDLE," she adds.

"If we're inside the FDLE, then what we investigate is left to your discretion," he replies.

"So what you're saying is that you want the UIU to be your own one-man operation?"

While George didn't tell me to keep my mouth shut at this meeting, I've tried to do so as a general policy, but Marquez's jab at him is too much.

"I think what my boss is saying is that, just like in the past, the FDLE doesn't have the resources to pay attention to everything that needs paying attention to."

"You haven't given me any examples," she says evenly.

I flash a sidelong glare at George. What's going on here? Does Marquez have more power than I realize? Is she on some kind of commission that has authority over us? Maybe that's it.

Andrew Mayne

"What about Pond 65?" I ask.

She thinks for a moment. "I already pointed out that's our case. We retrieved the car four days ago."

"I'm talking about the van."

"Van? There was nothing about a van in the accident report."

"No. I mean the van that was already in the pond. What are the FDLE's plans for looking into that?"

She looks to George. "What do I need to know about this van?"

"Exactly," he replies. "What do you need to know about the van, other than that McPherson referred it on to you and nothing has been done about it? The van is exactly why the UIU exists. While you're too busy taking over other investigations, you're ignoring evidence being handed directly to you. Like the goddamned van." He shakes his head in frustration.

"Can you excuse me for a moment?" She rises without waiting for an answer.

As soon as the door closes, George turns to me. "What the hell is this van you're talking about?"

Nobody can bluff like George Solar. He even had *me* thinking he knew about the van while he made a show of getting irate with Marquez.

"In the lake, I ran into a submerged van while retrieving the body. I told Highway Patrol."

"And?"

"They said there are hundreds of abandoned cars in canals."

"But you already know this. What makes the van special?"

"I don't know. A feeling. I didn't want to bring it up until . . ."

"Until they had a chance to do nothing about it?" He shakes his head like I just failed a test. "Sloan. You're not just a diver anymore. You're a detective now. You need to act like one. If your nose is telling you there's something there, then you should have told me."

"I . . ." *I didn't want to be wrong.* "You're right."

16

Marquez walks back in with a folder and reclaims her seat. "I spoke to Finick at Highway Patrol. He has high praise for you, McPherson. But he said that the van was likely abandoned and not worth the effort to pull from the water. It would be too far down in the muck."

I take my own folder out from my briefcase and lay a photo from Google Earth on the table. I've drawn a grid on the lake showing where the car was pulled from and where I ran into the van.

George inspects the map and lets out a laugh. "Finick is a good cop, but I don't think he paid much attention to this one."

"What do you mean?" asks Marquez as she stares at the map.

"You don't push a van into a lake and have it get out that far. You have to drive it. Fast," says George. "If there's nobody in the van, then someone has one hell of a story to tell. My bet is that we probably have a missing-persons case that could be solved and some family's minds put to rest if we put in the effort. And since you're too busy to look into it, I think you've made the case for the UIU."

"We'll see," she says.

As we walk back to George's truck, he mutters under his breath, "There'd better be a body inside that van, or it's gonna be mine."

"I didn't mean to . . ."

He waves off my apology. "You mentioned the van. Now we're stuck with the van. Speaking of stuck, how the hell are you going to get it out of the canal?"

"So now the van's my problem?"

"Well, you and your pirate father. He certainly knows a thing or two about pulling worthless debris out of the water."

Harsh, but true.

CHAPTER FOUR

WRECK

Big Bill is watching me, and he's pissed. My herpetologist friends would insist that an American alligator doesn't make the same kind of mental connections an ape like me makes, but as he sits there on the bank, his snout muzzled and body wrapped in the rope the Fish and Wildlife trappers used to snare him, he seems to know that I'm the reason for all this.

My hat is off to George for being able to pull the resources together to carry out this salvage operation. The only downside is, since word spread that Fish and Wildlife was going to trap Big Bill ahead of the van recovery, the media has shown up in force. There are news trucks and photographers lined up along the highway, taking photos and doing live broadcasts next to the giant crane we rented. But all their attention is on the massive reptile.

Poor Bill looks like a dinosaur in a museum display. The worst part is that, for Big Bill's safety, they'll probably have to relocate him so that opportunistic poachers can't hunt him as a trophy kill.

While Bill, George, and I are stressed out, my dad's having a field day. Having engineered this salvage operation, he's bouncing around and pep-talking the crew like an overly excited director getting ready to shoot his next feature film.

I guess it is a bit of a show for him. However, if we pull the van from the pond and find it's empty like the Highway Patrol claimed it will be, it'll be a terrible show for George and me in front of the media. The UIU got its start with a flashy case, but we could go out with a fizzle just as quickly.

My daughter, Jackie, asked if she could come. I regret telling her no, but I didn't want her to deal with the pressure of watching her mom swim in alligator-infested waters and god knows what else I might find. I also try to keep her dad—my boyfriend, Run—as far away from all this as possible. Which I've failed at spectacularly so far.

"You about ready, ma'am?" asks Scott Hughes. He's a former navy diver who did a stint with the Fort Lauderdale Police Department. He's also UIU's hire number three, as of yesterday.

A shade taller than me, he's squat and muscular and still sports the clean-shaven scalp from his navy days. He's also retained his southern manners.

"It's Sloan or McPherson," I tell him. "Pick one. Call me *ma'am* again and I'll stab you. Got it?"

"Yes, m—McPherson."

I turn around so he can check my tank, after which he spins so I can inspect the valves on his. Not surprisingly, everything is in perfect order.

I couldn't ask for a more ideal dive partner, which has me worried. Hughes is precise like a robot—a robot bound to notice that I tend to wing it more than I should.

I started breathing compressed air before I could read. Coming from a family of treasure hunters and salvagers, diving is second nature. It also means that my bad habits are deeply ingrained. I'm not sure how my new partner's military precision will work alongside my leap-first/ think-never mentality.

Maybe that's what George intended by hiring him. Perhaps Hughes is really here to be my babysitter and keep me from doing stupid things like free diving among giant gators. Or maybe Hughes is the expendable one who'll take those risks . . . I need to find out if George has a secret grudge against the man.

"Check," I say to Hughes, then call over to my dad. "Go ahead, Robert!"

Dad calls to the crane operator, who lowers the cable with the weighted straps into the water over the van. After he gives Hughes and me a thumbs-up, we start wading into the water. George is already in a flat-bottom Fish and Wildlife boat, along with Chris Kaur. While Kaur wields a rifle loaded with tranquilizer darts, George has his hunting rifle across his lap.

Just because Big Bill is tied up like Houdini on the shore doesn't mean that his friends we couldn't catch aren't still lurking about. Everyone's on edge. Even Dad's expression has changed now that I'm in the water . . . despite all we've been through. Or maybe because of it.

I downplayed the retrieval operation to my mother, like I do with everything else. After their divorce, she lost her enthusiasm for all things maritime, so I try not to get her too worried about my misadventures.

"Ready?" I ask Hughes as we reach the drop-off.

"Affirmative."

"Just an FYI. We're on an outcropping. If there's a gator den in this pond, right below us is the likely location."

"Noted."

When you think of burrowing animals, alligators don't come to mind, but they're probably the largest animal—next to bears—that alters their environment to create a habitat.

Alligators will dig into the dirt below the waterline and tunnel as far back as fifteen feet, creating a chamber large enough for them to turn around inside. With a gator the size of Big Bill, that's a serious lair.

When we pass by the lakes and waterways where alligators live, we tend not to think about what's really down there. There could be an entire network of underwater caverns beneath our feet. Some days you go out with a tracker and don't spot a single alligator. It's not because they're somewhere else—it's because they're sitting on the bottom or resting in their burrow, digesting their latest meal or watching over their brood.

We dive in and start swimming toward the floats over the van. Nothing grabs us from behind . . . not that I really expected that to happen. The den is a place to retreat to, not generally a hiding spot to attack from.

Visibility is still garbage, but it's much better in daylight than when I first dived into the lake.

Hughes is to my left and keeping pace with me. Periodically he rotates and checks behind us. This is a sign of a diver who has swum in shark-infested waters. Big ones like great whites or bulls like to ambush when you're not looking. When I tell people that a shark knows if you're looking at them, they tend not to take me seriously. I've seen it firsthand. Some divers even paint eyes on the back of their masks. I'm not sure if that gives the sharks pause or makes them laugh so hard they give up.

While we don't have to worry about sharks this far inland, there are other threats, like unaccounted-for alligators, large constrictor snakes, small venomous snakes, and the occasional American crocodile. Even the much-rarer Nile crocodile. Of all reptiles, venomous snakes excluded, I'd least like to encounter the Nile crocodile. They kill more people every year than just about any other animal that's not a snake. Fortunately, we've found only a handful of them in South Florida. Most likely they were escapees from a private zoo—of which Florida has more than its share.

Hughes holds his hands out and glides to a stop. The bright-yellow material of one of the lifting straps is floating before us. Beyond it, the brown hulk of the van has become visible.

I point to my right, and Hughes follows as we swim around the van to get a look at the whole vehicle. Its surface is covered by algae, making it impossible to see through the windows. The doors all remain tightly shut, and the van's stuck in the muck past its hubcaps. We make our way to the back of the vehicle, and I start to dig in the mud above where its trailer hitch would be located.

The plan is to use the crane to lift the rear of the van high enough to get the straps around the vehicle's body, then pull the whole thing ashore, where the FDLE forensic team can open it and examine the interior.

While I pull handfuls of mud away, I wonder how the van sank so deeply with all the windows and doors shut tight.

Hughes taps me on the shoulder and takes over the digging. As he burrows, I grab the rails of the ladder on the back of the van and peek over the top.

There's my answer. The van has a small bubble dome on top that's been cranked open a few inches. That's all it would take. As the water rushed in through the pressure-relief valves designed to keep your ears from popping every time you slam your door shut, the air was pushed out through the top of the van, causing it to sink quickly instead of float.

When I look back, Hughes has the trailer hitch exposed. I hand him a yellow strap, and he attaches it to the frame. We swim back a few yards and surface.

"Tell Robert to lift it," I say to George after pulling the regulator from my mouth.

The crane's motor shifts into gear, and the cable grows taut. The operator, an old friend of my dad's named Mel Bracket, who has a mustache like a walrus, is a pro at this kind of thing and doesn't force it.

After moving it a few inches, Mel lets the cable go slack for a moment, then revs the crane again. The marker on the cable rises a few inches as the lake bottom starts to lose its grip on the van and whatever secrets lie inside.

After the cable has risen another half meter, Hughes and I dive back down. I grab one end of a strap, and he grabs the other. We slide it under the back and to the front of the van in unison instead of one of us swimming underneath. That would be stupid—the kind of thing a McPherson does when nobody's watching.

We get the strap into place, and Hughes cinches it tight while I get the next one ready. Two minutes later the van is wrapped like . . . well, like Big Bill.

Hughes and I surface and swim away from the van. Dad gives the signal, and the crane slowly begins to lift the entire vehicle. I catch a glimpse of the parting water out of the corner of my eye. It reminds me of a submarine surfacing.

Once we get to shore, Hughes and I have our fins and tanks off before anyone can reach us to lend a hand. We turn back around in time to see the van emerge from the water.

Mel lets it hover over the lake for a few minutes. Muddy water gushes out from the undercarriage as the van begins to drain. Suddenly Big Bill is no longer the most interesting photo op. Camera operators and reporters line up against the barrier to watch the old vehicle as it floats over the lake, ready to reveal its mysteries.

I tell myself that the best outcome is an empty van, because that means nobody died. But the cruel reality is that, from a professional standpoint, there'd better be a body in there to justify this massive expenditure of state resources.

We finally get the van over land, and Mel sets it down gently on a large blue tarp. Two technicians in white hazmat suits go to the back doors with crowbars and start to pry them open.

Strategically, the van was placed so that its back faced away from the news crews and cameras. Hughes and I walk around to get a better look. A crowd of law enforcement officials gathers around us at the edge of the tarp.

The doors swing open. There's not *a* body inside. There are *four*.

CHAPTER FIVE
SALVAGE

Although I'm the one who found the van, pushed for it to be investigated, and helped pull it from the water, I'm simply another bystander now as FDLE's forensic unit swarms over it, taking photos, looking for the VIN, and cleaning the muck from the license plate. While UIU is an independent agency, we don't have a forensic unit. We have to rely on Marquez's good graces to give us the help we need.

Thankfully, despite our contentious meeting, she's made a sincere effort to supply us with the needed personnel. And right now it looks like it was a good bet on her part.

The moment the techs opened the van, the four sets of skeletal remains on the floor were unmistakable for what they were. Despite having spent years underwater, clothing, hair, and even shoes remained visible on some of them.

Sealed inside the van with only the small vent open at the top, they weren't predated upon by larger animals or shifted by currents. Instead, they were left to slowly decompose over the years in their metallic tomb.

You normally make such discoveries only in sunken submarines or ships with sealed compartments. Even so, those almost always occur in salt water, in which entirely different ecosystems govern decomposition.

To be clear, these bodies have decomposed, but not in the way a body normally does when submerged in a Florida canal.

Our state's history is replete with stories of bodies being found underwater in odd circumstances. For more than a century, human remains have been found in Lake Okeechobee, sometimes several dozen at a time. The bodies appear to have been buried when parts of the lake were above water, suggesting that they came from a much older civilization. Which, considering that there are Florida artifacts dating back over ten thousand years, means they could have died at any point over a ridiculously long period of time.

Unfortunately, the heyday for finding skeletal remains in Lake Okeechobee came long before modern forensic methods of dating existed, let alone DNA technology. Sooner or later a body will turn up and someone like my PhD adviser, Nadine Baltimore, will give us a fuller picture.

"What's going on?" asks George as he appears next to me.

I point to the techs in their white suits. "They're not saying anything."

A kneeling technician is using a brush and water bottle to clean the mud off the rear license plate. We all lean in as the letters and numbers are revealed.

George already has his phone to his ear. "Sierra Quebec Tango four one three," he recites into the phone.

Leave it to George to already have someone from the DMV on the phone. Or is it? I look over at the pool of reporters for his girlfriend, Cynthia Trenton. She's not with them. Instead, I find her on the side of the crane that's away from the crowd, typing on her laptop with her earbuds in. She glances over in our direction and gives George a thumbs-up.

"Leaking to the press already?" I ask George.

"Asking Florida's best crime reporter for background," he corrects me. "FDLE will use the new database system, and it'll take them an hour to realize they need to use the older system. Meanwhile, I can already tell you the names of the victims." He pauses for a moment, then speaks into the phone. "You know, honey, you can't run their names until we talk to the families . . ."

I can hear her blistering response and see the look on her face from a distance as she explains to George that she doesn't need a lecture in journalistic integrity from him. Watching an award-winning journalist chastise George is one of the perks of the job.

George puts down the phone and mutters, "That woman."

Scott Hughes tries to pretend he didn't overhear the whole exchange. The poor guy has no idea what he's gotten himself into with the two of us. God knows what George told him to lure him from Fort Lauderdale PD to our unit.

"Well," I ask George, "what did she say about the van?"

George points to the bodies being photographed by the techs and says in a low voice, "Four teenagers went missing in February 1989, in a van with these plates, after going to a rock concert. It was in the news for a few weeks, but eventually investigators decided the kids ran away. They'd had a couple of drug-possession charges and came from dysfunctional homes. Except for one. Straight-A student, but rumors of depression."

"Just like that?" I ask. "Case closed?"

"They'd executed Ted Bundy a month prior, and I guess people were sick of those kinds of stories. It was easier for the parents to believe the kids would come home than that something bad happened. Although something like this wasn't ruled out. Hold on." George checks his phone. "She sent some more stuff. Police searched the canals between the concert and their homes and found nothing. Hmm. I think I remember that."

Pond 65 is between here and nowhere. "What venue?"

"Black Coral Amphitheater. They shut it down years ago. It's probably a Walmart now." He takes another look at the bodies in the van as a tech starts to cover the back opening with clear plastic. "Anyway, assuming that's them. Oh, look who decided to show up." George nods to the road, where Janet Marquez is climbing out of an SUV.

"How much you wanna bet she was waiting at the nearest Starbucks to find out if there was a body?"

"You're learning. Oh crap! Follow me. She knows too." George grabs me by the arm and starts pulling.

I'm about to ask why, then realize that Marquez is making a beeline straight for the reporters. *Damn it.* She's about to put the FDLE stamp all over this.

I'm still in my dive suit and booties, which aren't meant for jogging, but I do my best to keep up with George. Scott Hughes is somewhere behind us, probably trying to figure out what kind of mental cases he's working for.

Heading off Marquez isn't about claiming credit. Well, it's not *only* about that. Now that bodies have been found, FDLE will want to take the credit and the investigation away from us, which would be okay in theory . . . but in reality, it'll pretty much mean closing the case and moving on. Which is probably what we'd do anyway, but UIU needs the credit for this one.

When George has to go before the state senate and explain who the hell we are, we need some wins on our record—especially because we put some of their major donors behind bars.

Marquez is nearing the press. We're not going to be able to intercept her in time without it being awkward. I briefly consider yelling to Mel to use the crane to knock the woman into the lake—better yet, drop her next to Big Bill, who only has the attention of two Fish and Wildlife trackers.

Just as Marquez is rounding the base of the crane and stepping onto the grass in front of the press, a miracle happens: Cynthia Trenton materializes out of nowhere and stands in front of her with a recorder.

Marquez stops cold. Trenton's a recognized journalistic figure, after all. Before Marquez can tell her that she'll be making her statement to the whole crowd, Cynthia is throwing a barrage of questions her way. I can't hear them from here, but from the look on Marquez's face, I can assume that Cynthia asked her point-blank about the missing kids—something Marquez probably doesn't even know about yet.

George pulls a pair of reading glasses from his pocket and hands them to me. "Put these on."

"What?" I ask.

"Just shut up and put them on."

I oblige, and he takes a brief second to assess the look. Through blurry lenses, I see him nod his head. "Good enough. Your hair is wet, and you still got a red mark where the mask was . . . but I think it'll work."

"For what?"

"If I'm going to put you on TV, I still need to use you for under-cover work."

"Wait, what?"

George is ten yards away from the press and already has his hands up in the air, calling attention to himself while Cynthia runs interference with Marquez. His gravelly voice booms, "Ladies and gentlemen, the Florida Underwater Investigation Unit will have a fuller statement later today, so I can only give you a brief comment about Inspector McPherson's case. First off, the UIU would like to thank the Florida Department of Law Enforcement for their forensic assistance. The facts are that we have recovered bodies in the van. We believe we know their identities but are awaiting more forensic testing. If that's confirmed, we won't be releasing that information until we've had a chance to talk to the families. I hope you understand. We can't risk any leaks, given the sensitivity of the matter. I think you can all relate. The last thing any-one wants to hear is some bureaucrat on TV telling them their family member is deceased."

Marquez's eyes widen as she realizes what George just did. If she'd planned on announcing that she and the FDLE found the 1989 runaways, he just killed that. George also managed to get the UIU's name in there twice, along with my own, which clearly has her seething.

George pushes me toward the lights and microphones. "Inspector McPherson will answer any questions she can."

I turn back to him and whisper, "What can I tell them?"

"Use your judgment," he says under his breath.

I'd ask for clarity on that, but he's already walking toward the furious Marquez. Words are about to be exchanged, and I'm not sure I want to be around for those.

Okay, Sloan, now what?

Um . . . what does Dad do in these situations? I could ask him, since he's leaning on the crane tread, watching me.

"First off, I'd like to thank the FDLE and Fish and Wildlife for their help, along with the Highway Patrol. I'd especially like to apologize to Big Bill for the disruption." I point to the alligator on the other side of the lake.

Oops, was that too flippant?

"As Director Solar said, the Underwater Investigative Unit doesn't have a full statement yet." *Wait, are we the Underwater Investigative Unit or Investigation Unit?* "What I *can* tell you is that we became aware of the van when responding to a Highway Patrol request for assistance when a separate motor vehicle crashed into Pond 65."

The rest of my moment in the limelight becomes a blur as I do my best to not mention what I'm not supposed to mention. I get a few shouted questions and stumble through answers. Thankfully, George returns to my side.

"If you have any questions, please contact us through our website," George concludes. "In the meantime, we'd again like to thank the FDLE for their forensic assistance to the UIU. Here to talk about that part of the investigation is Janet Marquez."

"We have a website?" I ask in a whisper.

"I hope so. We'd better get Hughes on that."

"Can he . . . code?" He strikes me more as the physical type.

"Yes, ma'am," says a voice behind me. "I mean, McPherson. I have a CS degree."

Hughes managed to rejoin us in a rather stealthy manner. I need to find out what exactly he did in the navy. I'd know if he was a SEAL, because he would have told me in the first two minutes. But the navy has other underwater covert-ops groups besides the SEALs.

Marquez makes a vague statement, the air already sucked out of her balloon by George. It was a ballsy move on his part, but I suspect a necessary one. He's not the limelight kind of guy, so there must be more scrutiny aimed at the UIU than I realized. By bringing down the judges, wealthy citizens, and politicians that we did, our fledgling organization already has its share of enemies who would love to see us fail.

I'm not sure if those poor kids in the van are enough to keep that from happening.

But there's no way to know until we learn exactly how they ended up in the middle of Pond 65.

CHAPTER SIX
UNDERCOVER

George Solar pretends to take a drink from his beer while I do my best to pretend I'm not watching the crowd of Nulty's Oasis and hoping that nobody I know recognizes me. While we're not exactly undercover, we're definitely operating below the radar as we try to get information on the New River Bandits. The Oasis is a hotel bar near the Fort Lauderdale marina frequented by crews from the megayachts docked nearby.

At any given time, you'll hear Australian accents, Italian, Polish, and a dozen other languages as suntanned men and women in polos and shorts chat each other up. The crowd leans heavily male, and the women tend to be above average in attractiveness, but all have the steely nerve of Vegas cocktail waitresses accustomed to handling a stray hand on the ass.

The dark secret about yachting culture is the number of people employed on yachts for the purposes of sex work. Yachts mean money. Money means horny men.

The crews here mostly work on sport-fishing boats, which tend to be more about the fishing . . . mostly. But it's not uncommon for those vessels to have "massage therapists" and no massage tables.

We're not here to look into that, and I pray to god the UIU never gets into that area of policing.

And technically, since our jurisdiction is supposed to be what happens underwater, it seems unlikely. But who knows? We're investigating this particular theft ring even though it's outside our jurisdiction because one of the governor's friends and donors is upset by the lack of response to his boat getting robbed.

George argued with the governor's chief of staff over the case, if only to make a show that we shouldn't be disposed for political purposes, but he only put up a token fight because he knows how badly we need political allies. Having a Florida billionaire who donates across the aisle in your debt couldn't hurt. It's kind of sleazy but something we have to do.

Right now, that means watching the crowd at the Oasis for anyone mingling with the crews who looks like they might be working them for information. The current theory is that the Bandits are scouting out what kind of gear's on the yachts and what kind of security they have at night.

When they robbed the *Bountiful*—the governor's pal's yacht—they managed to slip aboard and steal an entire satellite navigation console and radar mast while the crew slept belowdecks, somehow evading the ship's alarm system.

While the first suspects were the crew themselves, their stories checked out. A late-night fisherman spotted a small black boat leaving the harbor around the time the thieves would have been fleeing and said he saw three men aboard.

A month ago, the Bandits were caught in the act of robbing a yacht. Florida Marine Patrol dispatched a boat to the scene and gave chase but lost them when the weather turned rough. So here we are, an underwater policing unit on dry land, picking up a case nobody else wanted because the crime scenes are spread across the state and no one can figure out if they should be looking on land or at sea.

"What do you think?" asks George after he gives the bar a bored look.

"This is bullshit. I'd rather be talking to the crew of the burglarized yachts," I reply. "I'd say we should talk to whoever's fencing the gear, but I bet it's going overseas." I leave out my other concern: that the fence could be someone my dad or uncle knows.

"Yeah. It is bullshit. You don't need to talk to these sea monkeys to know what's onboard these boats. That idiot Cal Romero had twelve pages of glossy photos of his boat published the month before it got robbed. Same for that Saudi asshole." George has little regard for ostentatious displays of wealth. "Anyone can pick up those magazines and see what's onboard. You can even figure out where the safes are from the photos."

"Maybe we should be talking to the photographer . . . ," I murmur.

George puts down his untouched beer. "You're an idiot, McPherson."

"I know. It was just a joke."

"No. I mean the other kind of idiot. The kind that's actually smart but thinks she's dumb. Why didn't you mention the photographer angle before?"

"Probably because I just thought of it?"

He shakes his head. "I don't think anybody thought about going back that far. The photographer or whoever was doing the article would know a lot more than what's in the articles. They'd probably be able to capture security codes and all that. Hell, they could make sure things *don't* work. Next time I ask you for your theories, speak up."

"Sorry. I'm still getting used to the investigator thing. I kind of thought you'd handle the brain stuff and I'd be the one who jumps into the water."

"That'll be Hughes's job, if I have my way," says George. "I need your mental powers now."

"God help us." I look out the open window of the bar at the shimmering black water of the Intracoastal.

"What is it?" he asks.

"The van."

"I'm impressed. I didn't think you could go an hour without talking about it." He checks his watch. "Whoops. Never mind. Almost. What about it? Forensics will have their formal report tomorrow. But we know the teeth are a match for the missing kids. The press already figured that out. I was going to wait until it's official to say it, but job well done, McPherson. Their families will finally have peace of mind."

"Will they?" I ask. "If, god forbid, Jackie went missing, the best thing I could hope for thirty years later would be that she was out there alive and well, just clinging to a grudge against me. But to be told she's dead?"

"They know their kids are dead, Sloan. They've known for a long time. They didn't have any hope. This just gives them closure. Something to bury."

"Does it give them closure?" I reply. "We don't know how the van got out there."

"Four dysfunctional kids with substance issues end up inside a canal after leaving a rock concert. It's not hard to figure out."

"I guess. I'm not the expert on that. Still, why so far away?"

"They got lost, maybe on purpose to get high. I don't know. Call me harsh, but I don't care all that much. You want to worry about unsolved cases, dig into the files. I've got missing children's cases with patterns nobody else picked up on. As far as our jurisdiction goes, we know somebody's been dumping bodies in the Everglades, and nobody has a clue as to why. There're a lot more immediate things that need our attention."

"But shouldn't we be addressing what's in front of us?"

"Should I bust the bartender for dealing coke? I've watched him make three transactions in the last hour. The guy in the maroon hoodie at the table at the far end? He looks like he's buying for the owners of a boat. The two women on the other side of the bar trying to take the perfect selfie? They walked up to two different crew members, probably trying to see if the owners were looking for yacht girls. So, no, McPherson. We don't always address what's right in front of us. We worry about the living and don't get into other people's business unless our superiors tell us to. Unless . . ." He trails off.

"Unless what?" I ask.

"Unless your nose is telling you there's something more to the van. Is it?"

"My nose doesn't even tell me if I have a nose."

"Sooner or later you're going to have to find out if you got instincts for this." He gets up from the table. "Let's go talk to the bartender."

"You think he knows something about the Bandits?"

"No. But I'm sure he knows something about something. I'm bored. Let's see what he has to say."

While George Solar isn't exactly the old-school movie cop who'd drive his vehicle up on the sidewalk to hassle a pimp for information, he has no qualms about starting shit just to see what people say.

There's a lot to learn from him, good and bad. The hard part is telling them apart. I'm not sure if his outward indifference is a strength or a weakness, but I do know that my nose is telling me something about the van.

CHAPTER SEVEN
FINAL REPORT

While George and I were chasing down false leads in the New River Bandits case, Marquez and the FDLE were working overtime, more than making up for us hijacking their press conference. They've assembled an impressive presentation in the forensic warehouse lab in Miami. The van is center stage, up on blocks, while tables and signs surround it with the evidence gathered from its interior, along with maps, photos of the victims, and a timeline printed on poster boards.

The moment George, Hughes, and I walked into the lab, we knew the investigation was effectively over. While FDLE was limited to forensic assistance, they've pretty much closed the case, as far as the public is concerned.

While we wait for the head of the lab, Dr. Felix Aguilló, to present his results, I lean over to George and whisper, "What the hell? Why all this?"

George shakes his head. "I don't think they've ever gone to this much effort for a vehicle recovered with bodies."

It could simply be a big PR push for the FDLE. For all we know, they're about to ask for a budget boost and want to make sure there's good coverage in the press. As it stands, most Floridians don't even realize the agency exists.

Aguilló, a tall, thin man with gray hair and a deep tan, walks over to us in his lab coat. "There she is!" He holds out his hand to me. "Great work." He looks to George. "Is it 'Detective'? I'm not sure what your employees are called."

"'Detective' is fine," says George.

"Or Sloan," I reply, trying to be as cordial as possible.

Aguilló nods to Hughes. "Thank you as well. I have to tell you that this has been an amazing opportunity. We don't get a time capsule like this very often."

"Especially one with bodies," I reply, a little miffed at his glee regarding four tragic deaths.

He switches to a somber voice. "Yes, yes. Of course, very tragic." He says it with the believability of someone on a heart transplant list who just found out a motorcyclist with their blood type had a fatal accident. He checks his watch. "Let me go over what we found before the press conference begins."

Press conference? I'm about to blurt the words, but I see George displaying restraint. I try to follow his lead. But what the hell? This was *my case.* How is the FDLE having a press conference without my input?

Mind your temper, Sloan, and don't get territorial.

I remind myself that it's about the kids—whose faces are in front of me now as Aguilló leads us to four poster boards displaying their blown-up yearbook photos.

"Tim Kelly, seventeen; Grace Sandalin, seventeen; Caitlin Barrow, eighteen; and Dylan Udal, nineteen, were all students or former students at North Plantation High School. On February 18, 1989, they went to a concert in Udal's van. Caitlin Barrow was the last to be picked up. She'd told her father that she was going to go see a movie, while the others had told their parents they were going to a rock concert sponsored by a local radio station. The last confirmed sighting of the four teens was by Barrow's father."

"What about the concert?" I ask.

"We have no reason to doubt that they went there," Aguilló replies. "Nor evidence that they did."

George gives me a small look, not exactly telling me to shut up, but warning me not to push Aguilló too far.

Aguilló points to a map that shows all the homes for the kids and the likely route that Udal took to pick them up and then drive to the concert north of where they lived. "Either after picking them up or after the concert, they headed farther north and ended up in Pond 65 off Northlake Boulevard, where you found the van. We believe that Udal was under the influence and probably became disoriented, traveling north and ultimately losing control of the vehicle. The search area's widest zone ended ten miles to the south because investigators had no reason to suspect they went any farther."

Aguilló takes us over to a poster showing several X-rays. "Udal's neck fracture implies he was behind the wheel. The other three show consistent injuries to suggest that they were in the back of the vehicle, possibly sleeping or under the influence of alcohol or narcotics, when the van plunged into the canal. We can reasonably assume it was a peaceful death."

"Peaceful?" asks Hughes.

Aguilló directs his attention to Hughes. "There was no sign of any kind of struggling. The ceiling liners, seats, and placements of the victims suggest that they didn't try to escape the van, and Udal would have gone instantly. Like I said, peaceful. Or as close to it as possible under these circumstances."

He says this with a doctor's calm demeanor, but I'm pretty sure no physician has ever walked into a waiting room and told the family that their loved one died screaming in agony, begging for life.

Aguilló is smart; that's clear to me. But whenever I deal with forensic experts who have their salaries paid by the same people making the arrests, I have to wonder if what they're telling me is what they really think or what I need to hear to find the most expedient path to a conviction. In my schoolwork, I've studied a lot of fractures and broken bones and seen the signs of violent injury, but never anything like a car crash. There weren't a lot of minivans and SUVs roaming around when my archaeological subjects died. I have to take him at face value that what he's telling me is what's really there.

I walk over to a map of the lake. There's an outline of the van where it was found. I point to the actual van. "How did this get all the way out there?"

"We estimate Udal was going at least seventy miles an hour when he went off the road. The embankment probably had a sharper incline back then, acting as a ramp." He points to the rocky outcropping.

"Like Evel Knievel," I reply.

"Yes, I guess so."

Hughes stares at the map and says what I'm thinking. "It's almost like he aimed for it."

"We have no reason to believe that," says Aguilló.

George speaks up. "Translation: Who wants to tell the families that the kid may have intentionally gone in?"

"Like I said," says Aguilló, "we have no reason to believe that it was intentional."

"Unless you have evidence to the contrary," says the voice of Marquez from the entrance to the lab. She walks over and stands between us and the van, using it as a backdrop. "What do you think?" she asks George.

"Best fifth-grade science-fair exhibit I've ever seen," he replies.

She blinks, not sure how to take the comment, then brushes it off. "Well, we're only here to provide the forensic side of things. But I think science tells the whole story. Don't you?"

Andrew Mayne

"We'll see," I reply for George, lacking a better comeback.

Hughes has wandered over to a table and is examining items in plastic bags. "Is this from inside the van?"

"Yes," says Aguilló. He picks up a bag with a dented beer can. "Beer bong, cassette tapes, clothing—the things you'd expect to find in a van driven by a teenager."

I pick up a bag holding a plastic casing. It looks a lot like an old Polaroid camera film cartridge. "Any photos?"

"No," replies Aguilló. "No camera. Just one more bit of debris that was inside. We found a disc camera in Caitlin Barrow's purse, but there was no film in it. A shame she didn't have it loaded. I would be curious to see more information about their last night."

"So now what?" George asks Marquez.

"Well . . . I was thinking we do a press briefing about what we found. And unless there's anything you think we're overlooking, we close the case."

"Aren't you missing something?" says George. "Shouldn't we speak to the families before we talk to the press?"

"Actually, I just did that. I got off the phone with the parents right before I came here."

"You did what?" George glances at Hughes, then starts to walk between Marquez and the van. He's not normally a pacer when he's angry.

I think he's about to yell at her for doing it over the phone. Instead, he thrusts a finger in my direction. "Didn't you think maybe you should have included McPherson on that? She is after all the one who found the bodies."

"Technically, our people found the bodies," she replies.

"Are you goddamn kidding me?" George snaps. "We find the van, pull it from the lake, and just because your lab monkeys pry open the doors, you decide *you* found the bodies?"

40

I'd tell George to let it go, but I'm too pissed to say anything. Marquez just steamrolled right over us. The FDLE's going to get the credit for this one. The worst thing is, it's not that big of a deal in the grand scheme of things. It'll do little for them. What it's really about is denying the UIU credit when we need it most. She stepped on us because she could.

"You're more than welcome to make a statement at our three o'clock press conference," says Marquez.

"No, thanks," says George. "We have more important things to get to."

I realize then that Hughes was taking photos of all the exhibits with his iPhone while George went on his tirade. He and George are up to something. How the heck didn't I realize it? Maybe that was the point.

"Come on, McPherson," says George. He doesn't bother acknowledging Hughes, because he doesn't want Aguilló and Marquez to realize what he was doing.

The moment we get to the parking lot, I ask George point-blank, "What the hell are we up to?"

He opens the door to his SUV. "Climb in. Hughes, can you email everyone on the contact list Cynthia gave us and tell them the press conference has been moved up and relocated?"

"Sure, where and what time?"

"Five minutes from now. Um . . . North Plantation High School. Then call the principal and tell him to have the auditorium ready. Also, we need a video projector set up for the photos we took."

"Wait," I say. "Just like that, you're going to call a press conference at some school that doesn't even know we're coming?"

"Principal Trammel will love the attention. He wants to run for superintendent. We'll let him say a few words about finally putting the students to rest, and he'll get his TV time."

"You're a mercenary."

"No. That back there? *That* was mercenary. Someone's telling Marquez to squash us like a bug. She couldn't care less about us on a personal level. They didn't go through all that effort just to swing a bigger . . . um . . . thing. She's getting pressured to make sure the UIU has a very short life. So we have to fight just as dirty. Dirtier. Anyway, help Hughes figure out what he's going to say."

"Me?" says Hughes.

"You're our chief spokesperson. It can't just be McPherson and me on camera all the time. Especially if we're doing surveillance work."

"Yeah, but it's McPherson's case," he replies.

"It was the UIU's," I point out. "We're a team." Well, in this case we're a team, because I'd much rather Hughes be on camera than me.

"This job is weird," says Hughes as he starts typing a note on his phone.

My gut tells me it's going to get weirder.

CHAPTER EIGHT
Relationship Status

Run, the father of my daughter and, I guess, my boyfriend, knows how to throw a party. He has since high school, when we first met at the private academy I briefly attended before my family fell back on our natural state of hard times. There are more than a hundred people out on the deck at his house overlooking the Intracoastal.

Officially it's a housewarming party, but Run is treating it like a celebration for me as he parades me around by the hand and proudly tells people about how I found the van with the missing kids. The press conference was two days ago, and the newspaper ran it as the headline story. It's hard to miss tonight, as Run has spread a dozen copies around the tables and bars on the deck.

"Hey, Mrs. Steinberg," he says to one of his mother's friends as she and her husband watch the dancing and partying from the railing. "How you doing? You remember Sloan?"

"Of course," she replies. Eyeing me up and down.

I'm sure she does. As one of Run's mother's friends, she's no doubt heard an earful about me. Run's mother isn't exactly the head of my fan club. Partly for good reason, partly because she's a snob. Her one saving grace is that she absolutely adores our daughter, Jackie.

Right now, Jackie is splashing around in the pool with her cousins and their friends. She's getting taller. She still looks like a skinny boy, but I can tell that's about to change. *Lord help me.* She's got Run's good looks and charisma in a girl's body.

I pray she doesn't turn out like me or him. Not to say either one of us ended up in a bad place, but we sure as hell scared our parents. Run's parents, especially.

My own parents only gave me passing disapproval when I told them I was pregnant and Run and I had no plans to wed. We're a big family, and I could see the look in my dad's eyes as he realized he'd have yet another McPherson to induct into our little cult. For her part, Mom had been hoping for a granddaughter to fill the role I never quite did, as I was more into spear-fishing than Saturdays at the Galleria Mall.

"Congratulations," says Mr. Steinberg. "Your father must be proud."

"You can ask him," I reply, nodding to my father, who's sitting in a chair on the deck drinking a beer and talking to a couple of other people.

Huh, Mom's sitting next to him. I guess they're on speaking terms this week. "There she is!" says a woman behind me in a cheery voice.

I spin around and get blindsided as Run's mom plants a kiss on my cheek. "I read the story in the *Tribune*. Those poor children. My god, what their parents must have felt!" She takes my hand and presents me to the Steinbergs. "Have you met Sloan?" she asks. "You might remember how she went after those drug runners before. Well, she's done it again!"

I glance over at Run, who has a sly smile on his face. Now I understand. This whole operation was his way to win his mother over. I've gone from one PR maneuver to another.

She doesn't let go of my hand and drags me around the party, introducing me to people I've met half a dozen times before. We all go along with it. It's her moment. She dealt out plenty of snide comments when her son knocked me up, but now she gets to parade me around as her proud . . . um . . . mother of her granddaughter, as she says to someone, making me sound like a surrogate. It's fine. I'll take it. She loves Jackie, and that's all that matters.

After she's made the rounds with me, I find myself over by the railing where Hughes is watching the party with his too-cute-to-be-real blonde wife, who's holding a baby that looks like a miniature version of him.

"McPherson," he says. "This is Cathy. Cathy, Sloan McPherson. Thank you for inviting us."

Cathy swings the baby to her other arm and shakes my hand. "Beautiful place you have here," she says, admiring Run's mansion.

"Me? Oh no. See that marina down there?" I point down the waterway. "My place is a little boat out there. This is my boyfriend's house."

"Oh," says Cathy, trying to sort out our relationship. I hope she tells me when she figures it out.

Run has kind of invited me to move in, but I've held off. I'm still trying to figure out what our future is supposed to be. Part of it is ego. Part of it's fear.

We share custody of Jackie, which pretty much means letting her set her schedule with us. I'm worried that if I move in with Run and Jackie gets to live here full-time, and if things don't work out between Run and me, Jackie won't want to go back to living with me.

It's selfish, I know. But Run and I are complicated people. He's settled down since his wilder days, although I was probably the wildest part of them. Still, I don't know how we'll function together as grownups. That's why I'm taking things slowly—glacially slowly. I'll sleep over occasionally, and we've taken trips as a family, but we're still living separate lives.

"Calvin told me all about the case," says Cathy.

I'm about to ask who the hell Calvin is, then remember that's Scott Hughes's actual first name. "Well, we couldn't have gotten the van without him. We're lucky to have him on the team."

"I have to say I was worried when he took the job. We just had Callie, and I wasn't sure if it was a good idea. But now that I see what you're doing, I think it's the best choice ever."

First, *Callie? Drop it, Sloan.* Second, we now have an infant and a new mom dependent upon the success of our flea circus of an operation. My worst-case scenario is sleeping on my mom's couch while Run watches Jackie. Theirs is . . . I don't know.

I wonder what George said to get Hughes on board. Does *Calvin* have any idea how tenuous our job is?

The pitter-patter of wet feet comes from behind me, and suddenly I'm wrapped in thin, drenched arms. I look down at my soaked dress and see Jackie's grinning face.

"Hey, Mama. Oh my god! Your baby is so cute!" she squeals.

Oh my god, please believe babies are hideous troll monsters for at least two more decades.

It's too late. Jackie is already shaking little Callie's hand, and the baby is smiling in delight. It's adorable, but I'm getting flashbacks of my swollen belly.

"Is there a restroom we can use?" asks Cathy.

"Sure. You can use mine. I'll take you there," Jackie replies before leading the mother and child away to visit the largest bathroom any twelve-year-old has ever owned.

"It's like looking at a miniature version of you," says Hughes.

Please don't say that. "I hope not," I reply. "Although your daughter certainly looks like you."

"They say she'll grow out of it. I hope she turns out like her mother."

I hear the sound of Run's infectious laughter echo across the party. "Well, I hope Jackie turns out like . . . actually, she's pretty awesome, so, exactly who she is." I decide to change the topic. "So, what do you think of the UIU so far? Overwhelmed by all the new faces?" I joke.

"It's what I hoped for," he replies.

"Really?"

"Yeah. When I decided to get into law enforcement, I wanted to make a difference, but that's hard to do when you feel like you're standing still."

"I see. Can I ask you a question? You seem normal . . . I mean, highly qualified. Unless there's some baggage I don't know about, you could have worked for anybody. We're not even a sure thing yet. Why did you say yes?"

"I didn't sign up for the UIU. I signed up to work with you and George Solar. I followed the Bonaventure case. I was on a task force at the time. I read about what you went through. I knew what George had gone through. I told myself, those are the kind of people I want to work with. The kind of people I served with back in the navy, when I felt like I mattered. That's why."

Oh jeez. No pressure, now. "We're just trying to do the right thing."

"Finding those kids was a great start," he says.

"Yeah, well, we're thirty years too late to really make a difference."

"Are we?" asks Hughes.

"What do you mean?"

He reaches into his pocket and pulls out a small plastic bag and hands it to me. Inside is a silicone rubber ring shaped like a broken number eight.

"What's this?" I ask.

"A friend gave it to me. Someone at FDLE. Let's leave it at that. It was missing from the evidence pile."

"Because they took it?" I reply.

"No, because they excluded it. Do you know what it is?"

I recognized it immediately. "It's a snorkel ring to keep it attached to your mask."

"My friend thought you or I left it in the van," he says.

"But we were never inside the van."

"You sure?" he asks.

"Sure I'm sure. You saw the van when we raised it. It was intact," I reply. "Sealed."

"Maybe it came in through the vent in the top?" he suggests.

I examine the ring. "Possibly. It's the only explanation that makes sense."

"The only one?" Hughes asks.

He's a lot smarter than he looks, but I don't think what he's implying could be true. "I mean . . . someone could have been in there before us. Maybe opened the door or went through the hatch and replaced it. But why? Maybe Udal scuba dived? I mean, that's the obvious answer, right?"

"Yes. That's the obvious answer," he replies.

But not necessarily the *correct* answer. I groan inwardly. "You show this to Solar?"

"Nope. I wanted to check with you first."

"Okay. Let me think about this. I went out on a limb with the van, and I don't know if we need to do that again just yet. Marquez is clearly looking for opportunities to put us in our place."

Hughes nods knowingly. "Mum's the word."

CHAPTER NINE
GOLDEN MERMAID

The Golden Mermaid is a two-hundred-foot-long megayacht owned by a Hollywood producer who has an average-guy demeanor in interviews but lives like a Saudi prince in private. Last night, the captain of *The Golden Mermaid* reported a suspicious boat without lights watching the big vessel in a marina in Palm Beach.

This wouldn't necessarily get our attention if it wasn't for the fact that three nights earlier masked gunmen robbed a boat docked off the coast of Miami. That has every state and federal agency with armed agents and boats out patrolling the water.

George and I are no exception—we're watching the *Mermaid* with night-vision goggles from a twenty-foot Boston Whaler across the channel.

"Did you see this guy's last movie?" asks George.

"Yeah . . . *I* feel like robbing the yacht," I reply.

"Smart-ass. What about the profile? Does this fit the Bandits?"

"Maybe. Hesher—the photographer—he hasn't done a photo spread on this one yet, has he?"

Greg Hesher was the one common link between the other boat robberies. Our current theory is that he or someone he knew was connected to them and provided them inside information.

Presently we have him under surveillance, with an assist from the Broward sheriff's department, since UIU lacks the manpower to do that kind of work and get anything else done.

We toyed with questioning him but feared it might make him clam up. That would not only get us nothing on the New River Bandits but also possibly turn the trail cold. Truth be told, though, given the armed robbery, it could still be the more prudent decision. We don't want to wait until someone gets killed to pounce on our best lead.

"I don't want to sound judgmental, McPherson, but it feels like your head isn't exactly in the game. Something else on your mind besides the violent gang of pirates that may be about to attack *The Golden Mermaid*?"

"They're not attacking tonight," I reply. "If they're smart and have eyes, they know everyone and their aunt is out tonight looking for them. Especially since the robbery's hit the news."

"Whoever said thieves were smart?" replies George. "But, yeah, I get your drift."

"I also think we're overlooking something. There have been a dozen linked robberies, yet the case files from the other agencies haven't turned up anything. Isn't that kind of weird?"

"Weird how?"

"Like there's an angle we're not seeing. We have one boat chase and that's it."

"They searched a hundred boats going from the crime scenes and found nothing," he says.

"Isn't that telling us something?"

"Like they're not using a boat?"

"Maybe. I don't know. Anyway, I was thinking about the van . . ."

George sighs. "Because a van that went into the water three decades ago is more urgent than this?"

I shrug. "Your boy Calvin showed me something interesting."

"Cal . . . oh, Hughes. What was it? Your turn, by the way." He hands me the night-vision goggles and tripod.

"A diving mask ring. The thing that fastens your snorkel to your mask. FDLE found it in the van but didn't report it."

The only lights on the *Mermaid* are on the mast and in a porthole near the waterline at the bow. Right now, Hughes is aboard with two Palm Beach sheriff's detectives, waiting to see if anyone pays a visit.

"Since you were never inside the van, I'm guessing one of the kids dropped it at some point," George says.

"Maybe. But I took a look at the FDLE report. There's a problem with it. I didn't want to say anything until I was sure." I pull back my sleeve and show him the watch on my wrist. "I found it in a vintage store."

George uses the light of his phone to examine the watch. "What is that? A Swatch?"

"Yeah. Just like the one Grace Sandalin was wearing when the van crashed."

"Now you're creeping me out, kid. This better be leading somewhere besides asking you to submit to a psych evaluation."

"Look closer." I keep my wrist in front of him while watching the yacht.

"It's stopped. You bought a bad watch."

"It's stopped at four fifteen," I reply. "Same as Grace's watch."

"Okay, now you sound like a *Twilight Zone* episode. You intentionally stopped the watch at the same time as hers ran out?"

I lean back from the scope and rub my eyes for a moment. "I stopped it at the same time she died."

"But aren't those waterproof? In fact, I think I read that on the FDLE report. It's why they couldn't determine what time they went into the water."

"They are waterproof. Unless you get into an accident and crack the casing like this one . . . or the one Grace was wearing. Then it only takes about a minute for the watch to stop."

"Okay, now you have my interest. What else?"

"Well, the mask ring might just be what it is, something the kids left, but I read deeper into the report. The van still had half a tank of gas. The report speculates that they died a little after midnight, about an hour after leaving the concert and getting lost. That's how long it would take for them to get to Pond 65. But if Grace's watch is correct, they didn't die until five hours later. And the half-full tank suggests they weren't driving around in circles."

George follows the thread. "In '89, they pulled all the gas-station footage they could find. They didn't spot the kids. So, they didn't fill up?"

"Right. They were doing something for five hours. FDLE glossed over that part because it doesn't fit the simpler narrative."

"So what are you saying?"

"Saying? I'm asking. What were the kids doing for five hours?"

"Two boys, two girls. Do the math," he responds.

"Five hours? What kind of teenager were you? Besides. They were supposed to be high as a kite at the time. Was Udal just driving his stoned friends around, waiting for them to wake up? He was the one with the substance-abuse history."

"That's not an implausibility. Kids do weird stuff."

Don't I know it. I think Jackie was conceived on a golf course. But she doesn't need to know that.

"All I'm saying is that the forensic report intentionally leaves out anything that contradicts the simple story. Aguilló knows this, but he probably thinks it doesn't much matter whether it happened at midnight or four in the morning."

"Okay. They did sloppy work. Now what?"

"I want to look into this some more," I reply.

"It sounds like you already have."

"I mean I want to talk to Aguilló. I want to get all the notes. I want to see the van again."

"Okay. Marquez will be annoyed, but I'll deal with that. Anything else?"

"Yeah. I want Hughes to help me. He's smart. He pointed out the ring in the first place."

"Nope. You can work on this, but I need his attention on the Bandits. In case you forgot, this is our priority right now. The van is as cold a case as they come. I'm treating it as a training exercise."

"Fine. But I wouldn't be too sure." I don't know why I blurt out that last remark.

"Now what?"

"Nothing. It's just that if someone else saw those kids before they died, they never told anyone. Why?"

"So now you're assuming they saw someone?" asks George.

"Maybe they parked on the side of the road for five hours while they got it on. Maybe not. Maybe they were up to something else. Like I said, it's just odd. That's all."

There's another factor I haven't mentioned to George. I don't dare say it out loud, because I don't want word to get back to the families unless it's corroborated. But the one note I saw in the confidential report that wasn't given to the press, which was removed from the final report filed by the coroner, was a tiny detail with huge implications.

Both Caitlin and Grace had their underwear on inside out—which is one of the signs of rape and murder being covered up.

CHAPTER TEN
SECRETS

I glance over the top of my laptop screen and tap on Jackie's world history textbook on the table in our kitchen galley. She's sitting with her knees up, playing on her phone—a phone she wasn't supposed to have until next year but that her father decided she could have on her last birthday.

I would have put up a protest, but it wasn't that long ago that two men tried to kill me aboard my last boat. I have no reason to think my daughter is in any kind of danger, but you never can be sure. When I weighed the risk of that handheld electronic portal to a parent's nightmares versus the man who tried to drag me into the bow of my own boat to murder me, I decided to leave it to Jackie's judgment as to how to use her phone responsibly.

One of the conditions for having the phone was that Run and I could inspect it and her text chats at any time we chose. While neither of us wants to invade the privacy of our child, she's still a child.

She thought she'd be clever by using a texting app and burying the icon in a folder on the second page, but I showed her how I could pull up her most frequently used apps and find what she'd been using. I also explained that if she pulled a stunt like that again, she'd have to retrieve her phone from the bottom of a canal.

She's a great kid, but she's entering that phase of life in which she has secrets. When I tap on her textbook and tell her to put the phone aside, she places it so the screen is facing down. I also notice that she always holds the phone so I can't see who she's talking to.

I try to remind myself that not every secret a twelve-year-old has is something I need to know about. I've got to give her room to be herself with her friends and do their goofy things without being too worried about parental judgment.

"What are you working on?" she asks me, trying to turn the conversation away from schoolwork. She's a good student, but she just got her first C. It doesn't seem coincidental to me that happened at the same time the girls' and boys' swim teams started practicing together. I can only hope that boys are a mere curiosity to her for now.

"Just schoolwork," I reply. I close the PDF viewer with the details about Caitlin Barrow's forensic exam and open my browser window with a research paper about Paleoamericans. I experience a brief moment of self-consciousness as I realize that I'm keeping secrets from my daughter as well.

The biggest one that I feel guilt over is not being truthful about why I sold my last boat and bought this one instead. It's almost the same model and actually a year older. But nobody was ever killed on this one.

While I don't lose much sleep over having had to defend myself and fatally wounding the man who tried to kill me, even after all the blood was cleaned up and the boat looked new again, there was no way I could keep living on it and not recall what happened every day—me clawing at the carpet, grabbing anything I could to avoid getting dragged belowdecks . . .

The sensible thing would have been to move into the apartment at the marina that was mine to use for watching the place. But the apartment went away when I no longer had the time to play superintendent.

In theory, I could have rented an apartment somewhere else, or moved in with Run, but there's salt in my veins. I like the gentle rocking of the boat at night, and for some reason I feel safer at sea.

When I bought this craft, *The Comet*, I decided to keep it docked in the marina where Dad keeps *Fortune's Fool*. It's nice to have him around to look after Jackie—and keep an eye on me as well, I guess.

"Anything exciting?" asks Jackie.

"Nadine sent me some articles on minimally invasive archaeological excavation. She wants to know how much of it can be used underwater."

My PhD adviser, Nadine Baltimore, has cut me a tremendous amount of slack as I've taken on the workload of the UIU. When I told her I might have to drop out of the program, she had a few choice words for me. After she consulted with the academic department heads, a compromise was reached: I could use my investigative casework as credit toward my doctoral requirements. At first the other professors balked, but then Nadine pointed out that they risked losing the one candidate accumulating more underwater archaeological experience than anyone else in the state, or possibly the world. This was an exaggeration, but maybe not that far off.

I've been asked to do an interview for the alumni magazine, detailing my recovery of the Pond 65 van—something Nadine told me will go a long way toward shutting up my critics.

We'll see.

Jackie cracks open her textbook and stares at the pages. I reopen Caitlin's forensic report, then pull up the police reports on Tim Kelly and Dylan Udal. Neither appeared particularly rapey, but what does that mean? Reading between the lines, both couples had probably been sexually active for a while, and since both Caitlin and Grace had their underwear replaced inside out, it would suggest that Tim and Dylan were the perpetrators.

Or, more simply, there could have been some innocent teen activity and the girls put their clothes back on in a hurry, both of them managing to get their underwear on inside out. I've done that more than a few times.

Although, the forensic report indicates there may have been tearing at the bands, suggesting that they may've been stripped and redressed by someone else. The problem is that thirty-year-old forensic data is mostly fuzzy guessing.

The other curious point is what's *not* in the inventory list: condoms or condom wrappers.

Sexually active kids in the late eighties wouldn't have had any trouble getting access to them. At the height of the AIDS crisis, schools were handing them out in nurses' offices like college pamphlets.

The more I read into the report, the more sympathetic I am to Aguilló and Marquez censoring the final version—I disagree with the choice, but I understand where they're coming from. If the girls were raped by the boys but there's no way to prove it, whom does it help to put that information out there? The perpetrators are dead and the families of the girls would be left to deal with a horrible truth, while the parents of Dylan and Tim would be made to feel guilty for something that wasn't their fault.

I place the mouse cursor over the close button. Maybe I should just let it go . . .

Jackie giggles, and I see that she's placed her phone in her textbook. She glances up, her cheeks flushing at the realization that I've caught her in the act.

"If I were to look at your phone right now, what would I see?" I ask.

Jackie pauses, her eyes glancing down at the screen. She then picks it up and swipes a finger across the display, erasing the conversation. "Nothing," she says and tosses the phone on the table, where it skids across and hits my computer. She knows her phone privileges are over for the foreseeable future. "Can I go see Grandpa?"

I close my laptop, take a deep breath, and try to recall what mommy blog had the right advice for this situation. None comes to mind. No matter. McPhersons aren't known for conventional parenting.

Jackie is a good kid, most days. Maybe it's time for some of that unconventional parenting. She's an exceptionally bright and mature twelve-year-old, but she doesn't understand how scary the real world is and what keeps her mother up at night.

"You asked what I was working on. I lied. I was looking at the forensic report about the kids in the van. Maybe you can help me with an ethical question."

I then horrify my daughter and probably commit some form of child abuse by giving her the details of the forensic examination— slightly sanitized, but not sparing the horror of what might have happened.

Fifteen minutes later, tears are welling in my daughter's eyes. She's seen R-rated movies and senseless violence, but she's a deeply compassionate soul. While she'd heard the general news about the kids in the van, they didn't feel real to her. Now they do. And I made her cry, traumatized by that kind of first-person empathy young girls can turn on or off like a switch.

"Those boys . . . Dylan and Tim . . . do you really think they could have done that to their friends?" she asks.

I shrug. "I don't know. I'm not sure if we *can* know. I was thinking I should just let it go."

"You can't, Mom!" she blurts out and pokes my closed laptop. "What if they did it? Or . . . or . . . what if someone else did it?"

Hearing her mention the possibility of someone else sends a shiver down my spine.

"There was nobody else in the van. Just the four of them."

"Their parents need to know," she says with certainty.

"If you were Caitlin's mom, what would you want me to tell you? That her boyfriend may have harmed her before she died?"

She shakes her head. "No. I'd want someone like you to find out first. I'd want someone like you to find out the truth. It's what you do. I'd want you to tell me what you find out."

The plaintive sound of her voice moves me. She's speaking out of pure empathy. This was probably the voice I needed to hear.

"Okay," I reply.

"You're going to look into it? You're going to find out?"

"I'm going to try." In an act of justifiable parental manipulation, I pick up her phone. "What would I find if I pulled up the backup of your messages?"

Her mouth opens at the thought that I might still be able to see her messages. Her eyes drift away as she mutters under her breath. "Stacey said Conner needs to start shaving his pubes because they stick out of his swim trunks during practice."

Horrified but relieved, I slowly hand her phone back to her. "Let's never talk about that again." I also make a mental note to call her swim coach and make sure they're giving the kids proper personal grooming advice—and to keep this Conner kid as far away from Jackie as possible.

CHAPTER ELEVEN
CAITLIN

Diane Morera, formerly Diane Barrow, sits next to her husband on the patio of their Sunrise town house. She's aged well, and I can see traces of her teenage daughter in her tanned face. Her husband, Benson Morera, is sitting by her side, not too close, but leaning into her, watching his wife's reactions.

I can't imagine what she's going through. How do you deal with grief you tried to put away thirty years ago? For me, at least, half of dealing with grief is trying to figure out what I'm supposed to show the outside world.

"Thank you for coming in person," says Diane. "It was a little jarring to get a phone call about Caitlin's body being found."

"Yeah. That was . . ." I decide now is not the time to go into agency rivalry. "That's not the best way to handle these things."

"Did you see her body?" she asks. "The coroner recommended we shouldn't because of the state it was in."

"She was down there a long time," I reply. No mother should see what I saw.

"I kind of imagine her down there looking the same, frozen in time. But I know that's not the case. The doctor said she died painlessly. Is that true?"

Time to be circumspect. "I don't have any reason to think otherwise."

She nods. "It's been so long. She wanted to be an actress. I used to hope that she'd just run off to Los Angeles and I'd see her someday on a soap opera. Silly, I know. I used to tape them. She loved those shows. At first, I taped them because I wanted her to have them when she came back. Then I did it so I could watch them when I got home, watch and look for her. I never saw her. I finally gave up." She glances over at her husband.

"As a mother," I reply, "I can't tell you how sorry I am for your loss."

"It's the past. I knew she was gone a long time ago. The first time she ran away . . . well, it set a precedent."

"I read that in the original police report. She'd run away a few times?"

"Yes. Things were difficult. After her father and I broke up. And she didn't exactly adjust well to . . ." She pauses. "She didn't adjust well to having Benson around."

"Diane . . ." Her husband puts his hand on her arm.

This is new. "I didn't realize you two were seeing each other back then."

"After her husband left," Benson clarifies.

Diane shakes her head. "No point now. We were seeing each other before Caitlin's father and I separated. That was part of the stress."

I'll say. Her mom goes out with this guy while still married to her dad? Arguments in that house must have been intense. The police reports mentioned a pair of domestic-disturbance calls prior to Caitlin's disappearance, but they weren't specific.

Benson seems uneasy about the entire discussion. Understandable, although I'm not seeing any kind of guilt from the guy.

"I'm trying to get a little more background on the kids. Is there anything more you can tell me?"

"Sure. I didn't keep much, but I still have an album. Let me get that." She excuses herself and goes into the house.

"What was her boyfriend like?" I ask Benson Morera.

"Dylan? I never really talked to him. He'd pull up in the van, and Caitlin would hop in. The few times I talked to him, he was all 'Yes, sir' and 'No, sir.' Some kids do that as an act," he adds.

"You weren't bothered by an older boy taking Caitlin off in a van?"

He makes an apathetic shrug. "Caitlin was Diane's kid. I wasn't her father."

Way to step into the role. Either he legitimately feels no emotion regarding Caitlin, or he's concealing something. Out of curiosity and while Diane is still in the house, I decide to probe a little. "Did Caitlin ever act inappropriately around you?"

His shoulders tighten and his jaw clenches as he leans forward. "What the fuck is that supposed to mean?"

Well, asshole, if you never crossed boundaries with the attractive teenage girl you were living with but deny any parental connection with, you'd shrug off the question—but if you'd said something or acted in a creepy way, you'd react exactly like you just did.

What I say instead is, "Did she have violent outbursts? Tell you she wanted to kill herself? That kind of thing?"

"Oh." He sits back in his chair. "No. Nothing like that."

Diane walks back onto the patio and sets a large Trapper Keeper portfolio on the table. "This was hers. I put a photo album in here." She opens the Velcro flap and turns the pages to face me.

Caitlin's life in photos is revealed as I flip through the album. I see her first birthday. A bath with her mother. Riding a bike with training wheels. Hugging Chip and Dale at Disney World. When I get to the teenage years, I see the same experiments with too much eye makeup that my mother suffered through. Caitlin has short hair and baggy shirts for a while. Then she's wearing concert T-shirts and flipping the peace sign.

In these later photos, she seems less interested in the camera. Probably because the mother she disapproved of was holding it.

I turn the page and see a photo of all four kids dressed in tuxedos and cocktail dresses. "What was this?"

"Dylan's older brother got married. Don't they look adorable?"

They do. The girls look mature beyond their years, and the boys look like they're trying to be men comfortable with themselves.

"What did you think about Dylan?"

Diane sighs. "That boy. They knew each other since middle school. He could be a handful. Always polite. He treated Caitlin like a princess. She wasn't always nice to him, to be honest. She took him for granted sometimes."

I wonder where she got that from.

"But she always came back to him. He had his mood swings. When he was on his medication, he was fine. But that family of his." She rolls her eyes. "Anyway, he was a good kid. Good for her."

"Until he drove her into the canal," adds Benson. "Is it true he was on drugs at the time?"

"The bodies . . ." I almost say *were too decomposed*. ". . . weren't in a condition where we could determine that." But my money is on yes.

I pull out a stack of photos tucked into the binder's back pocket. Most of them are duplicates of what I've seen. I push through them and see a few others, including photos of her friend Grace in a park that I recognize. They're a teenager's attempt at glamour shots. I slide through them and find a Polaroid. This one is of Grace in a bedroom. Her bare back is to the camera and her head is turned toward it as she cups her breast with her hand. It's the kind of thing a lover might take, or two teenage girls playing around with an instant camera. At the bottom in magic marker is the word *Slut* in a girl's handwriting with a winking smiley face. I show it to Diane.

"Those girls. They were a two-person circus when they were together."

I catch Benson squinting out of the corner of my eye. I suspect he never looked through the album.

"They weren't . . . um?"

"If they played around, it wouldn't have surprised me. But no, they weren't, as far as I know. Like I said, Caitlin loved Dylan, but she caused him grief. She was a bit of a flirt."

Ah, got it. She was less than faithful to her high school sweetheart. No shocker there.

"Mind if I take some photos of the album?" I ask.

"Please. And you can take any duplicate photos if you want," she replies.

"Did she take any other Polaroids? Maybe some less risqué ones?"

"She didn't have a Polaroid. That probably belonged to Grace."

"Or one of the boys," adds Benson with a slight sneer.

I start taking photographs out of the album. "Did she have a diary?"

"You know, she did. But I couldn't find it when she went missing. I assumed she took it with her."

"We didn't find anything in the van." *Huh, diary goes missing after she does.* I glance over at Benson. "That's too bad. I'd love to know what was in there."

His eyes dart away from mine.

He's definitely got a secret. But is it the obvious one or something else?

CHAPTER TWELVE

GRACE

Randy Fulton, a classmate of the lost kids, is giving a touching speech at the lectern of Davie Methodist Church. He's got a beard, slicked-back gray hair, and the penetrating gaze of someone who writes about people—which he does, as a blogger for a political news site in DC.

"I didn't know Grace, Caitlin, Tim, and Dylan as well as I would have liked. They were their own crowd, which made them special. I can remember coming to school and seeing them across the street, smoking cigarettes and having a laugh." He glances toward the parents' section. "They looked a little rowdy to a nerd like me, but that was their way. I remember being jealous of them. Wishing I had friends like that. To this day, I don't think I've experienced that kind of camaraderie." He looks up from his notes. "You have to understand that when they went missing, nobody really thought they were missing. We just kind of assumed they decided to gas up Dylan's van and see how far it would take them. I remember thinking they were the same kind of free spirits that made the sixties happen. And truth be told, that was my personal wish—that they'd hopped aboard, leaving their troubles behind, and decided to go west, where the good music was happening. And I also remember wishing back then, as a shy senior who hadn't managed to make a real friend in four years, that I had gone off in that van with them. Laughing, listening to music with people who loved me. Truth be told, to this day, I still wish I could have been part of their group. That's what friendship was. That's what it's like to feel loved."

Fulton's speech generates a generous amount of applause and teary eyes from the parents. As a political writer, he's got his measure of bullshit and narcissism mixed just right. I know more about him now than I do the kids from his fairy-tale story of them singing along with the Mamas and the Papas as they headed west to resurrect the Summer of Love.

But in actuality, the foursome was more into Sisters of Mercy and Joy Division. Dylan's body bore several self-made tattoos of bands that embraced nihilism like a self-help philosophy. That said, Fulton's speech has done exactly what it was meant to do: made everyone feel better about a horribly tragic event.

After the speakers finish, none of them having had more than a passing relationship with the kids, I'm able to pull the other parents aside into a small meeting room.

I'd contacted them beforehand, telling them that I had some wrap-up questions for my report and the best time to talk to all of them would be here. They were happy to agree, and two of them told me that they had been wanting to meet me anyway, to thank me personally.

Tim Kelly's parents, Joyce and Peter, are much older than the others. Tim was adopted when he was seven. Which may explain why, with parents who were affluent and upper-class, Tim had trouble adjusting.

Grace Sandalin's parents, Nancy and Donald, appear blue collar. Her father, despite being retirement age, is wearing an ill-fitting collared shirt, and her mother has on the kind of orthopedic shoes I've seen on older waitresses.

Dylan's father, Grant, wears a nondescript suit over a muscular frame. The report said that he owned an auto-body shop that had had trouble in the past with stolen parts. Dylan's mother died the year before he went missing.

"Thank you for talking to me. This has to be very difficult," I say to start things.

"Thank you for finding our angels," says Nancy Sandalin, still wiping away tears.

"You're the one who dived in and found the van?" asks Grant.

"Yes. I was assisting with another case when I discovered it."

"Hmm. And what kind of condition would you say it was in?" he asks.

This gets a look from Peter Kelly. "That's your first question? Are you planning on reselling it?"

Grant faces him and growls, "Actually, I'm having trouble understanding how my son ended up in the middle of a lake, asshole."

Oh shit. "Whoa." I hold up my hands. "We're in a church. Let's all act . . . um, churchlike."

Good lord, I had no idea what kind of tension existed between these people. Here I was thinking it would all be tears and group hugging.

"First, to answer your question, Mr. Udal, the van was in working condition minus the water exposure and didn't appear to have suffered any malfunction that could have caused the accident."

"So you were saying he was fucked-up when he went in?" He shakes his head. "Dylan messed around with shit. I know that. But he knew I'd beat the shit out of him if he ever did it behind the wheel. That was the rule."

"That was the rule?" says Peter Kelly. "No wonder our kids ended up at the bottom of the lake. With your son driving."

"You wanna talk about this outside?" says Grant, getting up.

"Please sit down. Do I have to remind everyone that I'm a cop?" I turn to Peter Kelly. "To be honest, we don't know what happened. It could have been road conditions. He could have been swerving to avoid another car. And to Mr. Udal's point, despite Dylan's less-than-spotless criminal record, he was never accused of being under the influence while driving." And just to shut him up: "Something I can't say for everyone else here. These were kids. Kids have accidents. They sometimes exercise poor judgment. Now, I'd like to get to the matter at hand, and hopefully you can answer some questions for me."

"Like what?" asks Nancy Sandalin.

I make a dramatic point of holding up a folder from the original investigation in 1989. "First, can someone tell me why they did such a shitty job with this case? It reads to me like the cops decided that the kids had run away before they even looked into it."

"Because they'd done it in the past," says Peter Kelly. "A few months before, they went to Disney World without telling anyone."

"And then they came back?"

"Two days later. We called the cops when it happened. False alarm."

"I see. So when they didn't come home on February 18, the police assumed they'd gone off to Disney again?"

Joyce Kelly speaks up. "It's what we wanted to believe. We didn't even call the police until Sunday afternoon, and they told us to wait. So we did. Finally, on that Monday they started looking."

I pull out a map of the search area and hold it up. "They told you where they looked?"

"Yes," says Joyce. "They said they searched the canals too."

No doubt a visual inspection only. "So, after the search turned up nothing, what did they tell you?"

"They told us the kids had probably run away. They contacted Orlando police and sent out a bulletin about the van."

"Did the police tell you how they expected four teenagers to pay for gas and food?"

Peter Kelly points a finger at Grant. "Any theories on how your son could make money on the streets? Any at all?"

I raise my hands to stop him. It's not like his kid was an angel either. "Okay. I get it. According to the files, your son had a possession charge."

"One," says Joyce.

"One that you weren't able to get expunged from his record," I reply. Something tells me the Kellys used their money to try to keep their son's record clean.

I turn to Grant. "What did you think happened to the kids?"

He shrugs. "At first? Like they said."

"And after no contact?" I ask.

"Maybe he ended up in a ditch. I lost a brother that way." He gulps, then goes silent. What he doesn't want to say is that he also lost one of Dylan's brothers to a heroin overdose three years prior.

I look to the Kellys. "And you? What did you think after Tim didn't come home?"

Joyce sighs and looks at her hands.

Peter closes his eyes for a moment. "I can tell you that we felt relief."

"Peter!" his wife admonishes him.

"Our son was trouble from day one. We gave him everything, and he still treated us like strangers. Honestly speaking, we figured he was just another runaway. His mother was. God knows who his father was. Maybe it was genetic."

"But he didn't run away this time, did he?" I don't know why I say it. Maybe I can't handle Kelly's bashing of some poor kid who went from a broken home to a sterile one. "How about you, Mrs. Sandalin? What did you think?"

"I didn't think she ran away. Grace and I got along. Sure, it was rough sometimes making ends meet, and she was upset that we couldn't get her new clothes all the time and stuff like that. But we didn't really fight. I let her do her own thing. When she started seeing Tim, I didn't complain." She looks over at the Kellys. "We liked your boy. He was always sweet to me."

"He was a manipulator," replies Peter.

"He was an orphan who learned not to trust adults," I reply, defending a kid I never met. "They do what they can to survive."

"Survive? We had three cars and a maid."

"Emotionally," I reply. "Anyway. I wasn't there. I'm not here to pass judgment." *Not openly, at least.* I glance down at my notes. "Just a few more quick questions. Did any of the kids snorkel or scuba dive?"

I get headshakes all around. I cross that off the list. I don't want to be too obvious, so I have to pad the questions with things I already know.

"Did the kids tell you what concert they were going to?" Some did. Some didn't.

"Did they mention going with anyone else? Possibly meeting up with other friends?" Negative.

"Had any of the kids ever reported being the victims of any kind of violence?" I ask.

"Like spanking?" asks Nancy Sandalin.

"No. I mean by somebody else. A boyfriend who was violent?"

"Why are you asking that?" says Peter Kelly.

"Just part of the background." I look to Nancy. "Anything?"

"No. Nothing."

"No sexual mistreatment?" I ask.

"Does a pervert gym teacher the boys had count?" asks Grant. "Did they say anything about him?"

"Is he still breathing? Then the answer is no," I reply.

"Noted."

"Seriously, what are you getting at?" asks Peter Kelly.

"I'm just trying to get an accurate understanding of their lives. Okay. One more." *Be subtle.* "I'd love to have any photos of the kids, if possible." I turn to Nancy Sandalin. "Any Polaroids Grace may have taken?"

She gives me a dumb look.

"Did she have an instant camera?"

She glances at her husband. He shakes his head.

"Do any of you know if your child had a Polaroid camera?" Negative. Everyone seems certain.

This has gotten interesting. I have one highly suggestive photo of Grace in Caitlin's album, and nobody in the tight-knit group owned a Polaroid camera—or at least not as far as the parents know.

I'd dismiss it as an unimportant detail if it weren't for the fact that one of the items we found in the van was an empty Polaroid film cartridge.

Just how tight-knit was their group, really? "Ms. McPherson?" says Joyce Kelly.

Her husband shakes his head. "Drop it, Joyce."

"What is it?"

She ignores him. "I was wondering. It's a silly thing, but I'd like to get all Tim's stuff back."

"Most of it's pretty decayed," I reply.

"I know. They gave us what's left of his jacket. It's just that we'd like to have a private ceremony. And I'd like to get the other shoe." She turns to Grant Udal. "I'm happy to give you Dylan's other shoe, since they mistakenly gave it to us."

He gives her a confused shrug. "What other shoe? They sent me the rags of Dylan's Nikes. What are you talking about?"

"Tim was a size ten. They sent us two shoes. One was his Reebok, the other was a size-twelve Adidas. He didn't wear Adidas."

I flip through the inventory list in my notes. There it is, plain as day. Aguilló reported the belongings of each kid. Tim's corpse was missing a shoe, but they found one in the van. The problem is, the shoe was the wrong size. And brand, it turns out.

"What size did Dylan wear?" I ask Grant.

"Not twelves, I know that."

Kids keep all kinds of odd stuff in their vehicles . . . but the odd stuff here keeps adding up.

It leads me to one obvious conclusion, which George is going to hate.

CHAPTER THIRTEEN

ADIDAS

George Solar's frustration fills the warehouse of our run-down head-quarters as he glares at the documents I've placed in front of him. Hughes is sitting next to me at the table and is giving me his best blank stare while paying close attention. I roped him into this with an email explaining my findings, saying that I only wanted to "loop him in." I knew it would capture his curiosity while not exactly violating George's request that I not pull him into the case. Hughes responded with two words: "I'm in."

Our HQ was formerly a marina warehouse that was seized during our last case and turned over to us for the use of the UIU. While the main building has shoddy air-conditioning and is better suited to fiberglassing boats than doing office work, it has a convenient dock and suits our purposes fine. There's even a large aboveground pool that I can test dive gear in. I just have to forget the fact that someone I knew was murdered in it.

George holds up a photo of the worn Adidas sneaker. "A shoe? A shoe, McPherson? This is your best evidence?"

"No. It's one of several pieces. First, we have the girls showing signs of possible sexual assault. We have the empty Polaroid film casing. We have a Polaroid photo of one of the girls that nobody knows the origin of, and none of the kids even owned a Polaroid camera. There's the dive-mask ring, and we also have a size-twelve shoe that appeared out of nowhere. It's a lot of evidence that doesn't add up."

George isn't having any of it. "We once arrested a drug dealer in Homestead. Jamaican guy. When we searched his house, know what I found in the closet? A horse saddle. Not some sex thing, but a full-on horse saddle. He didn't ride. He'd never been near a horse, as far as I knew. When I asked him about it, he refused to talk about it. To this day, McPherson, I still think about that horse saddle. Why . . . ? But it doesn't change a thing. Some people have weird stuff. Comb a crime scene thoroughly enough, you'll find something odd. It doesn't change what happened. It simply reveals the truth that we're all weird. We're all messy in our own way."

I can tell George is trying to convince himself as much as me that the odd pieces don't mean anything.

"Or . . . ," I reply.

He shakes his head. "Let's hear it."

He's painted me into a corner. He wants me to say it out loud so I can hear how ridiculous it sounds.

Fine. "There was a fifth kid. Possibly a fifth victim. Someone who got flung from the van before it rolled."

George's eyes narrow. "That's your claim?"

"My theory," I reply.

"I thought you were going in another direction."

I am. But not openly. "A fifth person makes sense."

"He's the one who messed with the girls?" asks George.

"Possibly. Maybe there was a fight. That could be why they went off the road. He was knocked unconscious and thrown from the van and drowned outside the van. Maybe he was a new member to the group. But a fifth person makes sense. And there's one other thing." I've been saving this for last. "Hughes caught this back when Aguilló made his little presentation, but he was afraid to say anything. Right?"

"What?" blurts Hughes, unprepared for me calling him out.

"The X-rays. You noticed something? Didn't you?"

Hughes seems profoundly uneasy. The problem is, he's not accustomed to bucking authority. George laid down the law, and Hughes doesn't want to contradict him.

"Let's hear it," says George, sensing the man's discomfort.

"I'm not an expert. I spent time working at some naval hospitals and handling combat trauma, so all I know is what I've seen. It's the Udal boy's X-rays. He had a broken neck but no sign of facial trauma. I've never seen that in a car accident where the driver died. I thought it was surprising that Aguilló concluded he was driving, but I deferred to his expertise."

George lifts a folder I'd placed on the table and slides out the X-rays of the kids. He places them side by side and stares at them for an eternity. Finally, he looks up at me. "Damn it, McPherson. Damn it."

"Don't pull this," I reply. "You knew something was off from the start. Before Hughes and I did. Aguilló did a rush job, and things didn't fit. Yet you ignored them."

"It's a cold case, McPherson. I said this before." He points to a filing cabinet against the wall. "We got a bunch of them."

"And now we may have a fifth victim," I reply. *Or at least a fifth person who was in the van,* I think to myself.

"Who, correct me if I'm wrong, nobody is looking for."

"Take a look at the stack of papers under that folder. It's two hundred young men who went missing on or around that date."

George flips through the photos and descriptions. He turns one toward me. "Nikolaus Healy went missing in *Idaho*." He holds up another. "Terrell P. Irwin went missing in *Alaska*."

"Ever heard of hitchhikers? Maybe the kids met up with Nikolaus or Terrell or any one of those other young men. Maybe that's our fifth victim."

"Did any of the parents mention another person?" asks George.

"No. But I never told my parents about all my friends—especially not the sketchy ones."

"All right. So you want to do more background? You want to talk to anyone who knew the kids? Like the guy who spoke at the memorial?" asks George.

"Yes. I'd like Hughes's help to talk to teachers. People who were at the concert. Anyone else who might have information."

"Okay. As long as it doesn't interfere with the Bandit case." He looks to Hughes. "You know this is going to add to your workload. And you're allowed to tell McPherson no. At least in theory. Lord knows it doesn't work for me."

"I understand. It won't affect our primary case."

"Right," says George, unconvinced.

"One more thing," I say.

"No," he shoots back.

"You haven't even heard it."

"I know you. I know how you work your way from some simple request to asking for something ridiculous. You're already getting Hughes against my better judgment. What else?"

I try to say it like it's the simplest thing in the world. "I want to go back into Pond 65 to look for evidence."

If George had been drinking coffee, I'm pretty sure it would be all over the table by now. He shakes his head adamantly. "No. Fish and Wildlife trappers aren't going to go back out there and capture the gators. They're already getting hell from the environmentalist groups about their treatment of Big Bill."

"No Fish and Wildlife," I reply. "Just me in the water. You guys in a boat."

"Oh, why didn't you say so?" he says sarcastically. "That makes so much more sense. I'll scare away dozens of agitated reptiles. Brilliant plan." He turns to Hughes. "See what you signed on for?"

"I have a plan," I reply. "Actually, it was something my dad suggested."

"Oh, even better. Your pirate father with shark-bite scars has a plan. This I got to hear."

CHAPTER FOURTEEN
CAGED

My dad's brilliant solution to going into Pond 65 and not getting eaten by Big Bill or any of his scaly cousins is something he used in his younger days, when he and his friends were treasure hunting off the coast of Cuba—in waters that were most definitely Cuban *and* shark-infested.

To avoid the Cuban navy, they'd drift into Cuban territory at night and dive while it was still dark. Because this was prime hunting time and territory for bull sharks, they had to be on constant lookout for the creatures—and even then, looking out for the predators only confirmed what you already knew: bull sharks roamed the area and could bite you at any moment.

While speargunning a large shark can sometimes discourage others, bull sharks will devour each other if they're bored, and killing a bull shark is just as likely to spark a feeding frenzy in which humans are the easiest pickings. Although it's true that sharks don't generally want to eat humans because we're too bony, bull sharks bite and maim for the sake of it.

Dad's solution was a kind of mobile shark cage. Actually, it was two large crab cages bolted together with an open floor. Weighted at the bottom with a small float on top, the cage would stay upright and allow the diver to pick up the cage and walk across the ocean floor as they shoveled and probed for treasure.

When I asked him if it worked, he didn't exactly give me a specific answer, but he suggested that my private school tuition and his divorce from my mother may have in part been paid for by that expedition.

He also hinted that the maps they got of the wreck may or may not have been supplied by the CIA, which wanted to prevent the Cuban government from benefiting from the treasure.

Morally complicated is a phrase that describes much of my childhood.

While I like to think I walk a straighter ethical line than my dad and grandfather, I can't claim I have more common sense. I'm at the bottom of Pond 65 in my "dog cage," as George called it.

Big Bill was nowhere to be seen when we rolled up to the pond in our trucks with George's boat on a trailer. Hughes spotted a small nest at the far end of the lake, and I noticed the telltale bubbles of an alligator not too distant.

Alligators like to keep their distance from each other, but with the warm outflow from the power plant, this territory is a little like a dog park: open to anyone—until a crazy dog shows up.

I'm searching the area around where the van came to rest. The best-preserved remains I'll find would probably be underneath the van itself. Even though we pulled the van out of the water a week ago and currents and sediments have begun to shift, finding the rectangular indentation in the muck where it came to rest isn't difficult.

Muck—in a word, that's the challenge of underwater archaeology. Nadine Baltimore would not approve of the haphazard way I'm searching the pond. It's more scattershot than procedural. I'm sticking a pointed pole in the mud, trying to feel for anything solid—like the sole of a shoe or a skull.

Sticking pointy things into the ground may not sound like the most scientific process, but I've become quite good at it. Grandpa actually taught me this technique. He learned it from Peruvian grave robbers. At a party, he once demonstrated the method using a ski pole in the host's backyard. It took Grandpa ten minutes to figure out where they'd buried their cat. "Feel that *crack*? That's a thin skull like a cat's. Just an inch farther down? That's a spine. If I move the pole over and tap on it, you can hear an echo in the gas-filled stomach."

My childhood was both traumatizing and amusing.

I make enough holes in the van's indentation to be satisfied that the only way to know for certain that nothing is there is by vacuuming up the muck—something George would never go for.

I decide to extend the radius.

"I'm going to move out from the van and toward the shoreline, over," I call into the radio.

"Dolphins up by six," replies George.

He and Hughes are evidently watching the football game on the boat. I can only hope that they're keeping at least one pair of eyes on the water.

My pole hits something hard. "Got something."

I reach into the mud and feel what seems like a large chunk of rubber. I put it into the nylon bag clipped to the inside of the cage.

Already I've found a woman's sandal, fourteen beer cans, and items too encrusted with sediment to know what they are at this moment. All of them have gone into the pouch. I've already sent three pouches to the surface.

The pole hits something metallic. It takes me a minute to pull it free. It's a side mirror. The van was missing both.

"I think I found a side mirror. Looks like the van may have rolled. Over."

"Send it up with the rest," says George.

I put the mirror in the bag and attach it to a nylon cord that goes up to the boat and give the cord a tug.

The bag gets pulled up and through a hatch on top of the cage. I watch as it ascends into the light at the surface. George's boat is a shadow floating on a shimmering mirror.

As the bag nears the surface, I see a long shape glide past.

Looks like I'm not alone.

"I just spotted an alligator," I call into the radio.

"Bill?"

"Negative. A small one. Maybe four feet. Probably curious about what we're doing." This guy is barely an adult. I'm a bigger threat to him.

"I don't like curious alligators," says George.

Fair point. But the funny thing about alligators is that they actually look kind of adorable when they swim. At least I think so. It's that toothy smile and those dangling legs. I mean, when I have a close call, they seem far from adorable. But as this one swam by, I could make out the grin and the pot belly. Baby alligators would be almost cuddly if it weren't for the fact that their mother would snap you in two for being in the general vicinity.

I try to find the right balance between adoration and fearful respect for these creatures when I'm underwater. Anecdotally, and speaking more from my grandfather's and dad's experience, thinking about sharks and alligators as big, goofy dogs that will bite you out of fear or curiosity, not malice, helps you handle a crisis better when something does take a bite. Like a big dog, they can kill you, but panicking only escalates the encounter. And the surest way to panic is to imagine these creatures as aquatic serial killers, waiting to murder you. Some are; most aren't.

I start pushing the cage toward the shelf that Hughes and I dived from when we pulled the van from the water . . . the overhang that seemed like an excellent spot for an alligator burrow.

I push the pole into the bottom, hit a few rocks, and keep moving. The rocks indicate that this end of the pond is more geologically stable and not the mud pit the rest of the pond resembles.

CLANK! My pole hits something metallic. I dig into the mud and retrieve sideview mirror number two. Now it's a matching set—and in a completely different place from where the van came to rest.

"McPherson, we see you've moved," says Hughes over the radio. They can follow me from the surface via a floater attached to a cord.

"Affirmative. I found the other mirror."

"We'll bring the boat closer."

I shove the mirror into the bag and look up at the wall of the shelf. There's a dark spot about five feet below the surface and level with the top of the cage.

I pick up the dog cage and move closer for a better look. It's a three-foot-wide hole. When I aim my flashlight into the opening, it fades after about six feet.

This is an alligator den. From the rocks around the side and the size of it, an old one.

Lots of alligators have lived here over the years. This is also where an alligator would drag a large carcass to consume at their leisure.

If there was a fifth victim and they somehow landed outside the van, this burrow might be where they ended up. There wouldn't be much left of a thirty-year-old eaten corpse, except maybe clothing, a backpack, or a shoe . . .

All right, Sloan, how badly do we want to know what's in there?

I'm already strapping my flashlight to the end of my pole like a bayonet. That way I can push it ahead of me into the tunnel. If Bill or some alligator renter from their version of Airbnb is inside, I'll see their toothy face and be able to back out.

Um, great plan.

"Hey, fellas, I'm going to check something out. I might have a few minutes of radio silence," I say into the microphone.

"McPherson?" asks George.

"Just give me five minutes."

I open the door to the cage and pull it close to the wall face, making it easy for me to retreat if I need to do so in a hurry.

I pull myself up and push my spear into the cave and follow the light into the darkness.

CHAPTER FIFTEEN

LAIR

Get my father a little buzzed—basically catch him anytime after three in the afternoon—and bring up strange things he's seen in the ocean, and he'll tell you stories until the sun comes up. He's a hard-ass skeptic about what other people have experienced, but he'll shake a sinewy finger in your face if you dare question a single detail about the strange green lights he saw drifting over the ocean off the coast of Venezuela or the incredibly long tentacle that snaked across his ship's deck in the Philippines.

Even if I believed only 10 percent of what he says, that's still an incredible amount to believe. I give him added credibility because, ever since he was a boy sailing around the world with his father, he's explored some extremely unexplored places.

Sometimes all it takes is the right perspective to understand how something that sounds impossible could be perfectly plausible. Crocodiles are known to dig burrows like alligators in order to survive the cold. In the Roman era, when the climate was warmer for a period, it wouldn't surprise me if more than a few of them made it north to European rivers and perhaps inspired early legends of dragons.

I don't feel like a brave knight as I swim into the burrow. I don't know if it's fear or anxiety. The two kind of blend for me. I usually define fear as the thing I feel when the unexpected happens. Anxiety is when I'm doing something that I already know is stupid.

This tunnel is long. I'm at least ten feet in, and my light hasn't hit the end. While it's tall enough for my air tank, it's not that wide. I'm not sure if I will be able to turn around without slipping it off. Thankfully, I'm well practiced at that maneuver.

My bigger concern is making sure that I'm alone in here and don't have to pull my tank off to escape in a hurry. If Big Bill's sitting back in this tunnel—which I really, really doubt—I'll see a flash of silver light as it reflects from the backs of his eyeballs. He'll then either retreat or snap at my pole, giving me enough time to pull back. Theoretically.

I remind myself that this burrow is designed as a place to hide . . . well, that and make a sneak attack on any large fish that swim near the entrance. But mostly to hide.

The walls of the tunnel are thick dirt with roots and rocks, kind of like what you'd expect Bilbo Baggins's house to look like—or Gollum's.

Damn, this tunnel is long.

"McPher—" George's voice is cut off by the interference of the cave walls.

I focus on the floor of the tunnel, looking for anything resembling a bone or a human artifact, but all I see is rocks and dirt.

My light reaches the end of the tunnel abruptly. I guess this was a pointless exercise . . .

Wait a second.

There's a shaft branching to the left. I stick the light to the side and wait for the bone-jarring experience of an alligator snapping it in two, but . . . nothing.

I poke my head around the bend. This branch of the tunnel widens into a much larger chamber. This must be Bill's turnabout. I move the light around. The water here remains muddy and hard to see through, but there's no telltale sign of scales or gleaming eyes.

I'm pretty sure nobody is home.

Good . . . The chamber's floor is littered with fish skeletons, beer cans, and a thousand other pieces of debris.

My hand brushes something ridged and hard, and my heart jumps. It's only half a car tire.

Jesus. What happened to the other half?

I glance up and realize that there's a reflection on the ceiling. I push myself up from the bottom, and my head pops into an air pocket.

Holy cow, this is a pretty big little cave. Mentally, I try to place where I am. I'm guessing I set up my tanks and equipment directly above this location.

I've never heard of an alligator den like this before— or one containing this much crap. Bill or whoever made it is one odd gator.

Okay, no time to speculate on the inner psychology of alligators. I need to gather anything that looks like a clue and do it fast.

I go back underwater and start shoving cans, mysterious blocks of metal, and more chunks of rubber into my bag, feeling along the floor with my gloves. As I do this, my spear slips free and floats to the surface. The flashlight at the tip of the spear illuminates the entire chamber.

When I poke my head up again, I notice a section I didn't see before. There's a shelf above the waterline about as large as Big Bill.

Thankfully, there's no Big Bill there. Although the reflection of a glass bottle nearly gives me a heart attack.

Why couldn't my parents have raised me in the desert?

I aim my light at the nest and notice something white. Something long and white. It's a bone. A large bone.

I move close to the ledge and shove my pole into the nest, praying that a bunch of baby alligators don't come crawling out and cry for mama.

I'm pretty sure Bill is a guy, but it wouldn't be polite to assume. A fun fact about alligators is that the temperature of the nest determines the sex of the babies. Warm nests produce males; cold ones produce females.

I use my spear to lift the white bone. Yep. It's a big bone, but it's covered in grime and cracked on the end, so I can't tell what kind of animal it came from. It's definitely going in the bag, because it looks about the same size as the femur of a certain two-legged ape that inhabits Florida.

Nice job keeping things light in the dragon's den, Sloan.

With it, I find a clump of fabric clotted with dirt. I shove that into the bag as well. My probing doesn't reveal anything else, so I turn back to the main body of the chamber and resume pushing the pole along the bottom.

"SLOAN! YOU . . ." The radio cuts in and out again.

The water level in the cave suddenly surges . . . like something just entered the mouth of the cavern.

Oh damn.

I was so worried about finding Big Bill in here, I didn't think about what would happen if he came home.

And it looks like he just arrived.

CHAPTER SIXTEEN
UNDERGROUND

I'm deep inside an alligator's den that its owner has just entered. In about three seconds, he's going to round the bend and enter the main chamber. Chances are he's coming in hot, because he knows his territory has been violated.

I have one long, pointed pole; a dive knife strapped to my ankle; and a backup knife on my tank. None of which will make much difference against an angry reptile that weighs as much as a small car.

I back up to the shelf and pull myself out of the water. He'll have the same physical advantage here as in the water, but at least I'll see him coming.

Now what?

When he comes, it'll be all teeth. He'll rip right through my arms like steak knives through veal. I feel underneath me for something to shield myself but find only small bones and sticks.

Damn it.

Think . . . my tank!

I slip off my buoyancy compensation device and swing my scuba tank in front of me as I wedge myself against the chamber wall. The flashlight on my stick dangles over the edge, illuminating the water, which suddenly surges and overflows the ledge. A huge, scaly tail flips above the surface and into my light.

Bill is in the roundabout.

He's spinning around, frothing up a storm. He is *pissed*.

He's also trying to figure out what's in his chamber. Alligators don't possess imagination or much of a functional memory. They mainly operate on senses and instincts.

Right now, he's probing the water for the intruder. Sooner or later, some part of his reptile brain is going to whisper—

Splash. Bill's head pops above the waterline. His mouth opens for an instant before snapping shut. He spins, and his tail whacks my spear light, knocking it into the water, where it creates a green glow as it descends.

Bill's massive body eclipses the light.

Thrash. His head pops above the waterline and bites the air over the far end of the ledge.

He knows I'm up here.

I wedge myself farther back and wrap my fingers around the straps of my BC. I don't want him to hit it and knock the tank free, leaving me completely defenseless.

Splash. Bill's head pokes up again. His head twists, and he lunges toward the corner where I'm cowering.

Clang! His teeth make contact with the tank.

Bill doesn't like that. He sinks back into the water.

Think fast, Sloan.

I slide to the edge of the shelf closest to the exit, where Bill is still spinning around, blocking any chance of escape.

I need a plan.

Thwap. Bill's massive tail slams into the wall as he spins around, leaving the entrance open for a split second. He does it again.

What the hell?

My only chance to leave is to time it between his gaping mouth and his tail, which will knock me unconscious. It's like some goddamn video game.

Supposing I get past him and into the tunnel, I still have fifteen feet of passage to swim through, where he could overtake me at any moment. Plus, once I'm free of the lair, he could still snatch me in the pond before I reach the shore or drag me in as I try to climb in the boat with George and Hughes.

Worst idea ever. I'm such a damned fool.

Some part of my brain tells me to stop going over the minutiae of my stupidity and simply act.

Now!

I jump into the gap, spin around, and push my BC in front of me, blocking Bill from entering the tunnel with my tank.

Bam! His snout hits my tank and pushes me backward. What *now?* Hold him here until he gets bored? That ain't gonna work.

Bam! He pushes again. *Think, Sloan.*

I need to slow him down . . . The inflatable vest!

I pull back a little deeper into the tunnel and squeeze the air valve. A cloud of bubbles appears, and my vest fills up like a balloon, hitting the top of the chamber and dangling the tank downward.

I yank the regulator from my mouth and turn for the exit, swimming as fast as humanly possible—which is nowhere near as fast as a leisurely alligator.

The exit's a small green glow ahead. I swim faster.

A *clang* reverberates through the tunnel.

Bill just hit my tank. Did he slide past it? *Let's not stop and ask.*

I'm almost at the exit. A current pushes me ahead—his massive body entering the tunnel. I kick harder.

I reach the end of the tunnel. My dog cage has been knocked to the side. I'm not even going to try to make it in there. Nor am I going to swim for the boat. Instead I arch my back and swim straight for the shoreline shelf above me.

My fingers claw into the mud as I kick, and I pull myself up through ever-muddier water. When air touches the back of my head, I realize I'm only in two feet of water.

Not far enough.

I crawl desperately on all fours until I hear voices. When I finally roll over, knife in my hand, I see Hughes about to jump out of the boat in his scuba gear.

"Don't!" I yell.

There's a surge, and Big Bill's tail thrashes in the pond between me and the boat. And then everything goes quiet.

A moment later, the water surges again, and my tank floats to the surface, attached to my inflated vest. The hoses have been sheared off and thrash around like angry snakes as air escapes.

George's calm voice calls from across the pond. "Great plan, McPherson. Great plan."

I pull myself into a sitting position and realize that I still have my sample bag attached to my waist, an ivory patch of bone visible through the netting.

CHAPTER SEVENTEEN
ELEMENTARY

Nadine Baltimore probes at the bone on the specimen table as she sprays water on it, clearing away the sediment. Hughes and George are sitting on stools by the lab bench while I lean over the fragment, getting the occasional look from Nadine that tells me to back away.

"You found this where?" she asks.

"You can tell her," says George.

After he and Hughes joined me on shore, George spent a good ten minutes chewing me out and making me feel guilty because he almost sent Hughes into the water after me.

"He's a parent, Sloan! How am I going to tell his wife that he got eaten by an alligator chasing after your fool ass?"

"I'm a parent too!" I snapped back.

"Apparently not a good one."

That was the blow that ended the conversation. He knew he'd struck low. It was the worst kind of insult—one based in truth.

It's one thing for a younger version of me to go chasing after stupidity. It's another when I have a daughter at home who looks up to me, sort of. In the moment it seemed like a good idea. That's the problem with us McPhersons—we do all our best and worst thinking in the moment.

The bone fragment shut him up, but it really comes down to what Nadine says. I know a fair amount about physiology, but the markers I look for to identify species weren't present. I needed someone smarter than myself.

We could have taken it to Dr. Aguilló, but I'm concerned that it might not be a human specimen—which technically would be a good thing, because it means that nobody died a horrible death getting eaten by an alligator. But my credibility with George and everyone would take a huge hit.

Through all this, Hughes has been helpful but kept his opinions to himself. I'm trying to get a read on him and still can't quite figure the man out. George likes him and thinks highly of his skills. Part of me wonders if Hughes is here to take my place when I screw up again, terminally.

"This appears to have been exposed to the air for a while," says Nadine. "Where'd you find it, again?"

"In an underground chamber," I reply.

"A limestone formation?"

"Not exactly. It was more of a burrow."

"Oh." She points to several indentations on the bone. "That would explain the alligator-teeth incisions."

And that's the extent of her reaction. This is Nadine.

George, frustrated that the other authority figure in my life isn't admonishing me, decides to provoke the discussion. "Did McPherson tell you that the alligator was in the den when she retrieved the bone?"

Nadine looks up at me. "That was stupid." George gives me a sly smile.

Wait for it, George . . .

Nadine continues, "Next time you should bring a video camera and some other equipment. That's really a rare opportunity. How did the alligator react?"

"Angry. It spun around and tried to block the entrance."

"Very interesting. I wonder if that was because it knew you were a mammal or that was its normal response. You should let me know next time you do something like this." Nadine examines the bone with a magnifying loupe. "My estimation is approximately two to three years old."

"It's been down there a lot longer," I reply.

"No. I'm talking age."

"That's one big three-year-old," says Hughes.

Nadine shakes her head. "Not at all. I'd guess it was a midsize breed of horse. But I'm not an expert."

"Horse?" asks George.

Nadine takes off her gloves. "Yes. I'm sure Sloan told you. This is clearly part of an equine femur."

George gives me a sidelong glance. "Um, no. Your student forgot to mention that."

Nadine turns to me. "Clearly you could tell? Just look at the thickest diameter. That's from an animal that carries considerably more weight than a human."

"Well, I was holding out for your professional opinion," I offer weakly.

"Hmm." She moves over to the plastic bins where I've deposited the contents of the bags from the excavation. They're soaking in water to keep them from decomposing. "Why don't you all put on a pair of gloves, and we'll see what we have here."

"Shouldn't we send this to the FDLE lab?" asks Hughes.

"Really?" asks George. "After what Ms. My Little Pony just pulled, do you really want to do that?"

"Well, if we find something . . ."

"We'll bring it to *them* and not just Aguilló." George looks down at the box of latex gloves. "I'm going to go work on our other case. Hughes, you're with me."

The pair leaves me alone with Nadine in her lab. She's already removing mud from a piece of fabric. "Solar seems rather frustrated," she observes.

"Yeah. I kind of pushed the limits on this one."

Nadine lifts a denim pant leg from the water basin. There are no obvious bite marks on the fabric. Next, she pulls out a gleaming hubcap. "Where did you find this?"

"In the mud by where the van was found," I reply.

"Then it stands to reason this came from the van."

"It does."

She removes a clump of mud and sediment and places it into a plastic bag. She then reaches into the tub and pulls out an L-shaped tire iron. It makes a clanging sound as it hits the counter.

"Near the van?" she asks.

"No. Close to the shore."

She washes off several beer cans and sets them in a clean tub, then holds one up in the light. I lean in for a closer look. It's a Pabst Blue Ribbon special.

"What do you see?" I ask.

"Oh, just thinking about an idea for a research paper. Comparing historical middens with modern ones. How much does the quality of the alcoholic vessel tell you about the socioeconomics of the people who deposited them?"

"You mean like tracking the Egyptian economy by their wine jars?" I ask.

"Something like that. While we can't reliably count on court records for minor economic fluctuations, the size and quality of the vessels might tell us if there was economic hardship at that time."

That's my PhD adviser. She's not exactly scatterbrained—more like a laser beam that obliterates things at random with incredible precision.

She reaches the last tub and reveals a small lawn-mower wheel. "What exactly are you trying to establish?"

"I don't know. I was chasing a theory."

"Was this helpful?"

"Well, it didn't exactly support my premise. It didn't falsify it."

"So your theory has precisely as much supporting evidence as another theory that has yet to be falsified."

"More or less."

"So now what?"

"I guess I just drop it."

This draws a "hmm" from her.

"What?"

"Maybe that's the right response. I don't really understand your police work. But if this was a research project, I'd suggest that you try not to make your hypothesis too narrow."

I'm sure there's wisdom in that statement. But I'm not in the mood. I'm in the doghouse with George and myself for my stunt. I'm not sure which feels worse—his disapproval or my self-loathing.

I gather up the tubs and stack them. "May I leave this here for a few days?" I ask.

"Sure. And next time you go into an alligator den, make sure he's not coming home anytime soon—that's unless you want to make Jackie my permanent lab assistant."

CHAPTER EIGHTEEN
MISFIRE

Halfway between the university and my boat, I get an urgent text message from Hughes:

Meet us at new winds marina asap

That's a luxury yacht dock in Palm Beach—which suggests his message is related to the New River Bandits. I put the blue light on my dashboard and drive as fast as safely possible at this time of night.

The marina is filled with police cars, and I see two hovering news helicopters. I flash my badge—which is actually an FDLE badge and another reason they want to absorb us—and make my way through the police line, where George and Hughes are talking to a Marine Patrol captain.

Behind them stands a 150-foot yacht, *The Storybook Princess*. Palm Beach Sheriff's Office forensic technicians are aboard, taking photos and dusting for fingerprints.

I listen in as George talks to Captain Buckley about a search perimeter and pulling surveillance videos from the area.

Hughes takes a half step next to me and explains in a quiet voice, "An hour ago, three men robbed the boat. It belongs to some internet gaming guy. Apparently, he kept a lot of cash on board. It looks like the bad guys barged in, zip-tied the crew, and stole the money."

"I see."

"Highway Patrol stopped an SUV a half a mile from here for running a stop sign. The driver had ID; the two others didn't."

"Well, that's interesting."

"No guns. No money. Palm Beach Sheriff's Office thinks they might not be connected. It's been suggested the crew staged the whole thing."

"What about the marina cameras?" I ask, looking up at a security camera on a post.

"Funny thing—they were all off-line."

"That benefits either the crew or their alleged robbers. Are they here?" I ask.

"Yes. Palm Beach Sheriff's Office is talking to them in the restaurant at the end of the pier. Want to see what they're saying?"

"I trust you guys on that one. Think I can have a look at the boat?"

Hughes turns to George and Captain Buckley. "We'd like to have a look at the boat." He directs his question to George, reinforcing the idea that this is our case.

"Your people have an issue with that?" George asks the captain.

"Be my guest. But other than the prints we're pulling from the latches and the safe, there's not much in the way of evidence." He glances at me. "And we searched the crew quarters."

"There are a lot more places to look," I reply.

"DEA already ran a dog through that can smell currency."

"And?"

"She barked at the places where the money was kept. That was it."

"How much money?"

"Dustin Sanchis, the owner, was kind of hesitant at first. Then he realized that he'll never get it back if he can't put a number on it. He said it was between six and eight million dollars."

"Between?" I'd love to live in a world where a two-million-dollar rounding error is no big deal for me. "All right. Let's go find this jerk's cash."

Hughes and I pull gloves from our pockets and walk up the gangplank to the yacht. At least Sanchis knows his boats. He decided on more deck space and a garage underneath for Jet Skis and dive gear instead of using all the space to build a floating mansion with huge cabins and less room to enjoy the ocean.

Some yacht owners forget that their boats are meant to go out to sea and basically turn them into floating hotels with little to do.

Hughes and I walk into the main salon and then down a corridor leading to the owner's cabin. It's huge. A king-size bed stands against one wall, with three massive flat-screen TVs—one on each side—suspended from the ceiling.

"Three screens? What's that about?" I ask.

"Porn," says Hughes, attracting the attention of a forensic tech dusting the cabinets. "Um, I mean, I guess."

"Okay. But three?"

Red-faced, Hughes points to a small camera on top of a television. Each screen has one. They're all aimed at the bed.

"For crying out loud . . . you mean he was filming himself?"

"Not necessarily himself," replies the technician.

"I don't suppose the cameras were on when this place was robbed?"

"Um, no," replies the tech. "Not then . . . but . . ."

I hold up my hand. "I don't want to know any more. Where's the safe?"

"Follow me." He leads us to the bathroom behind the bedroom. It's bigger than the master bath in Run's house. "Here you go."

I look around. All I see is an empty closet behind a mirrored wall. "Wait? That's the safe?"

"Yep. The cash was supposed to be in duffel bags inside there."

"Good grief." I inspect the latch that held the door closed. While the wall of the safe is thick metal, the frame where it was bolted has an aluminum edge. All the thieves or crew had to do was use a small pry bar to pop the door. Anybody could have busted in there.

"What do you think, Hughes?"

"Anybody could have broken in," he replies.

Smart minds think alike. I turn to the technician. "I'm not asking directly. But hypothetically, if someone reviewed the footage those cameras recorded . . . are we talking local talent?"

"In every port of call," he replies.

"So Game Boy was probably paying them out of the stash in the back. Which means everybody knows about this safe. That certainly doesn't narrow things down. Assuming it's not the crew or the three gentlemen they stopped. Any word on that?"

"I'll call Solar," says Hughes.

"Okay. Let's go have a look at something else."

We walk back down the corridor and onto the deck of the boat. At the far end is a set of steps that leads to the wet locker, the large, garage-like room on the back of the boat that opens up to the diving platform.

Inside the room there are three Jet Skis, an inflatable raft, a small powerboat that can pull a water-skier, and a bunch of pool toys and life jackets. Fishing gear hangs from one wall. On the other, racks of scuba equipment.

Hughes and I use our flashlights to probe into the dark spaces. As we do this, I hear sounds on the steps and turn to see a Palm Beach detective.

"We already searched down here," she says. "But you're welcome to it. There's also storage lockers under your feet."

Hughes nods. "I was here."

"Oh, this is your second time?" I ask. "Why didn't you tell me?"

"Another pair of eyes is another pair of eyes. Maybe you notice something we didn't."

"That hasn't been working out so well lately for me." I inspect the diving BCs, tanks, and regulators. All the kind of equipment you'd buy if you walked into a dive shop and flashed a bunch of money. It's not bad stuff, but it's not what I'd use. The masks are pretty good. The fins aren't bad. Although I've been trimming mine down for inshore diving.

I run my light along the gear and inspect the lockers. Inside one of them I find five pouch weights that you slide into the vests to adjust buoyancy. I go back and inspect the vests.

Hughes walks over and aims his light at the vests as I count them. There are eight total.

Eight buoyancy compensators and only five weights. Each vest holds at least two. Plus there should be some weighted dive belts.

"What's up?" asks Hughes.

"Tell them not to let the crew leave." I call to the detective, "When you searched the boat, did you search the water below it?"

"Did we put a diver in the water?" she asks. "Negative. We thought that's what you did."

"You bring your gear?" I ask Hughes.

He nods.

Thirty minutes later, we're surfacing and handing two duffel bags to George and Captain Buckley on the dive platform.

"You've almost redeemed yourself," says George.

"Almost? We got the New River Bandits," I reply as I strip off my gear.

"No. I think we caught a couple of opportunistic crew members who were hoping we would blame the New River Bandits. But still, good work." He weighs the bag. "That's at least eight million dollars between the two of them."

"Great. Then I want more time on the van case."

George looks around at the other police and Hughes. "Are you"—he bites back a curse—"effing kidding me?"

"Nope. While I was down there, I had a realization."

"While you were underwater and your brain was starved of oxygen, you had a realization?"

"To-mah-to, tomato, but yeah. Just give me one more day. If I'm wrong, I'll never mention it again."

"I doubt that. I really doubt that."

I don't. Because this time I'm really, really sure I'm not wrong.

CHAPTER NINETEEN
RESIDUE

Dr. Felix Aguilló's wife, a short, trim older woman with bleach-blonde hair, answers the door in a bathrobe and stares at me for a moment, trying to figure out who the hell I am. It's almost ten p.m., not the most unreasonable hour to talk to somebody in my opinion. But my judgment can be suspect.

I tracked the doctor to a suburb of Miami and decided talking to him at home was the best approach, given the limited time George allowed me. And to be honest, I wanted to catch him a little off guard.

I show her my badge. "I work with your husband. I wanted to ask him something."

"Felix, one of your work friends is here." She doesn't let me step inside.

A moment later, Aguilló comes to the door in an untucked collared shirt and shorts, holding an iPad at his side. He locks eyes with me. "You . . ." Over his shoulder, he says, "It's okay, honey, I have this."

His wife walks away, mumbling something about his working hours. Aguilló regards me for a moment, then holds up his iPad.

"I just saw the news about the bust. Please tell me it's about that."

"No. It's about the van."

"You come to my house at . . ." He realizes his watch is missing, so he checks his iPad screen. "At ten o'clock at night to bother me about *that*? Case closed. Or rather, it is as far as we're concerned."

"I understand that. It's just that . . . I had some more questions."

"I should call your boss right now and complain. But, to be honest, I'm impressed you're here this late. I can't get the people in my lab to stay late without them complaining about overtime." He steps away from the door. "All right, come in."

I follow Aguilló to the kitchen table, where various scientific journals are spread around. I stop to look at them.

"I take my work home too," he says.

"And then some." I take the seat he indicates. "Listen, forget for a moment about our departments."

"You barely have one, so that's not hard," he replies.

He sounds like Marquez. "Forget about that. Forget we're police. Forget what we've determined."

"That's a lot of forgetting."

"I'm trying to frame this," I explain.

"Poorly."

"I know we stepped on some toes. But can we put aside the politics for a moment and just think about those kids? I don't know what Marquez wanted you to write, but when I went through your report, it was much more thorough than the summary. It felt like there were conclusions you held back on because . . . well, I don't know. My point is . . ."

"Please get to it." He yawns.

"I pull odd things out of the water all the time. Evidence. Bodies. Weapons. Just give me your honest opinion. Forget there was a van. If I brought you the bodies of Grace and Caitlin and only told you that they were found in a canal, what would your assumption be?"

"They died from traumatic injury and were dumped there," he replies.

103

"No. That's not what your report would say."

"Excuse me? Who's writing this?"

"The same guy who made a note that their underwear was on inside out and ripped in a manner implying someone tried to redress them. I've looked at other cases you've handled. Good ones, where your evidence got convictions. I've even read courtroom testimony where you've called similar discoveries 'emphatic evidence of sexual assault.'"

Aguilló's eyes narrow as he realizes I've trapped him with his own words. "So what?"

"So what? Your final report didn't mention that. Not even a hint. Just a clinical description. You wanted to say something, but you didn't. Instead you just reported all the facts you thought were suspicious but without interpretation. I thought that was because you wanted someone like me to find them. Now I realize it was a matter of ego. You didn't want us to take the bodies elsewhere and have someone else call you out for missing it."

"You're making a lot of assumptions there. But let's play this game for a moment. Let's say that it looks like the girls were raped before they died. Then what? Their rapists are dead too."

"Are they? It sounds like you're assuming Tim and Dylan assaulted the girls. Maybe someone else did. Like, at the concert."

"And then we're back to where we started," he replies.

"No. We're not. Then we have a rapist who may have killed them but didn't die in the van."

"And no DNA evidence. And no case. We can't prove rape. We can't single out a suspect."

"But what about a murderer?" I reply.

"What?"

I take a pair of X-rays from my bag and set them on the table. "Both boys had neck fractures, not just the one driving, right? What's this on the back of Dylan's head?" I point to a small fracture.

"Probably caused in the accident."

"Okay. What about here on Tim's temple?" I point to a fracture on the left side of his head.

"Another fracture from the accident."

I shake my head and peel a label off the bottom of Tim's X-ray. It reads, "B. Guillaum." I pull a label off the other and reveal the name T. Ridden.

Both of these victims came from other cases Aguilló handled. They were taxi drivers who were assaulted and, in Ridden's case, killed by a robber.

I showed the doctor images he identified in another case as clear examples of a fracture from impact with a blunt object, not trauma from a car accident.

Aguilló realizes my trick. "Clever."

"Tim and Dylan had almost the exact same injuries. That's why you confused them. Both had the same fatal injuries. It's impossible to tell which one was driving—or if either was behind the wheel at all."

"Okay, Ridden and Guillaum were assaulted with a blunt object, but the van was clean," he says.

"Yes. The van was clean." I reach into my bag and pull out a large plastic evidence bag and let it fall on the table with a clang.

The tire iron.

"I found this near where the van came to rest. I didn't think much of it until another case triggered something. If we'd just found Tim's and Dylan's bodies floating in the canal, we would have looked for these injuries. Same with Caitlin and Grace. The van was a self-contained package. We didn't care what was on the outside, because we assumed the whole story was inside. It wasn't."

"Caitlin and Grace didn't have similar injuries," he replies.

"Because they were drugged. Did you do a chemical analysis of the beer cans?"

"No. I didn't need to." Aguilló looks out the window and into his own reflection. "Item number sixty-three on the list. It's listed as a metal alcoholic container."

"A beer can?"

"No. A flask. We found residue," he replies.

"What kind?"

"Inconclusive."

"Cut the bullshit!" I snap.

"It could have been Rohypnol. Or not. It was thirty years old," he says weakly.

"Two girls are drugged and violated. Two young men are killed or knocked unconscious, and their vehicle is driven into the water. What does that look like to you?"

"Marquez said it was too tenuous."

"You ran this by her?"

A nod. "I didn't know about the tire iron. I only suspected the possibility that there was another assailant, but to be brutally honest, I convinced myself that Dylan and Tim did it."

I'm about to tell him that his insight would have saved me a trip into the alligator den looking for a fifth victim. But there wasn't a fifth victim. There was a murderer who covered his tracks and got away.

"I can't believe I let her convince me to drop it," he says after a long pause. "I used to be better than that."

"It's okay. I understand."

"No. You don't. Hold on a moment." He leaves the table and goes to a different part of the house.

I try not to judge Aguilló too harshly. He has tons of cases to handle and isn't free to choose which to pursue. If his bosses tell him to drop it, he doesn't have much choice—especially in a case this old.

Aguilló returns with a thick folder. "If you mention me in connection to this, I'll deny everything. I won't testify for you. You'll get nothing. Understand?"

I shrug. "Fine."

"You don't understand. This is my reputation on the line."

"I said fine. I get it."

He slides a photograph across the table of the body of a young woman lying in the grass near a thick copse of trees. Her clothes are torn, and there are ligature marks around her neck.

"October 1990. Sia Krimmer. She was a student at Miami-Dade Community College. She went missing at seven p.m. She was found like this four days later." He pulls another photo from the folder. This one shows a red-haired young woman on a floor with a wire around her neck. "Amanda Wiseman. She and her boyfriend were killed in 1992. I have eight others like this, going through 1997."

"Okay . . . ? Florida has over a thousand murders a year. What's the connection?"

"This doesn't leave this room," he says softly. "At least my involvement I can't be attached to the theory." He pulls several typewritten sheets from the folder. "This is the evidence inventory. Either from what was found near the body or at the scene of an abduction."

I scan through the sheets and find that he has highlighted certain words and phrases:

instant film casing

Polaroid film cartridge

box tab from instant film package

"You saw the inventory from the van?" he asks.

"Yeah. Hughes actually noticed the cartridge."

I flip through the pages of other items found in relation to the murders. In total, they number in the thousands. That's why the film-related items weren't obvious.

"I even checked to make sure this wasn't material left behind by our own forensic team," he explains.

"All these cases . . ."

"We had suspects in some. But no convictions. All are unsolved."

"So you think that there is some serial killer taking Polaroids of his victims?"

"Nope. That's what you're saying. But if it were true, then our victim zero would be the kids in that van."

"And our killer stopped in 1997?"

"Could be. Or maybe he went digital."

CHAPTER TWENTY
WALL OF SHAME

"Here we go," says George as he walks into our headquarters and sees the large map of Florida I've stuck to the wall, alongside a grid of twenty mug shots. "I'm going to guess this has nothing to do with the New River Bandits?"

"Um, no."

"Not even tangentially?"

"Not a chance. I didn't know our policy was one crime at a time."

He looks at my map. "You know they only do this in movies. It's the kind of thing a crazy person does to convince everyone else they're not crazy." He takes a seat by the table facing my map. "All right. Let's hear it."

"Where's Hughes?"

"Following some leads on the New River Bandits. Where I should be. Where you should be."

"If you're not convinced, then that'll become one hundred percent of my focus. But remember, you gave me one more day."

"And apparently you spent it making the biggest damn map of Florida I've ever seen. Anyway, proceed."

I walk up to the map and point to Pond 65. "This is where we found the victims."

"You mean the crashed van?" says George, trying to steer the conversation.

"I mean the four murder victims."

George's posture tightens, but his face remains inscrutable. "So it's murder now?"

"Tim and Dylan *both* had neck fractures *and* injuries consistent with blows to the head. And Hughes pointed out that Dylan lacked the kind of facial injuries a driver usually gets in a crash." I pull the tire iron out of a cardboard box. "I found this where the van was recovered."

"An angry motorist threw it," says George, challenging me.

"Okay. Possible. This is a Chevrolet L-bar that came in a standard tire-repair kit. There's nothing special or rare about it—except for the fact that the Chevy van we pulled from the water that was supposed to have been intact was missing exactly one thing from the tire kit in back."

George nods and leans in. I have his attention now. The skull fractures were compelling, but the weapon missing from the van and found outside the vehicle is the clincher for him. Not that he's convinced by a long shot, but now it's too much for him to ignore.

I step to the table to retrieve the folder with my other evidence. It's circumstantial, but it might be enough.

"I get it," says George.

"Well, I have something else to show you."

"Sure. But I believe you. I believe you're not insane . . . at least about this. Something fishy *is* going on here. We need to look into this." He points to the mug shots. "Who are those assholes? Suspects, I assume?"

"Suspects in other murders. Possibly related to this one."

"Other murders?" He shakes his head, not in disbelief but trying to change his point of reference, I assume. "Those dots on the map? More murders?"

"Yes. I think there's a connection. The last one was well over a decade ago, but I think there are probably more, because the evidence connecting them is . . . well . . . you'll see."

"Hold up," says George. "You're telling me you think this is a serial killer case?"

"Active," I reply. "I think there's an active serial killer."

"And what part of that is underwater?"

"Pond 65 is where it started. You think the FBI will take this on? Or any of the local departments?"

"No. We'll need to brief them, but they won't make a move on it unless we get some heat."

"Then great. If we can make a case, I'm all for handing it off to some other agency. But we can't ignore it."

"No, we can't. Okay, walk me through what happened."

"What I think or what I know?"

"What your gut tells you."

I smile. "Okay, I think Tim, Dylan, Grace, and Caitlin went to that concert. I think they met someone there. Maybe someone they knew peripherally. Not necessarily a close friend, but maybe someone who had their trust. Probably someone the girls already knew. They hung out. They all went back to the van to get high or to drink. That's when our fifth person drugged the girls with something in a flask. Check the lab report on that. There might have been an argument with Dylan and Tim. Maybe not. At some point our fifth person struck the boys with the tire iron. Possibly in the parking lot. Maybe at another location. Then he took the van to another location, and that's where the girls were undressed. Possibly violated before drowning.

"Our suspect then realized he had to do something with the bodies. That's when he went out to Pond 65, which was even more remote back then, drove the vehicle into the water, and swam away."

George considers this for a moment. "You think the suspect drove the van into the water himself? That seems like a dumb way to do it."

"Maybe. It could have been a failed suicide. Also, remember that he was probably a teenager himself, so it might've seemed like a perfectly reasonable idea."

"All right. I'm not fully convinced. But that's . . . plausible." He says the last word with some difficulty. "Now explain why you think he's an active serial killer."

"It's thin, I'll admit. But I'm not the only one who has thought along these lines."

"You've spoken to someone else about this?"

"Yes. An anonymous person who thought the case didn't add up but didn't want to go against the head of a certain four-letter law enforcement agency."

"Got it. So what did he or she say?"

"This is a map of other crime scenes. Mostly in South Florida. The victims are almost always younger, attractive females. Sometimes there are males with the females. But never a male alone. In each case the male appears to have been incapacitated and the woman violated, but no DNA is ever left behind."

"That's not exactly a narrow profile," says George.

"There's one other factor. In every single one of these murders, a piece of packaging from instant-camera film was found nearby and logged as evidence. Not always close by, but somewhere near the scene."

"He's taking photos."

I nod.

"Lots of people had those cameras back then."

"The majority of our victims didn't. We found a film cartridge in the van, but none of the kids owned a Polaroid camera."

"Tenuous," says George.

"It's a start. And there's one other thing." I pull the bag with the half-nude Polaroid of Grace from my evidence box. "This was in

Caitlin's belongings. When I first saw it, it looked like a little joke between them."

"You think our killer took the photo?"

"Or they did it with his camera sometime before the concert. I think he may have been a guy they knew but their boyfriends didn't. Maybe a little older. Maybe a little more interesting."

"Maybe a little more psychotic," says George. "Okay. What are the next steps?"

That catches me off guard. I've been so worried about persuading him that I haven't really thought through what happens after that. "I . . . um. Well, there's this list of suspects in the other cases. We could start by interviewing them."

"Sure, we could see how they respond to questions about the other cases. Might help rule them out. But what's the main plan?" he asks. "What are we going to do that the other investigators didn't? It can't be brute-force, nose-to-the-ground background checks. We don't have the resources."

I contemplate this for a moment. "Well . . . we should start with the Pond 65 case. That was his first kill, as far as we know. There's a good chance it's also where he was at his sloppiest. I guess I can start by looking into who the kids knew and talking to their classmates. Maybe someone noticed a creepy serial killer type."

"With a penchant for Polaroids." He shrugs. "You might be surprised. You know why Jeffrey Dahmer didn't stand out in high school even though he was a classic weirdo that liked to kill animals? Because he wasn't the weirdest kid in school. Find out who the other weirdos were. Not just the obvious ones. They don't have to be people that were known to hang out with our subjects."

"You think a classmate could have done this?" I ask.

"Probably not. But here's the thing about weirdos—they're the best at telling you who the other weirdos are."

"Okay. I'll start with the guy who spoke at the memorial."

"He a weirdo?"

"More of a busybody narcissist."

"All right. I'll give Amelia Teng a call and see if she wants to stop by."

"Teng?" I've never heard him mention her name.

"Criminal psychologist. One of the good ones. She worked with us on profiling. Not the voodoo kind. Solid statistical stuff. She reminds me of your professor. All about the numbers."

"Okay, great." I nod at the mug shots on the wall. "I'll also track down some of the suspects."

"With Hughes. I don't want you talking to them alone," says George.

"That's a bit . . ."

"Sensible. Complain all you want, but that's gonna be our policy with potential sex-offender interviews. Got it?"

"Yeah." I tell myself I could take any of those losers in a fair fight. But it's never a fair fight.

"Good. Now, in your extra time, I still want your brain on the New River Bandits. Got it?"

"Got it."

CHAPTER TWENTY-ONE
Weirdos

Randy Fulton is already waiting for me at Lester's Diner when I arrive. He's wearing a polo shirt and a sports coat, a look I've seen on journalists before. It kind of says, "I tried." My own professional attire consists of slacks, a polo, and a jacket that I wear over my gun when it's not too hot. I kind of miss the beat-cop uniform.

"Detective McPherson," he says as he tries awkwardly to get up from the booth.

"Please, sit." I slide in across from him and ask the waitress for a cup of coffee.

"We didn't get a chance to speak at the memorial," he says.

"Yeah. I was talking to the parents."

"Oh, and how did that go?" he asks with a reporter's curiosity.

"It was emotional. Anyhow, I wanted to ask you a few questions."

"And I, you," he says pulling out a notebook.

"Um, are you writing an article about this?"

"No. A book, actually."

Okay. "I see." He's got a probing look in his eyes, like he's already writing this scene in his head. "Anything we talk about will have to be off the record."

Fulton makes a show of snapping his notebook closed. "Then I'm afraid we have nothing to talk about unless you come back with a subpoena. And let me assure you that I have excellent counsel."

I can't stop from rolling my eyes. "Are you for real?" I gather myself. "Let me put it this way, Mr. Fulton. There are two sets of questions I can ask. The ones where I trust you and you find out a little bit more about the case but don't source it back to me. Or the smaller set that you'll find pretty boring."

He pauses for a moment. "Is this about the fact that Tim and Dylan raped the girls?"

He's wrong about that, but he knows something. I almost ask him how he got hold of the coroner's full report. Instead, I take a breath and try to play it cool. Maybe he knows something else. "What are you talking about?"

"You're not a very good liar."

"How would you know? I asked you a question. I didn't say one way or another if what you said was true."

"I'm a political reporter. I deal with the best liars in the world every day," he replies.

"If they're so good at lying, how come everyone thinks 'lying politician' is a redundancy? But you're right. I'm not a good liar. Which is why I don't bother trying. So why don't you tell me what you're talking about."

I need to know if he's talking about a recent revelation, possibly from the internal report, or something he knew from back in high school.

"I have my sources, off the record."

Okay, so it's a recent revelation. "No rumors about that back when you were in high school with them, then?"

He blinks at my question. "Well, they were an odd group."

"Did you even know them? I'm beginning to think your only connection was seeing your old high school in the news."

"Of course I knew them."

Time to call his bluff. I check my watch and start to slide out of the booth. "You're wasting my time. I have other people to talk to."

Fulton watches his single best source for his book get up to leave. "Hold up, Detective. We might be able to help each other."

"It sounds pretty one-way. I don't think you know anything about anything."

His nostrils flare. "Really? Did you know that Caitlin was sexually abused by her stepfather? The same man at the memorial?"

I sit back down. "And how do you know this?"

"Sources."

"Thirty-year-old sources? New ones? I'm not asking for names. Just a shred of credibility."

"She had a peer counselor. An older student she could confide in. She told her that she'd been abused."

"The peer counselor told you this?" I ask.

"Among other things. Caitlin begged her not to tell anyone, so she didn't at the time."

"I see." Okay, Fulton knows more than I realized. I have to keep stringing him along without divulging the real thrust of my case. "I'm trying to track down a diary that belonged to her. It went missing after she did. It wasn't in the van."

"Interesting," He makes a note of this.

"Who did the kids hang out with?"

"Themselves, mostly. There were a few other lowlifes that would hang out across the street from the school in the morning and smoke before class," he says.

"Did anyone stand out in particular?"

"There was one kid, Ethan Rafferty. They called him Rattery. Tall kid. Long, curly, blond hair. Looked like the overweight member of a heavy metal band. He drove an old beat-up Buick to school. Sometimes I'd see Tim and Dylan with him. Once or twice, the girls. Caitlin may have dated him for a month or two after Dylan dropped out."

"Was there anything unusual about him?" I ask.

"He was a big LSD user. I think he had issues to begin with. His dad was a cop, funny enough."

Yeah, hilarious. "Did he have any kind of record?"

"Besides possession? They all did. But it was a joke. The juvenile court judge would let them go with a wrist slap—more like a hug."

"Nothing violent?"

"Like fighting? Not then. Not that I know about."

"What do you mean, 'not then'?"

Fulton makes an unpleasant smirk. "Rattery developed a bit of a meth habit. Quite the record now."

The glee with which he says this annoys the heck out of me. What's his problem? Was he the guy who could never get laid in high school and is still bitter about it? Maybe there's something more. Of the two girls, Caitlin was the more conventionally attractive one . . .

"Tell me about Caitlin. You said that you really didn't know the group. But what about her? Did you have a connection?"

"You mean, did we . . . ? Oh no. She wasn't my type." *Human?*

"Did you talk?"

"We had a couple classes. I helped her with some homework."

Bingo. Teenage Fulton had a crush on her. I wonder if he tried to act on it? What happened?

"I met Dylan's father. He's a piece of work."

"That whole family was," replies Fulton.

"The dad came across as a bit of a bully."

"Like father, like son."

Here we go. This might be why Fulton seemed almost gleeful calling Tim and Dylan rapists. "You ever have an encounter with him?"

Fulton's eyes narrow. "Both of them. They weren't nice people."

"What happened?"

"I don't want to talk about it."

"Let me guess: Dylan caught you talking to Caitlin, so he and Tim jumped you." I try to make it sound like it's not a big deal.

"Something like that. They could be mean."

"Yet you said nice things at the memorial."

"I've tried to forgive."

By writing a book accusing your teenage enemies of being rapists?

"Anyone else they hung out with?"

He shrugs. "Nobody worth mentioning."

Man, Fulton's childhood trauma runs deep. I'd try to coax more from him, but I think I've reached the limit for today.

"So, answer me this question, Detective: Why are you still asking questions about this case? Are you going to investigate Tim and Dylan for rape?"

"Nope."

"No? Because it's an old case or because you're afraid of the fallout from the families?"

"Neither. Because I have no reason to believe that Dylan and Tim participated in any kind of rape."

Fulton scrutinizes my face, trying to see if I'm lying. "I see." He looks dejected. "Thank you. I'm sure we'll be in touch."

As I walk out of the restaurant, I see a text message from Hughes:

get here asap
found a partial print match in an active crime scene

It's followed by an address.
I text back:

New River Bandits?

He replies a moment later:

No
a partial match between your cold cases and a new murder

CHAPTER TWENTY-TWO
DITCHED

At first, I think I have the address wrong. The GPS in my truck takes me to the northwestern part of Broward County and one of the last undeveloped parcels of land before you get to the Everglades. When I turn a bend in the dirt road, I see a line of police cars and a forensic van.

Hughes is talking to a woman wearing a Broward Sheriff's Office jacket. I exit my vehicle and walk over to them. Despite all the activity, the sound of the cicadas creates a constant hum.

"Sloan McPherson, this is Detective Hoffer," says Hughes.

She's a tad shorter than me and has auburn hair pulled back into a ponytail. Her grip is strong and confident. "I don't believe we've formally met."

I glance over her shoulder at a group of people standing on a berm overlooking what I assume is a ditch. If there's a body here, that would have to be the spot.

The roads look like they were carved out for eventual construction a few years ago. The brush is overgrown, and the grass is weedy and tall.

It's one of the last good places to dump a body in this area—if you're too lazy to go a hundred yards west and drop it in the Everglades.

"What's the situation?" I ask.

"The body belongs to Alyssa Rennie," explains Hoffer. "She was reported missing five days ago. We did a preliminary search of her town house and saw signs of a potential struggle."

"Boyfriend?"

"Missing too. The fight might have been between him and an assailant. We found some blood at the scene but haven't matched it to anyone we found yet." She gestures to the berm and the group standing on it. "Her body was found this morning by a trail biker. Strangle marks on the neck, although the preliminary exam shows minimal bruising."

"She was unconscious?"

"Possibly."

"What about the boyfriend? What do we know about him?"

"Jared Sanna. Coworker. They both work at Seagrass Financial Services. They started dating and spending time at one another's places a few months ago. No record on him."

"What's the connection?" I ask Hughes.

"They found a partial print in her place. It matched two of the crime scenes on your wall."

A chill runs down my spine. We found the van eight days ago. Did its discovery agitate our killer? Is this woman dead because of me?

"This one was five days ago?"

"That's when she was reported missing," says Hoffer.

"Don't even go there," Hughes says to me. "Chances are the killer already had her picked out. And we don't *know* when she was killed. It might have been before."

His words do little to make me feel better. Logically, there's no way I could have known, but emotionally I'm afraid I've opened Pandora's box. What if he'd gone dormant? Have I reawakened a serial killer into action?

"What else do we know?" I ask.

"Not much," says Hoffer. "We're still gathering evidence from the scene. If I had to guess, she's been here a few days. Assuming this is connected, what can you tell me about the suspect we're looking for?"

"Well, until a day ago, we didn't even know there was a killer in the van case. But if it's the same guy, he'd have to be in his late forties or early fifties now. He's from here, at least since he was a teenager. We're looking to see if he went to high school with them."

"That's a start. Let's keep talking and pool our resources."

"Can I take a look at the body?" I ask.

"Follow me."

She leads Hughes and me over to the berm and introduces us to her supervisors and the two other detectives on the scene. Some of them are familiar faces, but I didn't know their names.

The ditch is an unfinished storm drain that runs the length of the property. Yellow grass and crushed meadow fox plants partially cover her body. She's nude from the waist up and wearing pantyhose ripped at the sides. Her head is tilted to an angle with her hand near her chin. If it weren't for the decomposition, she could be sleeping.

Hughes glances at the body, then turns away. Probably seeing his wife or daughter in her place. I get it. I've been there . . . every time I look at a body.

I glance around the crime scene. Yellow tape marks off certain sections, while small plastic signs denote objects of interest like bent grass or partial footprints. Back on the road, forensic technicians are making castings of tire tracks.

"We've got several tread prints," says Hoffer. "That might help us narrow things down a bit."

I turn from the body and walk up the other side of the berm. It ends in a sharp drop to a tangle of mangroves and the water of the canal that runs alongside the Everglades Wildlife Management Area.

In places, the mangroves give way to patches of open, rocky shore. It's part of a fourteen-mile stretch of water carved out by the Army Corps of Engineers. At both ends there are boat launches and small parks.

I spin around and stare at the body again. "He dumped her from the canal," I say aloud.

This attracts the attention of the other detectives. "What makes you say that?" asks Hoffer.

"Because if he was in a car with the body, he'd have just gone out to Alligator Alley and dumped it there. I think he pulled into a boat launch, had her in his craft, and was going to dump her in the Everglades. Something spooked him, so he landed here instead. Maybe somebody saw him?"

"Like Fish and Wildlife?" asks Hoffer.

I was thinking an airboat tour, but that's a better idea. "Yeah. It's just a guess, but I think if you come this far, there's no reason not to go farther out unless you can't."

"Interesting," Hoffer murmurs.

"It also makes it look like the victim was dumped from a car here, without having to actually use a car. If he got spooked and wanted to get rid of the body away from the water, then hiking it up here makes the most sense."

Hoffer calls out to the other detectives, "Let's get forensics over there and check for footprints."

Realizing I might be standing on evidence, I tread a large, curving arc back to the others, avoiding the path between the body and the canal.

Hughes and I walk back to our parked vehicles to let the BSO techs work. Both of us have our eyes fixed on the ground, looking for anything out of the ordinary.

"What's next?" asks Hughes.

We both know the waiting game can take forever while forensics tries to find evidence, but neither of us is content to sit still.

"I think the killer had more than a casual connection to the victims. Or the night they died wasn't the first time they met . . . or at least not the first time the girls met him."

"Too bad we can't just pull up their Facebook profiles and see who they knew."

"Yeah—1989. I couldn't even find phone records. Let alone a social network. What did they use back then?"

"The mall? MTV?" Hughes shrugs.

Kids had to have expressed themselves in other ways. Communication wasn't just telephone calls and hallway conversations. What was the 1989 version of Facebook?

I slap my hand against my forehead. Of course. "What was the original Facebook?" I ask Hughes.

"Myspace? Friendster?"

"No, way before that. It was *yearbooks*. High school yearbooks."

"I think we have one back at the office," says Hughes. "It's where we got the photos from."

"I don't mean the yearbook itself. I'm talking about all the inscriptions kids leave in them at the end of the year. Who signed whose yearbook? What did they say? That was their Facebook back then. We need to try to get ahold of all of their class's yearbooks we can and try to create a map of who knew who."

"I'll get on it," says Hughes.

"Great. One more thing." I spot Hoffer talking to another detective. "Excuse me, quick question." I pull Ethan Rafferty's file up on my phone. "I'm trying to find a particular meth head. Any suggestions?"

Hoffer hands my phone to another detective. He thumbs through to the last arrest report. "Seventy-Two Hundred Pines Avenue," he says.

I think for a moment. "That's not a home. That's a street."

"Correct. It's also near a homeless encampment. The county won't let us shut it down. But if that's where he got picked up last, that's where you'll probably find him. It's right where the bus ends." He smirks. "Wear gloves. Double carry."

Great. "Well," I tell Hughes, "ready to visit hoboville?"

CHAPTER TWENTY-THREE
DISPLACED

You'd think a homeless camp would be easy to find since you always seem to run into them when you're not looking for one, but this encampment's elusive. It's after dark, and Hughes and I have been up and down 7200 for the last half hour, looking for tents, shanties, or cars on blocks. All we've seen are some rather large raccoons crossing the road. I'm beginning to suspect that we were misled. That or the county decided to dismantle the camp.

"What now?" asks Hughes as we make our fifth trip up the highway.

"Either it ain't here, they're using some Harry Potter cloak of invisibility, or they're nearby and we just can't see them."

"I've also noticed that there's a lack of homeless people coming to or from said camp."

"Hold on." I take out my phone and look at a map of the area. I search for bus stops and find there's one a mile down the road at the entrance to Butterfly Park. "Ah. We need to think like pedestrians. Go back to the park entrance."

Hughes drives us to the gate. "Now what?"

"Now we get out and walk."

We take out our flashlights and follow the fence until we come to a line of dense bushes and trees. When I shine my light at the base of the fence, I spot a narrow footpath along the outside perimeter leading into the woods.

I start down the path, using my light to keep from walking into spiderwebs or human feces. "If I was ten and didn't know there was a shantytown of drug addicts and felons at the other end of this path, I'd think this was a magical adventure."

"Just think of them as goblins," replies Hughes.

"That really doesn't help. You ever hear of sea goblins?" I ask.

"No. Is that a thing?"

"It was when I grew up. I was told that if I didn't go to sleep at bedtime, the sea goblins would climb aboard and take me away. One night I fell asleep reading. I was woken up in the middle of the night by my grandfather yelling. Which wasn't unusual. In this case he was yelling at something to get off the boat—which would have been traumatic enough if my bed wasn't covered in seaweed."

"Your family is weird."

"This is true. Aren't they all?" I ask.

"Not like yours."

The path begins to widen out, and we come to a small clearing. A small blue tent is at one end with a pair of legs sticking out and a man snoring inside.

"Sounds like a goblin," says Hughes. He kneels by the man's feet and taps them with his flashlight. "Excuse me."

The man doesn't stop snoring.

Hughes taps again, then shakes the tent. "Pardon me."

A suntanned face with a bulbous red nose over a dark beard pops into view.

"Who's that?" he asks blearily.

Hughes reaches into his pocket and pulls out his badge before I can tell him not to. The man in the tent squints at it, then yells, "Pigs!"

"Damn it," I mutter, getting to my feet as the sound of voices shouting and running footsteps filters through the woods.

"Stop him," I yell back to Hughes.

In the glow of my flashlight, I see bedraggled men running in every direction into the brush like raccoons darting away from car headlights.

The first person I see is a tall man in an orange T-shirt hauling ass in the distance. May be Ethan Rafferty, maybe not, but I give chase. Whoever he is, and despite whatever medical conditions he may be suffering, adrenaline and his long legs enable him to make quick strides.

I chase after him and shout, "I just have some questions!"

"Fuck your questions," he yells back.

Well, the first step of diplomacy is dialogue. I keep after him, ignoring the others. "I just want to talk!"

He darts through a tangle of twisted branches, clearly having navigated this briar patch before. I, on the other hand, find myself getting scratched by twigs and tripped by fallen trees.

I spot him again as he starts booking down a nature trail. I think I can catch him on the straightaway, but I try a different tactic: pity.

"I can't keep up!" I shout.

The man stops cold in his tracks and wheels around to stare at me, confused. He's not Ethan Rafferty. Damn, I chased the wrong one.

"Fuck!" shouts Hughes from somewhere in back of me. I don't think I've ever heard him swear.

A gravelly voice yells, "STAY BACK, FUCKER!"

I turn on my heel and race back toward the commotion and get tangled a second time in the thick brush. Behind me comes the sound of snapping branches. The man I was chasing is now following me.

"Keep your distance!" I yell, catching him in the beam of my flashlight.

His hands are up in the air. "Don't shoot, lady. That's Mad Mike. He's, uh . . . mad. He just needs to calm down."

"If he doesn't, he's going to get shot." I hurry toward another clearing and find Hughes with his gun aimed at a small, wiry man with unkempt black hair down to his shoulders holding a hacksaw. Blood is trickling from Hughes's wrist.

"You okay?" I ask, pulling my own gun on Mad Mike.

"Yeah. I grabbed him by the shoulder. He swung on me. I'll need a tetanus shot after this."

I call to the man with the saw. "Hey, Mike, put down the saw."

Crazy eyes stare back at me. I remind myself that this is a man probably suffering from some mental health condition and not a comic-book villain. Now inside those eyes I see only fear and uncertainty.

I decide to de-escalate and put my gun back in my holster. Hughes keeps his drawn but aims it at the ground. Mike watches us both, unsure if this is a trick.

The man I chased comes clomping into the clearing. "Hey, Mike. Settle down."

"What's his condition?" I ask.

"Dunno. Crazy, I guess."

Over to the left is a small lean-to made of cardboard boxes and plastic sheeting. There's a bucket and a shopping cart next to it piled high with clothing, cans, and children's toys.

"Why don't you drop the saw and go back inside your home," I tell Mike.

"I'm not going to jail!"

I glance over at Hughes. "Is he going to jail?"

"I don't know. It depends." He asks the man behind us, "Is he violent?"

"He doesn't like to be surprised. But other than that, no. PTSD from Iraq, some say. But I'm pretty sure he was nuts before then."

"What unit you serve?" Hughes asks Mike.

Mike seems confused by the question, then replies, "Eighty-second." The rusty blade doesn't waver.

"You're not going to jail," says Hughes at last, holstering his gun.

Mike drops the saw blade and stumbles back to his hut. Under his breath, he grumbles something about fucking cops not leaving him alone.

I pull a handkerchief from my pocket and wrap Hughes's wrist. We can do proper first aid in the truck. And, yeah, Hughes will want to get shots at the hospital.

My partner glances over at the other man. "Is this the guy?"

"No," I say, then ask, "Do you know where I can find Ethan Rafferty?"

"You mean Rattery? I think you ran over him back there," the man says, pointing to where we came from.

Hughes and I retrace my steps. Sure enough, the log I thought I jumped over is actually a man in a brown sleeping bag, still sound asleep and snoring loudly.

"Rattery?" I say, prodding him with my foot.

"What the hell?" he says, wiping his eyes as my flashlight beam hits him in the face.

"I have some questions."

He falls back down. "Google 'em."

"Want me to kick the shit out of him until he talks?" asks Hughes. I assume he's joking.

"Be my guest," says Rafferty. "Watch the balls."

Without warning, Hughes leans over and rips open the sleeping bag. Rafferty rolls onto the dirt and stares back at us, confused.

To be honest, I'm a little shocked by Hughes myself. He reaches down and picks something up. A foil packet gleams in the flashlight's glow.

"What's this?" asks Hughes.

"It's not mine," says Rafferty.

"It will be if you don't start talking."

Rafferty pulls himself into a sitting position. "Seriously, it's not mine."

I kneel down. "I wanted to talk to you about Dylan Udal, Tim Kelly, Grace Sandalin, and Caitlin Barrow."

He stares at me for a long moment. Wheels are turning in his head. "The Whack Pack? They died a long time ago."

Something tells me he doesn't get the latest news. "How do you know they died?"

"Because I know who killed them." Rafferty squints into the beam of my flashlight. "But you won't believe me."

CHAPTER TWENTY-FOUR
FIFTH WHEEL

Rafferty puffs at a vape pen as Hughes and I sit across from him at a park picnic table. The only light is the bright moon overhead. A cold breeze occasionally drifts across the grass and makes the humidity a little more tolerable.

"Like I said, you're not going to believe me. But trust me, everything I'm telling you is true."

Neither Hughes nor I say anything because we don't want to interrupt the man, but I have a feeling that when a meth addict tells you he's going to share something unbelievable with you, it's probably not an exaggeration.

"Back then in the late eighties, when we were teenagers, there was all this talk of Satanic worship, right? People blamed Dungeons and Dragons, music albums with backward lyrics, and stuff. So, because we were teenagers, we all started getting into that stuff. I mean, not all of us, but some of us, those of us into that kind of thing. A group of us started meeting up in parks to try stuff." He looks at us to make sure we understand what he's talking about.

"What kind of stuff?" asks Hughes.

"Satanic rituals," Rafferty says with complete conviction.

"Human sacrifice?"

"I'm getting to that."

Talk about burying the lede.

"Usually we'd do it after a concert, or a movie, or watching the planetarium show down in Miami."

"The science museum?" asks Hughes.

"Yeah. They'd do Laser Zeppelin or some shit like that. Laser shows where people would go get high in the parking lot then watch the show and trip balls. And then we'd meet up in a field somewhere and try to summon a demon."

My childhood suddenly seems boring. "Who was this? You and Tim and Dylan and the others?"

"I'm getting to that."

Okay. I'm hoping he does it soon.

"So, we're a bunch of kids that don't know what we're doing. It's not like today with the internet. We had to steal books from Borders to figure this stuff out. We'd make a bonfire, light some candles, and do the chants."

"What about sacrifice?" asks Hughes.

"I'm getting to that. We'd usually draw our own blood and put it into a goblet and drink it. Sometimes there were animals. One time a guy threw a cat into the fire. It came screeching out of there in flames and set the grass on fire. We had to stomp it out."

I really want to punch this guy in the face right now and knock out his remaining teeth, and I get the sense that Hughes is feeling the same. But we both know better and let the asshole keep talking.

"Sometimes people claimed they saw stuff in the flames. One night some of us saw a Balrog in the fire."

"A Balrog?" I ask.

"The big monster from *The Hobbit*," says Hughes.

"No. It was *Fellowship of the Ring*, and they're basically fire and smoke demons. Anyway, somebody, maybe it was Lane Howie or his brother Nathan, came up with this blood potion and threw it into the bonfire. It was made up of our blood and, uh, some other fluids, and gasoline. It made a big explosion, and we were all knocked back by the fireball. That's when some of us saw the face and the wings before it vanished into the sky. That's when I knew we'd summoned a demon."

"Were any of the missing kids there?" I ask.

"What? No. They weren't into that. They were more into that moody electronic stuff."

"So what does this have to do with them?"

Rafferty shakes his head. "Don't you see? We unleashed something that night. When they went missing, I knew it was the Balrog."

"I get it. Quick question: Were you high at the time?"

"Does somebody who isn't high try to summon a demon? Yeah. I was pretty much high all the time. That's why I'm a good observer. I can tell what's real and what's not because I have so much experience."

Oh lord.

Hughes is giving me a sideways glance. I already feel guilty for trekking out here and for the gash on his arm. This was a waste.

"Did anyone else see this demon?" I ask.

"Yeah. One guy, Sleazy Steve, was the closest. I'm pretty sure he got possessed."

"Possessed?" echoes Hughes.

"Have you been listening? I said I thought the demon got those guys. Sleazy Steve was the last person anybody saw with them on the night of the Metal Moon concert."

"The same night they went missing?" I ask, trying to clarify things.

"For cops, you don't listen very good. I saw Sleazy Steve talking to the chicks that night. Later on, all five got into the van, and that was the end of it."

Well, this just took a turn.

"You saw Sleazy Steve with them that night, getting into the van?"

Rafferty looks over at Hughes as if he's about to ask why I'm so slow, then decides not to. "Yes. Sleazy Steve was at the concert. He was also at our Satanic meetups. Ergo, he got the Balrog."

Hughes is furiously taking notes on a pad—quite an accomplishment in the moonlight. "Back up for a moment," I reply. "Who's Sleazy Steve?"

"Some guy that started hanging around us. I think we met him in Miami at a concert. He was a bit of a weirdo, but cool enough, I guess."

"Where did he go to school?"

"I don't know. He was maybe a year or two older. I think he was out of school."

I barrage him with more questions. "What else do you know about him? What did he look like? What was his real name? Where did he live?"

"Uh, very little. Average, I guess. What were the other questions?"

"Let's start with appearance."

"Average, like I said. White guy. Brown hair? Average height. Used to wear an army jacket."

"Eye color?" asks Hughes.

"I don't know. He almost always had on sunglasses."

"At night?" says Hughes.

"Those bonfires were pretty fucking big. He was kind of a loner. He'd just show up."

"What about his name?" I ask.

"Sleazy Steve? Nobody knew his name. He got that one because I think the first time we met him, we caught him feeling up Lucy Pell while she was stoned and then some other chick. That was Sleazy Steve for you." Rafferty laughs, coughs hard, and sucks on the vape.

I want to punch this man so badly, but I keep my calm. "What else can you tell us?"

"He always had a courier bag. That's where he kept shit like his flask and photos."

Goose pimples run down my arms and back. "Photos?"

"Yeah. That's another reason he got the name. He liked to take photos of weird shit. Sometimes it was crotch shots of girls. Dead animals. That kind of thing. He'd buy beer for chicks and get them to pose."

Hughes is staring at his notes, trying not to react. I, too, am trying to keep my composure. "What else?"

"He had a flask, right? I think he may have roofied girls with it. That was his MO." This is our guy. "In fact, he was the guy that threw the cat into the bonfire. Huh. Now that I think about it, he was kind of a sick asshole." Rafferty stares into the distance, finally getting some perspective on his teenage years. "I wonder what happened to him."

"You said you saw him get into the van."

"Oh yeah. Metal Moon. I figured he straight up killed them. That was the last I saw of them and pretty much the last I saw of him too. At least for a while. Things get hazy."

"Why didn't you tell anyone?" asks Hughes.

"I did. I told my guidance counselor at school everything. Well, just about."

"Did she have you speak to the police?"

"What? No. She called my parents and said I needed to go into rehab. And that was the end of that. Goodbye, Tim. Goodbye, Dylan. Goodbye, Grace."

"What about Caitlin?"

Rafferty gives me a cold stare. "Fuck her." *Jesus.*

"We're going to need you to come to our office and make a more formal statement," I explain.

"Yeah, sure. Can I get my stuff first? These assholes will take it if you're not careful."

Afraid of losing our single best witness, Hughes and I follow Rafferty back to the campground. We keep back a few paces to talk.

"That was . . . something," says Hughes.

"Yes, it was. And a spectacular fuckup."

He raises his wrist. "I've had worse."

"No, not that. I mean that Rafferty did the right thing and told the only authority figure he knew about a suspect."

"You mean an average-looking guy wearing sunglasses?" Hughes says sarcastically.

"Thirty years ago, there were a ton of people who knew Sleazy Steve. They could have ID'd him. They would have known there was a fifth potential victim or witness."

Hughes lowers his voice. "Did you listen to this guy? Would you want to be the one to take his report to the chief? How does 'I have a witness who says a demonic demon did it' sound?"

"Crazy. But crazy doesn't mean completely wrong. A good cop would have listened."

"Maybe. But his guidance counselor shut him up." Hughes stops walking and appears to think something over. "I wonder how many crazy stories she heard? Maybe she knows a little more about Sleazy Steve before he became Serial Killer Steve."

"Sounds good. I'm curious to know who else was at the Metal Moon concert. Maybe there are more witnesses out there. It's the last place we're fairly certain the kids and their killer were seen together."

"That's a heck of a long time ago to find witnesses. Where would we start?"

"Oddly enough, my uncle."

"The one . . ." His voice trails off, not completing the sentence with *who was arrested for drug trafficking*.

"Yeah, him. I just hope he's willing to talk to me."

CHAPTER TWENTY-FIVE
SMOKEY JOE

Shady Tree Villas has few trees and no villas, as far as I can tell. What it does have are lots of mobile homes in various states of disrepair and the highest concentration of sex offenders and parolees in South Florida. Like a tide pool that collects garbage, Shady Tree collects men—many of whom aren't allowed near children, schools, or places where children might congregate, which is pretty much everywhere. One of the few remaining spots in the county for them is this mobile home park.

We're here thanks to my uncle Karl. He doesn't live here—he's a mere drug trafficker—but the one person he said I should talk to does call Shady Tree Villas home. When Karl said I should find Joseph Raymond "Smokey" Viccola, aka Smokey Joe Ray, I wondered if it was a snide FU to me for not doing more to get Karl's sentence lifted. I'd already pulled what strings I could to get him out of lockup after he assisted us in our last case, but since half the people we had arrested still had friends on the bench, I'm amazed we were able to get that far.

Hughes glances out the passenger window at the rows of almost-identical mobile homes. The grass is uncut, and the men sitting outside in lawn chairs—talking, listening to the radio, or contemplating their situation in life—all look identical in some way. I can't quite place it.

"It's fraternity row with the most pathetic guys you ever met, forty years later," says Hughes. "A pervert tailgate party."

That's it. These men reek of pathos, but I don't quite know how I feel. Some are evil bastards who tried to lure children online. A few are men who hired prostitutes and either had terrible lawyers or didn't realize the sex companion they were hiring was underage. Some are here for "crimes" that don't exist in other states; some should be locked up and never allowed to leave.

Hughes and I spot a short man, almost clinically a dwarf, walking into a mobile home.

Would he have been here if he'd not dealt with a lifetime of insecurity? I don't know. It's not my place to psychoanalyze. My job is to find the people who did the crime and let the courts figure out what to do with them.

This is what I try to remind myself. But deep down, part of me believes that my own difficult childhood, caused in part by the actions of Uncle Karl, whose drug conviction put the family in a negative light, may have turned out differently if Grandpa had put Karl and my dad on a surer footing—or at least taught Karl by way of a better example.

As angry as I am with Karl, I can understand the moral confusion for a young man who knew food was put on the table because his father smuggled artifacts and pirated shipwrecks—not to mention the endless stories about our smuggler grandfather and great-grandfathers, who ran rum through the same canals I now patrol.

I check the address against the GPS and come to a stop in front of a double-wide mobile home at the very end of the road. A brown mutt is lying on the grass with the same sense of resignation as the men who live here. He can barely manage to lift his nose to look at us before going back to pondering his own fate.

"I wonder what he did to get sentenced here?" jokes Hughes.

I don't know about the dog, but in the case of Smokey Joe Ray, it was the third time he got arrested for being with an underage girl that the judge decided he should be incarcerated for a much longer time and remain on parole longer yet.

The story of Smokey Joe Ray's multiple trials was major news when the public learned that one of South Florida's most beloved radio DJs of the 1980s and 1990s had a problem with underage girls. What may have been acceptable in a different era finally had become recognized as child abuse or rape, but Smokey Joe Ray never got the memo.

His first conviction was a suspended sentence in the 1990s. He was fired from one radio station and rehired a couple of years later. Then came the second and third convictions. Also came the news that Smokey Joe Ray had been quite the pervert, with an enormous collection of pornography, both commercial and amateur. He tried to resurface again as an internet radio-show host interviewing porn stars, but that only lasted until a judge decided it was a parole violation.

Smokey Joe Ray's lurid interests aren't why we're here. Uncle Karl told us that, in the late eighties, Joe was everywhere in the South Florida music scene. He was emceeing concerts, producing them, and, as it turns out, partying hard with fans and rock bands alike. Everyone had a story about running into Smokey Joe Ray at a high school party or in a concert parking lot.

Hughes and I walk up the steps to the screen door. The interior door is wide-open, revealing a torn-up couch and magazines on the floor. The inside smells like cigarettes and sweat.

"Joe?" I call into the home.

There's a coughing sound, and the whole structure shakes as a stocky barefoot man with gray hair down to his shoulders and a half-unbuttoned shirt hanging over shorts comes to the door.

He glances at Hughes and wipes his eyes. "FBI?" he asks in a deep, deep voice.

"No," I reply.

He makes a melodramatic "Whew!" and wipes his forehead. He stares at me for a moment. "Hey, you're the lady cop that found those kids."

I point a thumb to Hughes. "We're the ones that pulled the van from the lake."

"What a tragedy," he says. "What can I help you with?"

"We'd like to ask you some questions about back then."

"Inside or outside?"

"Inside is fine." I really, really don't want to step in there and sit on that couch, but you always learn more when you're in someone else's space.

"Sure, sure," he says, motioning us inside. He gives me a look up and down. "You don't look like a cop. He does. Not you. You ever think about doing music videos?"

"Has that line worked this century?" I fire back.

"Sadly, no." He directs us to the couch while he takes an easy chair opposite of us in the small living room. "I was there that night," he offers freely. "The night the kids went missing. I introduced the bands, in fact. It's a strange thing to think that I saw their faces out there in the crowd."

"Did you ever meet them?"

He shakes his head. "I don't think so. I used to sign autographs in the parking lot before the shows. The kids loved that."

It was probably a great place to pick up underage girls too. "But you don't remember them?"

"I stared at those photos for a while, trying to. But no. And I'm pretty good with faces."

Attractive, young, female faces, I'm sure.

Joe seems eager to help, but there's a sense of unease about him. If I had to guess, he's concerned that we might find out about some parole violation. That could be anything from possessing marijuana to having a dead girl under the house.

"Do you remember anybody strange or odd from that night?" asks Hughes.

"You ever been to a rock concert?" says Joe. "The lead singer of Metal Moon had a tattoo of a snake that started at his Adam's apple and ended at the tip of his dick. Their manager was a former New York wiseguy who was a person of interest in three murders back in the 1960s. We had to kick a pro football player out of the backstage area because he was dealing out in the open to the stagehands. I'll tell you what would have been weird—someone who wasn't weird. That's why god invented rock and roll. It's an industry built on insanity."

"What about the crowd? What about when you walked through the parking lot? Or the kids you knew?" I ask.

"What about them?"

I realize we're not going to get anywhere without being more specific. "This is confidential, you understand?"

"Yeah, sure. What?" He leans in on the armrest.

"We think the kids were murdered and the van was dumped into the water to cover the evidence."

"Holy shit. Murdered?" He says it with a radio announcer's exclamation.

"You're the only civilian we've told this to," says Hughes. "If it leaks from you, we won't be happy." He makes a show of looking around the mobile home, as if to suggest we'll come back and ransack the place for something incriminating.

"Shit. These lips are sealed. Are you asking me if I saw a murderer that night? A few. Besides Metal Moon's manager, half the roadies probably. Maybe not that many, but more than a few had done serious time."

"What about among the kids? Was there anyone you saw at multiple venues who gave off a vibe?" I ask.

"A vibe?"

"There's a difference between someone who kills a man in a bar fight and someone who does it for fun. Think Ted Bundy—someone who seems especially creepy or just 'off.'"

He thinks this over. "No. Not like that. You have a description?"

"Nothing specific. Average white male with brown hair and possibly sunglasses."

"Shame. But we might be able to tell who he is by who he was hanging out with."

"How would we know who he was hanging out with?" asks Hughes.

"By who he was standing next to," replies Joe as if it's plainly obvious.

"And how would we know that?" I ask.

"From the attendance photo." He looks at us, confused. "You didn't pull that up? Skyshow, the promoter for the label? That was Skylar Bancman back then. She handled money for the band. She didn't trust the venue to do an accurate count—they were always undercounting the box office and screwing artists over. So at the start of every show, after everyone was inside and waiting for the band to start, she'd have a photographer go out and take a wide-angle photo, and he'd go develop it in a custodian closet converted into a darkroom while everyone was kept waiting."

"What was the point of that?" I ask.

"Skylar'd get the photo guy to blow up a poster-size print of the photo, and she'd use a sewing pin to poke a hole in every face and a clicker to count them all. If she counted so much as one extra person, she'd threaten to cancel the concert if they didn't pay up. You ever wonder why sometimes it takes forever for a music act to take the stage? It's not always because they're hungover or counting green M&M's. It's because their manager's backstage yelling at the local promoter to pay up or else they'll leave."

"Wait," I say. "You're saying there's a photo with everyone at the rock concert?"

"You're slow for a cop. Maybe you should take me up on that music video offer. But, yes. Skylar probably has all those negatives. She kept everything."

If Caitlin, Grace, Tim, and Dylan are in that photo, then there's a good chance Sleazy Steve is too—possibly right next to them.

Hughes is on his phone already, probably looking up Skylar Bancman.

I decide to probe Joe's memory a little more. "Did you ever hear of someone named Sleazy Steve?"

Joe smiles. "That's a hell of a nickname. I don't suspect it's one he gave himself."

Hughes's phone vibrates; he rises and moves out of earshot, putting it to his ear.

"No," I agree with Joe. "He had a reputation."

"That can mean a lot. What was his?"

"He liked to molest unconscious women," I reply.

"Jesus. That's when they're the least fun." Joe shakes his head.

"Uh, yeah. He had a Polaroid camera and took photos of them. Not always against their will, but often when they didn't know it. He also photographed more depraved things."

"On instant film?"

"Yes."

He makes a small headshake. "Never heard of that."

Hughes returns to us and tells me, "We can pick up the negative in an hour."

Joe whistles. "That was fast."

"I guess Ms. Bancman's pretty active on email. Ready, McPherson?"

We thank Smokey Joe and leave him in his dark, shoddy lair. Something's not sitting right in the back of my mind, but I can't figure out what it is. I have a feeling Joe knows more than he's saying, but to get those answers, we'll have to come up with the right questions.

CHAPTER TWENTY-SIX
Ruins

"It looks like a forgotten Aztec temple," says Hughes as we stare at broken concrete slabs poking out of the earth. The setting sun, visible through the trees that have grown over the remnants of the Black Coral Amphitheater, casts an orange glow, adding to the eerie tableau.

The roof of the Family Ford dealership that now sits where the parking lot for the amphitheater was located is barely discernible from where we're standing—on a small hill of dirt and rubble that used to be the stage. The band shell and everything inside, including the backstage rooms and offices, were demolished decades ago.

The only part of the amphitheater that's left is the broken concrete of the seating and the bowl-shaped landscape.

There are no physical clues to be found here. Years of graffiti, loitering, and vandalism have erased any evidence that could have possibly remained; Hughes and I still decided to come here to get a sense of the place and to understand the last hours of the victims. We also thought it might help in making sense of the audience photo we got from Skylar Bancman.

"How about here?" says Hughes, unfolding a stand to hold the blown-up poster of the negative.

I stand a few feet behind the spot and imagine the thousands of faces staring back. The sides of the hill line up with the edges in the photograph. "Yeah. This looks right."

Hughes sets the photo on the easel, and we both stare at it. Six thousand faces crammed into an amphitheater meant for half that, originally, but the photo's so detailed that you can make out the expressions of even the kids in the back row.

You can almost feel them cheering or jeering the photographer as he set up his large-format camera and snapped the image. Even though it's black-and-white and decades old, the image feels strangely alive. Especially where Grace, Caitlin, Dylan, and Tim are standing. Caitlin's on Dylan's shoulders, making the two-fingered, one-thumbed sign of the horns. Grace wears a half smile, while the boys are all grins.

I've seen dozens of photographs of these four kids, from yearbook photos to candid images. This feels the most real and the most . . . invasive.

This is their world, their night. This was their tight little group. And almost surely the last image of them alive—likely because of the young man standing a foot to their right.

Sunglasses, an army jacket, and a smirk on his face make him appear above it all. Dark, messy hair, slightly taller than average, he's maybe a year or so older than the kids next to him. I can't point anything out about his face any more than the last guy I saw in a car commercial, but there's something about the way he carries himself. He's watching the crowd, not the stage.

It's Sleazy Steve.

Before coming here, we asked Rafferty to identify Steve from the photo. It took him only a moment. He also pointed out his own stoned face at the outer edge, leaning over a railing, shirtless, not a care in the world.

I walk up the hill, stepping over cracked stone and broken bottles, climbing until I reach the spot where the kids stood. Hughes watches, unsure what I'm doing.

I don't know either. I just want to stand in this spot.

Why?

Because they were alive when they stood here. All I've encountered so far is their deaths. The van was a tomb, and the memorial ceremony an emotional release for their passing. Here they were happy, at least fleetingly so.

I stand here, visualizing the stage, feeling the crowd around me, trying to take myself back to that night. My imagination responds eagerly, and I can almost believe I'm there.

There's a snap of twigs, and I jerk toward the noise. George Solar walks through what would have been the mosh pit at the concert. He looks at Hughes on the berm with the poster and me standing on the hill.

I expect him to make a sarcastic remark, but he doesn't. Instead he walks up to the imaginary stage to look at the photo. His gaze moves around the trees, probably visualizing the amphitheater just like I did. What does he see?

Knowing George, it would be a dope deal taking place or a purse thief near the exit, waiting for his accomplice.

His eyes move to me, then alight on the spot where Sleazy Steve once stood. I nervously glance over my shoulder, almost afraid I'll see him there.

Actually, I wish he were here. So I could . . . what? Kill him? Arrest him? I don't know what emotion drives me more, my desire for justice or revenge. I didn't know these kids, but I know what it was like to be troubled. They may have been assholes at times, but so was I. When I went to private school and started dating Run, we were part of the cool clique. I was probably a snobby bitch. There was a time when I would have laughed at jokes directed at the sketchy kids who wore the same T-shirts every week. My desire to fit in and not be an outsider probably made me a mean girl, at least for a while. I can't judge these kids; I can only feel sorrow for what was taken from them.

"McPherson?" calls George.

I realize I'm still staring at the space where Sleazy Steve stood.

"Hey? Are you okay?" he asks.

"Yeah. Sorry. Just thinking." I erase whatever emotion's showing on my face and watch George scrutinizing the poster.

"We can get a pretty good simulation of what he looks like now," George says. "Mostly. The glasses don't help. But they can do some amazing stuff with the facial structure and extrapolate the rest."

"I've already requested yearbooks from all the local high schools," says Hughes. "We might get a name for him."

I hope that's the case, but I don't think it will be that easy. The face in the photo appears to be twenty or so. He might not have gone to high school in South Florida, and even if he did, if he dropped out or changed his name between fifteen and twenty, we might never place him, but it's worth a try.

Whatever the method, we *have* to find a way to track him in the present. He's still here, still killing. He could be living a mile away. I've probably passed him on the highway or been in the same shopping center he has. So close . . . yet so far away.

"How did it go with Fish and Wildlife?" I ask.

"They're pulling all the tickets and notes they have from around the time we think he dumped the body. Maybe somebody was an eyewitness."

"I'll bet it wasn't his first time out in the Everglades. We need to go back at least a few years," I reply.

"That'll take some work. I'm guessing it'd involve thousands of incident reports." He doesn't say this to complain, only to point out a fact.

I look back to where Sleazy Steve was standing and envision the smug asshole with his sunglasses on at night. Did he have an eye condition? Did he want to look cool? Or was it something else?

"The sunglasses," I say out loud as it hits me.

"What about them?" asks George.

"They're for control . . . because he wants to control things. He likes using his camera to see, but he doesn't want to *be* seen. We should tell Fish and Wildlife to prioritize tickets for people running boats without registrations or running lights."

"That could be half of them," says George.

"Yeah. But he'll have done it several times. Also, we need to check with Highway Patrol in case they've stopped anyone near the boat ramps with expired or missing tags."

Operating your car or boat without your tags is a minor offense and something Sleazy Steve might have been willing to risk rather than have eyewitnesses see him do something suspicious and take note of his license plate.

Also, running his boat at night without the running lights would allow him to avoid being seen if . . .

"We also need to look at all the cases of human remains being dumped out there. Even ones where they had suspects," I tell George and Hughes.

"Broward Sheriff's Office has already been doing that. We can go see what they've found tomorrow, if you want."

"Yeah. He has to have dumped more bodies out there, right?"

"That would make sense."

I get an uneasy feeling with my back facing where the killer stood. I catch myself nervously glancing behind me to make sure that he isn't actually there.

But if he were, I know what I'd ask him: How many people have you killed?

CHAPTER TWENTY-SEVEN
PIECES

Detective Hoffer slides a photograph of a severed arm across the table in the Broward Sheriff's Office conference room. "This was found ten years ago by a fisherman." She pulls another photo from a folder and shows it to Hughes and me. This one shows a leg from the knee down. "This was found a few days later, after they did a search for more remains."

"DNA?" I ask.

"Male. White. That's all they could tell. No match to a missing person." She pats the folder. "There are eleven other body parts, going back twenty years. All found within the same twenty-mile area."

Twenty square miles is a lot of area in the Everglades. "Serial killer?"

"We don't know. Ever since Al Capone, it's been a convenient dumping ground. Could just be gang related with no pattern, or one guy."

"Just dumping them?" asks Hughes. "How were they severed?"

"That's where it gets interesting. Most of them have saw marks."

"Seems odd," I reply. "To go through that much trouble to cut up a body and then not do a more thorough job of getting rid of it."

"I'll throw you an alternative theory," says Hoffer. "Maybe he is thorough but a little too prolific. These are just the outliers."

"You mean there could be a lot more victims?" asks Hughes.

Hoffer nods. "If he preys on people from different socioeconomic levels and switches things up, we might not detect a pattern. Except . . ." She taps the photograph of the arm. "There's a reason we didn't contact you sooner about this. We hadn't made the connection to the body in the drainage ditch because these are all male, and that body was female."

"And intact," I add.

"He cuts up the guys? But leaves the women?" says Hughes. "Why? I mean besides being messed up?"

"I asked Solar's behavioral psychologist consultant, Teng. I was expecting some kind of psychosexual explanation. She said it could be simpler than that. Males are larger and harder to carry. He cuts them up for convenience. And in the case of Alyssa Rennie, it might mean that her boyfriend, Jared, is somewhere out there in pieces."

"Do you have a map of where the body parts were found?" I ask.

"I can make one. Hold on." She leaves us and returns a minute later with a rolled-up map under one arm and a stack of folders under the other. "I brought a bunch of cases. These are ones that we marked as closed because we got a confession from someone. The trouble is, I looked back at a couple of them, and the guy who did the confessing was a pathological bullshitter. We ran a little different back then; closing cases seemed more important than actually getting the bad guys in some situations."

Hughes and I pick up the folders and start reading through them. They're filled with reports, photos, and transcripts of interviews. Some of them relate to the photos on the table.

Hoffer flattens the map with two coffee mugs and draws red circles where the body parts were found over the years. Most of them were strewn along the canal on the other side of the berm from where Alyssa Rennie's body was found.

"You can see they're pretty spread out here. It doesn't make much sense to me."

It does to me. "That's what happens when you throw body parts from a moving boat. The wake often pushes them ashore."

"Okay. But why along this canal? It only makes them easier to find."

"Same reason cocaine bundles wash up on the beach. A criminal would rather ditch them in a hurry than get caught with them. My guess is he went to go ditch the body somewhere else and saw Marine Patrol and got spooked. He didn't want to risk going back to the boat launch with body parts. So he dumped them. He probably weighted them down, hoping they'd get eaten before surfacing. But it didn't always work out that way." I wave my hand over the map. "This isn't what he planned. This was his contingency plan. And something he had to do more than once."

"So if this was what he did when he got spooked, what was his plan when everything went fine?" asks Hughes.

I search the map, trying to put simple shapes to features I remember from trips to the Everglades. For people who've never been there, it's hard to fully grasp. The Everglades is a sea of grass that stretches from one side of Florida to the other and runs right up the middle. Instead of a vast plain, it's shallow marshes, stretches of mangrove-covered islands, and mazes of small waterways that are almost impossible to navigate in some places. Boat propellers get caught in the grass, and paddling a kayak is exhausting. The fastest way to get around is an airboat that glides over the water, but even then, you can only make it so far.

The only way to fully penetrate the Everglades is on foot—which means trekking through chest-high water with alligators, cottonmouths, pythons, and a few hundred Florida panthers.

There are plenty of secret trails and hunting camps, but they're known only to the locals. It's easy to get lost out there, but it's also easy to hide something, if you know where you're going.

"He's got a burial ground," I announce.

Hughes and Hoffer don't need any convincing. They both nod immediately in agreement.

But agreeing isn't the same as knowing where the spot is located. We only know where the failed body dumps happened.

"So how do we find it in all this?" asks Hoffer. "We can't just go start looking."

"No, of course not. Maybe the Fish and Wildlife reports will tell us more?"

Hughes holds up an artist's rendering sketch from one of the files he was poring over. "Look familiar?"

It's Sleazy Steve's face—only older.

"When was that?" I blurt out.

"Fifteen years ago. After they found a foot, they interviewed fishermen and various airboat operators in the area. Three people said they saw a man matching this description in a small flat-bottom boat."

"Now we're talking," I say. "Anything else in there?"

Hughes flips through the file. "Just some vague descriptions. But it's pretty thorough. It looked like this even made it on the news for a hot minute."

"Are there locations?" I ask.

"Yeah. GPS coordinates."

Hughes makes a quick call to Fish and Wildlife while I put them on the map. Two of them are close to a boat launch. But one of them is in a much more remote part of the Everglades, about five miles distant.

"It's interesting," says Hughes, "but I'm not sure where it gets us."

"Hold on." I call George on my cell.

"What's up?"

"Can you do me a favor and search your internal reports for a few dates?"

"Hold on, let me get my computer. Go ahead."

I rattle off the six dates when the body parts were found.

"One second. Huh. What brought those up?" he asks.

"Body parts found in the Everglades. Parts we think our suspect ditched because he got spotted or spooked."

"Damn. Makes sense," says George. "So what do we do with it?"

Hughes and Hoffer are looking at me with the same question in their eyes.

"Those nights when he was out there? DEA and local drug enforcement would've had planes up and boats out looking for traffickers dropping loads."

Hughes nods, getting it. "Our guy could've seen the planes or unmarked vehicles and worried they were after him. So he ditched the body parts in case they had eyes on his burial ground. Damn, that's smart."

It's also discouraging. It means Sleazy Steve is highly suspicious by nature. We're never going to get within a mile of him if he thinks we're onto him.

"Hey, McPherson, I'm still here," George says in my ear.

I set my cell on the table. "Putting you on speakerphone."

"So, you think he may have a specific dumping ground out there?" he asks.

"It's a possibility."

"Hmm. Then we might have caught a break."

"What's that?"

"Some of those operations were military. They would've been using planes with infrared technology. One of those splotches they saw could've been our guy. Maybe that footage is still available. Let me make some calls."

CHAPTER TWENTY-EIGHT
MATERNAL INSTINCTS

I'm standing on Run's back patio, looking at police reports on my iPad as the sun sets in the west. The lights of the houses and buildings across the waterway flicker to life like a thousand fireflies. Boats drift across the channel, sending waves into the sea wall in a gentle drumbeat. It's a beautiful night outside my head, but I'm too absorbed in eyewitness accounts and forensic details to appreciate it.

I keep tabbing back to the three infrared maps George was able to get for us from the nights when we think Sleazy Steve may have seen DEA undercover units and bailed on going to his graveyard.

The idea of a graveyard was only a notion until we ran it by Amelia Teng, the Florida Atlantic University professor who has done some insightful research into criminal psychology. What I like about her is that she takes more of a zoologist's approach, focusing on actions instead of trying to mind-read suspects.

Her papers are filled with exhaustive databases of details that sound mundane but actually make sense: for instance, serial killers often stock up on energy bars and drinks when they're in their killing phases. Which makes sense if you realize that someone like Sleazy Steve might not want to stop at a McDonald's drive-through with a dismembered body in the back of his vehicle.

When we showed her Grace's Polaroid photo and the evidence of instant-camera use by the killer, she showed us a correlation between people collecting symbolic trophies, like photographs, before moving on to physical ones, like body parts.

She said something else that made sense: our suspect being so image-driven may suggest a strong attraction to pornography, especially anything explicitly violent or transgressive. This has us extending our potential suspects to men who have been cited for criminal violations relating to that.

It doesn't help us narrow potential suspects down, but it does help us understand who we might be looking for if he crosses our path.

Run leans in over my shoulder. "What are you doing?"

"Oh, work stuff."

"Huh," he says.

Tonight is pool, pizza, and movie night with Run and Jackie, but I've been too obsessed with this case to partake in the fun.

"Being a cop is a twenty-four-hour job," I reply.

"So is being a mom," he says, taking the iPad from my hands.

I'm about to snap at him, of all people, for saying that to me, when I feel slender arms gather around my waist and drag me to the edge of the pool.

"Incoming!" shouts Jackie as she pushes me in, fully clothed.

I float back to the surface and look up at her giggling face. "Jackie!"

She puts her hands on her hips and wags her finger at me like I've seen my own mother do a thousand times. "You know the rules."

Ah, yes. The rules of pool, pizza, and movie night: if you're not in the pool by seven p.m., you're fair game to be pushed in.

Whoosh! There's a huge splash as a squat figure jumps into the deep end. My dad's head pokes above the water. He's still wearing his clothes too.

"Oops!" he says as he swims to the side and places his phone, keys, and wallet on the patio.

"Moron," says my mother.

Huh . . . the two of them together again. I was so deep into my work, I didn't even think about it till now.

"Will your mom be joining us too?" I ask Run.

"I would say the odds are against it."

I hear more footsteps and see two blurs as my nephews come hurtling through the air over my head and land in the middle of the pool like meteors.

The waves pour over the edge of the pool, sending a small flood toward my mother. Jackie runs over to her. "Come on, Nana!"

Mom, always the last one to get in, lets Jackie walk her to the steps, where she can soak her feet.

Dad's in the middle of a splash war with my nephews. My brother Robbie takes a seat on the edge of the pool with a beer.

"Where's Marta?" I ask.

"Book club," he replies. "Basically, an excuse for a bunch of broads to drink wine and bitch about men."

"Where can I sign up?"

"You have to learn to read first," he fires back.

I splash him. He feigns a smile. I can tell he's stressed out, but he's never one to talk about what's bothering him. A genuine laugh escapes him as he sees his son Robbie Jr. try to splash Dad, only to have Dad duck, drenching Mom instead.

Run swims up next to me. "I figured we'd expand movie night tonight. I hope it's okay."

I nod. I can't remember the last time I got to be around everyone like this. Jackie's laughter crackles through the air, and it brings a smile to my face.

"Is our girl doing okay?" I ask quietly.

"She almost got suspended from the swim team," says Run.

"What?"

Run whispers, "She punched some kid named Conner for calling one of the other girls fat."

"Oh. And how do we feel about that as parents?"

"I yelled at her in front of the coach. Then I high-fived her in the parking lot," says Run.

"Was that the right way to handle it?" I ask, not doubting him, but truly unsure how you're supposed to raise a strong girl.

"She cried when she saw the black eye she gave him. So I think she's not a sociopath."

"Or she's really, really good at manipulation."

"God help us," says Run.

We both look over at the smiling face of our daughter as she uses a pool noodle to slap the backs of both her cousins' heads at the same time. "Nuck nuck nuck!" she calls out, like the Three Stooges.

"Did she get that from daddy-daughter homework time?" I ask.

"I blame YouTube."

"Right. Maybe I need to talk to her about violent behavior."

Run bites his lip. "Um, about that . . . She told me she had a nightmare."

Oh damn. My blood turns cold. "Because of what I told her about the case?"

Run nods.

"I'm so stupid." I can't believe I traumatized her like that. What was I thinking? Then I draw the connection to her hitting Conner. "She punched that boy because of what I said. Damn it, I never should have done that."

"It may have been a mistake," says Run. "But maybe not a bad one. She's not a victim, Sloan. Our little girl is tough," he says, trying to soothe me.

"I don't want to raise a bully either. Some people can't tell the difference."

"Give her some credit. She's a hell of a lot smarter than we were at that age."

Run slides his hand around my waist. I can feel his muscular forearm through my clothes as my body presses against his chest. All of a sudden, I feel less worried. He's still got it. Of course, that tingling, "everything is all right" feeling is how Jackie happened in the first place.

We climb into the hot tub while Dad and Mom play Marco Polo with the kids. Robbie Sr. sits on the sidelines, watching. I should probably talk to him at some point, one-on-one.

"How are *you* doing?" Run asks me as we settle in.

"This case . . ." I shake my head, at a loss for words. "This guy's still out there." I glance at the distant lights. "It feels weird to be here while he could be . . . killing someone."

"You can't run your engine nonstop. You'll burn out," says Run. He nods to the pool. "You need this every now and then."

"I need to be there for Jackie," I reply.

"She's doing fine. She knows she's loved. What I would have given to have had this when I was her age."

"A bunch of bathing apes splashing each other?"

"Exactly," he says. "I know you had it rough, real rough. I saw some of that. But your family, as dysfunctional as it was, was a family. *Is* a family. You'd kill for each other."

"More likely, lie, cheat, or steal," I reply.

"Yeah, family . . . I know things between us are, uh—"

"Complicated."

"That's one word for it. But no matter what, I'll have your back. And I'm not saying this as an excuse to get more time with Jackie. I'm saying this because I want the time you spend with her to be quality time."

"And not me traumatizing her with tales of teen rape and murder."

"No. Time spent where you're not traumatizing yourself with those stories. Jackie's tough. Her mom, on the other hand—she's vulnerable and tries too hard to hide it sometimes."

"Fair enough," I reply. "What about you? Are you happy?"

He waves a hand at the pool filled with laughing people and the mansion. "I have just about everything I could possibly want."

"Just about?"

His blue eyes look deeply into mine. "Just about."

CHAPTER TWENTY-NINE
WETLAND

Kell, an uncle of a friend of Run's, paddles his canoe ahead of Hughes and me, guiding us deeper into the swamp. We pulled the canoes out this far behind his boat, then boarded them to go deeper into this part of the Everglades.

Kell, a tall Miccosukee in fly-fishing clothes and a New England Patriots cap, grew up in South Florida hunting in the Everglades with his uncles and then went to school up north. Even during college, he came back to help them with their guide business during the summer.

He's crisscrossed the Everglades from one edge to the other and even traversed it from the Keys to Lake Okeechobee on foot and in a canoe. If anyone knows all the back trails and hidden spots, it's Kell.

When we first told him about a secret graveyard, he seemed skeptical, like we were describing a lost pyramid that had somehow managed to stay hidden for hundreds of years. He was also a bit concerned because of the uneasy history of white explorers in the Everglades.

Ever since Ponce de León, men have tromped their way through this land in search of treasure and lost empires, digging up cemeteries and destroying sacred places.

As an archaeologist in Florida, I'm acutely aware of the line between exploration and stomping on someone's history. While I think some indigenous peoples' claims stretch things a bit, I'm not the arbitrator of where that line should be.

When we discussed what Sleazy Steve's graveyard might look like, Amelia Teng said it could be something that wasn't obvious but symbolic. It would have meaning for the killer and could contain some kind of surface feature, like a tree or group of trees, that stood out. She added that some serial killers' dumping grounds have been discovered only a few yards away from public hiking spots. In fact, that's often what gave them the idea.

We based our search area on two things: glowing splotches from the military's night-vision photos and the frequently used paths of airboat tours. We decided on the latter because Sleazy Steve might have seen something he liked on a tour and decided to go back and investigate in his own boat.

The fact that he uses a boat suggests that the site is accessible from the water and wouldn't require trekking too far overland, given that he'd have to haul one or more bodies to their final resting place.

"This way," says Kell as he paddles into a small cut in the mangroves.

I could have paddled right by and never noticed the narrow waterway. We follow him in, careful not to hit the sides and get stuck.

"Could he get a boat through here?" asks Hughes.

"Probably not. This is a shortcut. Leaving the canal saves us almost two miles to get where we're headed."

"Did your uncles show you?" asks Hughes.

"No. Google Earth," Kell replies with a laugh.

The trees form a canopy overhead. Birds and frogs chirp and croak while things splash into the water or out of it as we drift through.

There's a moment when you enter the Everglades, leaving behind the tourist trails and man-made canals, when you realize you're in the wild—a wild as exotic as the Serengeti. You could fit two of Hawaii's Big Island inside here.

What makes it deceiving is the plain of sawgrass that stretches into the distance in the north. The flatness and apparent uniformity make it seem smaller than it actually is.

However, once you're on foot or in a canoe in the wetlands, you feel dwarfed.

It's like you've been shrunk down and dropped into your own backyard. Every tiny blade of grass is now a tree, towering over you.

In the sawgrass prairie, you can walk for an hour and feel like you've made no progress at all, unlike in a forest, where you have landmarks denoting changes in the landscape. Here, I feel closed in and can't make out any useful features at all. At least at sea, if you know the currents and the time, you can get a pretty good idea of where you are.

"This can get pretty spooky," says Hughes.

"At night it's amazing," replies Kell. "But also terrifying when you're a little boy. My uncles used to tell me stories of the Gator Men."

"Gator Men?" asks Hughes.

"You know, half-man, half-alligator monsters that roamed the Everglades," says Kell over his shoulder.

"Imagine if they teamed up with the sea goblins," Hughes says to me as we exit the trail and come to a wide waterway.

"You have any childhood monsters?" I ask him.

"Just one that would come home drunk and beat the living daylights out of me and my sister if our chores weren't done to his satisfaction."

"Yikes," I say.

"He's in a better place now."

"Oh."

"Sobriety."

My family certainly has its own challenges with sobriety, but my dad never lifted a hand against me. I saw him slap Harris and Robbie around a few times for outright stupidity—but never any harder than I'd have hit them myself.

Kell slows down his paddling and lets us catch up to him. He points to the shore, where the water gives way to low grass. "From here it's overland on foot, then through marsh."

"Could he have carried a body through here?" asks Hughes.

"We carried wild boar out of swamp like this on foot," says Kell. "Same difference if you know what you're doing. All you need is two sticks and a tarp."

Wild boar hunting? I wonder if our guy is a poacher?

"Would he go to the effort?" asks Hughes. "Or is that the point? A symbolic thing? Bringing a body out here?"

I pull out a marked-up, plastic-laminated map and compare it to the landscape. The military photos showed that someone with a high body temperature was within a mile of here on one particular night. Another, fainter heat spot indicates what might've been a boat motor that had been pulled ashore a few hundred yards from here.

This seems as good a place as any, but something's been bothering me. Dr. Teng said that we should look for a prominent visual marker. Sleazy Steve came here at night. Did he do it from memory? GPS?

I follow Hughes and Kell to the shore and pull my canoe next to theirs. We grab our gear, then start down a small trail, following our guide.

"Boar trail?" asks Hughes.

"Deer and wild hogs. Occasional panther too."

The trail leads us in a zigzag pattern through grassy landscape and sparse trees. The view doesn't change much, but I keep my eyes up, looking for something to pop out at me.

The trouble is, a serial killer graveyard could stand only yards away in the grass, and we'd never know.

Two hours go by, and we've seen a few alligators, heard a lot of creatures rustling in the grass, and had to cross knee-deep water at multiple points. I'm not sure what we were expecting, but this is a disappointment.

"Let's head there," says Kell, pointing to a cluster of cypress trees.

We have to walk around a small inlet to get there without swimming. When we finally arrive, we find an old lawn chair sitting in the shade with a pile of beer bottles.

Hughes and I stare at the items.

Kell grins. "Don't get too excited. It's a hunter's spot."

"Not a very tidy one," says Hughes.

"No. Probably someone hunting for a living."

I walk back to the edge of the shade and stare out into the Everglades. Maybe we should have used a helicopter. Or maybe this was a bad idea to begin with.

I pull out my maps again and sit on a dry patch of ground. The small glow we're reasonably sure was Sleazy Steve appeared only a few hundred yards from here; yet, much as in the ruins of the amphitheater, he remains elusive.

Where does he go when he comes out here? I scan the horizon for warped trees or anything else that stands out visually, but it all looks the same in every direction.

"What do you *see* out here?" I ask aloud, then stare back at the map and his spot.

What brought you here? Did some feature call to you? Or was it something you sought out?

I try to find a pattern but can't discern one. Okay, step back. This is a place he wants to find but doesn't want others to know is there. It's something he needs access to but doesn't want anyone else to discover. What does that remind me of?

Buried treasure.

But you can't bury something out here and expect it to stay buried for long . . .

Almost all the really old archaeological sites in Florida, the ones going back to the Ice Age, are underwater. Not all were flooded in the intervening centuries. Some tribes used underwater burial as a means of disposing of their deceased. They'd be placed in skin bags and staked into the water, or in some cases, their bodies would be held to the bottom by a series of poles trapping them.

Where were Sleazy Steve's first victims found? In a van, underwater.

Where was he trying to dump the last one?

In the water . . .

We're not looking for some aboveground burial site or shrine. What we're looking for is underwater.

I stare down at my map. He didn't choose the location from an airboat ride. He chose it the same way Kell found the secret cutoff. He looked at Google Maps or whatever reference he had back then and found a spot.

To the west of us is a collection of small, round ponds, as shown by the map. A dozen of them are spread across a several-mile-wide area. They have almost a ghastly look, like mouths screaming.

It's not the kind of thing you'd notice from the ground, but you'd see it easily enough in a black-and-white aerial photo.

I call to the others. "I think I know where we have to look."

"Great," says Hughes.

"Yeah, there's just one problem. I think we can only find it at night."

CHAPTER THIRTY
THE MAZE

Kell examines the aerial image of the "mouths," then looks out to the Everglades, where storm clouds are beginning to gather on the horizon. "Huh, I didn't realize we were looking for the Nexus of All Realities."

"What's that?" I ask.

"A bridge between our world and other universes," he replies.

"Is that a thing you believe in?" I ask.

Hughes starts to chuckle. "It's a comic-book thing, McPherson. Man-Thing."

"Oh, like Swamp Thing," I reply.

"That's DC," says Kell.

"Sorry, I'm not up on the great works of literature." I never took Hughes for the comic-book reader—he's full of surprises.

Kell hands me the photo. "That's a weird spot. Expect to run into gators. Lots of them."

We've all got hiking poles to poke into brush and try to scare away anything that can be scared away. If that fails, Hughes and I are armed with our pistols, and Kell has a marine shotgun. We're also all wearing waders.

I've used my waders before when I had to dredge things out of shallow water where diving didn't make any sense. I've also had plenty of experience in wetlands like this. My biggest fears out in the open aren't alligators—they're snakes and snapping turtles when I stick my hands into slimy spaces.

We march toward the small ponds, stepping on tall grass at some points and muck at others. Even in thick grass, it's hard to tell if our next step will be on land or in water.

Kell, who's a head taller than Hughes, takes long strides and clears a path for us. Occasionally he comes to a stop and gestures for us to hold back. This usually means he spotted an alligator sunning himself on land. Most of the time they get irritated and slip into the water.

When we come to a large gator that has its snout aimed in our direction, Kell taps his pole on the ground, making sure it knows we're here.

Reptilian eyes stare back at us; the gator shifts but doesn't move.

"I suggest we go around," says Kell.

"She's protecting a nest," I say over my shoulder to Hughes.

When we're what we presume is a safe distance away (hard to know when you're dealing with an amphibious creature that can outrun you), Hughes calls out to Kell, "Did McPherson tell you about her trip inside a gator den last week?"

"Inside?" asks Kell. "How'd you fit? And why?"

"It was a few feet across and about twenty feet deep. I was searching for clues."

"I call bullshit. I never heard of one that big," he says back.

"How much scuba diving have you done out here?" I ask.

"Fair point. I forgot you're the McPherson that doesn't need to exaggerate. But that was dumb. Real dumb. What would you have done if the alligator came home?"

"What *would* you have done?" Hughes taunts me.

"Shut up," I growl under my breath.

Kell raises his hand for us to stop and be quiet. His eyes are searching the ground for something. We remain steady like rocks but scan the area, trying to see what the tracker is seeing.

Hughes glances at me, then to a small trail in the grass less than a foot wide, directly ahead of us. Kell is looking into the distance for where the trail ends. He motions for us to stay put while he unslings his shotgun and takes small steps down the trail.

His lower body is lost in the grass, but we can see him aiming the shotgun toward the ground a few yards ahead of him. Kell moves a little farther, but slowly, so he doesn't make a sound.

In the distance, thunder rumbles, but the only sound around us comes from frogs and birds.

Suddenly it's interrupted by the noise of a shotgun blast. *BANG!*

Hughes and I both have our hands on our own guns, but Kell gestures for us to hold back. He steps forward, shotgun aimed in the grass, then stops and slings it over his back.

He reaches down and picks something up. A shiny, slick pattern of dark green and dark brown reflects the setting sunlight as Kell lifts the tail end of a python from the ground.

I assume it's the back end of the snake, because it's missing its head. The python—a Burmese python, specifically—is one of a hundred thousand of the invasive snakes that have been eating other animals and eggs and threatening the balance of the ecosystem out here.

"Grab the other end," says Kell.

Hughes and I come to him and help pick the larger end up. The thing is huge. We're each about four feet apart. It's not super heavy, but it's massively long.

"Sixteen feet?" asks Hughes.

"Fourteen or fifteen," replies Kell. "Let's move it back a little ways near the edge of the pond where we saw the mama alligator."

"Great," I reply. "We're Uber Eats for alligators."

"Will she eat it?" asks Hughes.

"Gators aren't that picky. More importantly, I want her babies to get a taste for python," says Kell.

"Ah, the circle of life," I say. "I can't wait to share this experience with my daughter." One more horror story to tell her. I feel a twinge of guilt.

We place the snake in the grass upwind from the mama alligator. Say what you want about people, but how many other animals leave food out for other creatures to eat? Dead mice your cat won't eat don't count.

We leave the snake on the shore and walk back toward the grassy path.

Hughes glances over his shoulder at the giant snake. "You mean we don't get to stay and watch it eat?"

"You want to stand between it and everything else that's going to come see what's for dinner?" asks Kell.

"Fair point." Hughes catches up with us. "What's the biggest one you've ever seen out here?"

"Officially or unofficially?"

"What's the difference?"

"They used to be stricter about when and how you could kill pythons. Back then, we knew they were a threat and took matters into our own hands. That's when some of the biggest ones were caught and killed, but nobody ran to the *Sentinel* or the *Herald* to tell them about it. They just had lots of snake meat for months."

"Oh," says Hughes. "So, what's the unofficial record?"

"Some friends of my uncle say they caught a twenty-two-footer without a permit."

"Twenty-two feet?" I reply. "That's five feet longer than the record."

"Do you believe them?" asks Hughes.

"Let me put it this way: Who do you think is the first to find the really big critters out here? Some eggheads from the university or hunters who come here outside of hunting season and go where the hobbyists don't? They got all the giant ones and left the runts for everyone else."

"Does that include alligators?" asks Hughes.

"My uncles say a trapper showed them a twenty-one-footer. They measured it themselves. He pulled it from a protected area. It supposedly weighed fifteen hundred pounds. I've heard about other big ones poached from state parks."

"Yikes," says Hughes.

"And the eight-hundred-pound eleven-footers all around us right now don't bother you?" asks Kell.

"Another fair point," replies Hughes.

The sun is beginning to sink below the horizon as we reach the foot of another pond.

Bubbles trickle up at the far end, telling us something is down there.

Kell comes to a stop. He takes a light from his pocket and attaches it to his hat. "What's next, Boss Lady? We're in the middle of your hell mouths."

While there are a few standing trees, I also see several felled logs and withered stumps. I look across the horizon for anything that could serve as a landmark. All I see is swamp.

The sun finally sets, and the stars begin to fill the sky. Birds make their nighttime chirps, and small bats flap their wings overhead.

"Okay, lights out, everyone," I call out.

Hughes and Kell flip theirs off, leaving us with the distant glow of the sun just beyond the horizon and the moon partially obscured by clouds.

We search the darkness for a sign of something out of the ordinary—a strange silhouette, a glow, anything.

I remember what my father taught me about orienting. Look for a large marker, then a small one. Find the mountain, then look for the valley, then the tree. Or in the treasure-hunting world, the breakers, the reef, then the cove.

We're all deathly silent, trying to concentrate. The Everglades feels different now. The frogs and insects of the daytime have given way to the nocturnal shift, and their tune sounds different.

The wind whips at our clothes, and large things splash into the water in the distance, yet we all remain still. I keep waiting for Kell and Hughes to speak up and challenge my theory. I almost wish they would. But they don't. They can feel it too. Something is different here. Sleazy Steve noticed this.

"There," says Hughes, almost in a whisper. "Can you hear it?"

I turn my ear to the wind. There's a distant melody. It doesn't have a pattern, yet it's pleasing . . .

"Wind chime," says Kell. He points a finger in the direction that it's coming from. We start to walk toward the sound; then I stop.

"Hold on. I think it's a trap."

"A wind-chime trap?" asks Hughes. "How does that work?"

"A siren song," says Kell. "Calling you to shore but dashing you on the rocks."

"Back in the old days, wreckers built fires that looked like false lighthouses to trick ships into crashing so they could salvage the cargo," I explain.

"Okay," says Hughes. He glances at the ground around him. "Speaking of traps, we're surrounded by alligators and other dangerous creatures."

"Not to mention animal traps that may have been placed to catch men," adds Kell. "What now?"

I listen more closely to the chimes. Something is off. With the wind, it's hard to know if that's exactly the right direction. In fact, it almost sounds like it's coming from two points.

Ah, that's it.

"There are multiple wind chimes."

172

"So which one is the right one?"

I take out my flashlight, the powerful one that could light up the moon if I had to, and slowly pan it across the area where the sound is coming from.

As it passes between one sound and the other, a brilliant show of sparkles ignites near the middle—my beam reflecting back at me in a dazzling array of colors.

"Holy cow," says Hughes. "I think that's the spot."

"Maybe," I reply. "But let's proceed carefully."

CHAPTER THIRTY-ONE
ABYSS

Kell uses his cap light to illuminate the way toward the distant shimmer. Hughes and I keep our own lights on the ground and in the distance, respectively, making sure that we don't step into an alligator hole.

Out here, they can just be a few feet across and look like a puddle. They help provide watering holes for other animals during dry spells, but they can also be a hazard if you're not careful.

Every now and then my light catches a pair of glowing silver eyes in the distance as it strikes an alligator. They have incredible night vision and can see us before we see them. At one point, I spot as many as twelve sets watching us from all around.

Kell stops and points to his ear. There's a guttural croak sounding in the distance. "That's a male alligator making a mating call."

"Do they do that at night?" asks Hughes.

"The deed or the call?"

Hughes shrugs.

"Do you want to tell him to stop?"

"Nah, I'll let him carry on."

"Spend much time around alligators?" asks Kell.

"Gators? No. Caimans and crocs, more than a little. But usually it was shoot first and ask questions later."

"Shooting them?" asks Kell.

"Military related. Sometimes we needed water superiority in a place where crocodiles were used to having it."

Kell shakes his head. "Saltwater crocodiles. You can have them. Nasty fellas. I prefer my alligators. They stick to the rules. For the most part."

As we draw closer to the shimmering light, we can see the separation between the reflections and the outline of a withered, leafless tree.

"Looks like fishing lures," says Kell, his keen eyes probing the dark.

We come to a pond about fifty feet across. The water ripples, sending splashes into the grass that lines the shore. Kell passes his light over the surface and lands on the snout of an alligator at the far end, not too far from the dead tree.

"Easy there, fella, we're just friends passing through," he says.

"Does that help?" asks Hughes.

"To be polite? It always helps." Kell starts to move around the pond, toward the tree, keeping his light trained on the alligator.

"Hey, Kell," I call out.

"Yeah?" he replies.

"Just one thing. I'm sure you thought of this, but if this pond is what I think it is, and that alligator is a local . . . uh . . ."

"Oh," Kell says, coming to a stop. "He's eaten human flesh."

"Probably has a taste for it," says Hughes. "But the dead kind."

"Either he's going to expect a treat from me or"—he points his light at my feet—"expect me to feed one of you to him."

I can't see his face behind the beam of light. Suddenly he begins to cackle.

"What's so funny, Kell?" asks Hughes.

"What if I was your killer?" he asks, his face still hidden. Hughes's hand slowly moves toward his gun belt.

"George Solar would drop you from a hundred yards back with his rifle," I reply. "He's been following us all the way here . . . just in case."

Kell laughs again. "That would be a convincing bluff if I didn't know how much George hated the swamp." The light flashes back to the alligator, and we get a view of Kell's profile as he faces away from us, studying the beast.

Hughes whispers to me, "He has no idea how close he came to getting dropped."

I, too, was a breath away from taking aim, but I play it cool. "Give him some credit," I whisper back. "If we weren't all armed, it would be funny."

"Get out!" yells Kell.

I turn right as he high-steps straight at the alligator and kicks the water near the beast. The gator snaps his head back, opens his massive mouth of nightmare teeth, and hisses at Kell.

Kell stands his ground and stomps again, slapping his stick against the shore. The gator jerks his head to the side and bites at the ground near where the stick hit. Kell taps him on the snout. The alligator slides onto shore and swats his tail in Kell's direction, just missing him, then stomps his stubby legs and vanishes into the grass.

"Don't try this at home, kids," Kell tells us.

"First the snake, then us, and now him. Is there anyone else out here left for you to terrorize?" asks Hughes.

Kell looks up into the sky and catches a bat with his light beam. "I guess I could try to catch one of them." He looks back at us, catching our faces in his light. "I figured we didn't want the alligator at our ankles while we looked around."

"Wise move." I reach into my bag and pull out a roll of yellow crime-scene tape. "Hughes, grab one end. I want to mark out a path for us so we don't stomp on anything important."

Kell stares down at his feet. "I guess I should stand still until you get some photographs of the mud here and by the tree."

"Good call," I reply. I take out my camera and start photographing the path and the dirt. When I get to the tree the fishing lures are hanging from, I take photos from different angles, catching what might be a footprint. I put a ruler next to it for comparison.

Hughes uses his camera to do the same, then places yellow flags in the ground next to anything that might be a clue—mostly patches of dry mud where there might be tracks.

"What's next?" asks Kell. "Do you get the crime-scene unit out here?"

"Not quite," I reply. "We have to make sure there was a crime here. All we have so far is an art project." I turn to the pond with my hands on my hips. "The real evidence is going to be in there."

I set my bag down and pull out my mask and a thin bodysuit. It's too deep to go in there with my waders. They'll just fill up with water and weigh me down. I need to explore this pond underwater.

"Detective," says Kell as he observes me stripping down to my T-shirt and shorts. "I don't want to tell you your business, or interrupt a show, but may I suggest an easier and safer way to do this?"

"God, I wish you would," says Hughes.

I give him a cross look. I'd call him lazy or afraid, but he's neither. He just has more common sense than I do.

"Okay. What you got?" I ask Kell.

He pulls a pouch from his bag, drops it on the ground, and pulls out a rope with a huge, three-pronged hook on the end.

"Are you going to rappel down there?" asks Hughes.

"Alligator hook," I reply.

"You can catch them on that?"

"You let them wrap themselves up and get tired," says Kell. "Then you get close and use a bang stick to put them out of their misery."

"We just used grenades and MP7s," says Hughes.

"That doesn't exactly sound humane," replies Kell.

"Those crocodiles were all members of ISIS. My commander told me so."

This trip's drawing Hughes's real personality to the surface. I can't tell if he's funny or a psycho—a term that could probably describe everyone here.

"The worst thing I ever saw was the bone crusher," says Kell. "In theory it's great. You have a huge steel pipe on your boat and just drop it on top of an alligator, crushing his skull. Only one time we used one and just hit some spot in front of his eyes, and the thing came to the surface and kept thrashing around in circles, sending waves so powerful the boat rocked. His tail hit two guys and sent them into the water. Shooting him didn't do anything—he was already brain-dead. We had to back off and wait until he just stopped cold. Fun times." He picks up his hook by the end and nods to me. "Okay to dredge?"

"It's got to come up sometime," I reply.

Kell throws the hook into the pond at one end and starts to pull it back. By the time it reaches his feet, the hook has amassed a clump of vegetation and mud.

"Hold on." I take a tarp from my bag and walk over to his side. "Let me spread this out, and we can dump that out on it."

Kell lets the muck fall to the blue plastic. I slip on my gloves and start sorting through the dead grass and wet dirt. I don't see anything of interest, although Nadine Baltimore might question that assessment.

Kell throws the hook out again and drags it toward us. He dumps the grass, mud, and roots onto the tarp, and I run my fingers through. "Nope."

Kell lets the hook fall just a few inches from the last spot and pulls it in. I sort through this muck, starting to doubt myself. If this was a body-dumping ground, I'd think we'd find something.

I let the mud fall through my fingers. Hughes's light falls on the tarp. "What's that?"

I spread the mud evenly across the plastic like the world's most disgusting cake frosting. A small metal disk reflects in the beam of his flashlight. I pull the wire attached to it from a clump of dirt and discover a small electronic device.

"It looks like a hearing aid," says Kell.

More precisely, a cochlear implant, the kind that's semipermanently attached to the skull.

Kell's arms drop as I hold the device up in the light. I know they can feel what I'm feeling; this doesn't belong here. This place feels *wrong* in the right way.

"Should I go again?" asks Kell in a somber voice.

"Yeah," I say softly.

We all watch as the hook hits the water and sinks. He starts to pull the rope in. Suddenly it grows taut. Kell pulls, and the rope moves but remains taut.

"I think I caught something." His voice is even quieter now. This is no longer a joke for him as he realizes what's on the other end could have been alive once—alive and walking and talking. It could be a person.

He pulls again. "This feels odd."

"Like bones?" asks Hughes.

"No. Like metal."

Hughes and I lean in, trying to imagine how deep the pond could be. "Like car metal?" says Hughes.

"No. Not like that. Hold on." Kell pulls, and again the rope moves while remaining taut.

"Need help?" asks Hughes.

Kell shakes his head. "Not yet. Just keep an eye out."

We're so deep in this mystery that we've forgotten we're surrounded by thousands of meat-eating reptiles larger than ourselves. I flash my light around the pond, looking for our original alligator, but see no sign of him.

Kell keeps pulling, struggling harder now. The black water begins to move as something is pulled from the bottom and dragged slowly ashore.

A broken tree limb surfaces, and the edge of something covered in mud and dead grass begins to poke above the water. Kell gives a mighty heave, and the thing cuts through the water and slides up onto the wet grass.

We stare at it, trying to make sense of it all. It's a three-foot cube . . . more precisely, a cage. Filled with dark-brown . . . bones.

Hughes aims his light at the round curve of a human skull.

The cage is filled with them. Lots of bones. More than one person.

He walks over and kneels to get a closer look. We stare at the bones, stripped of all flesh, and a thousand questions come to mind.

Splash! We jump as Kell's alligator hook sinks into the pond again; then our attention returns to the remains, trying to get a count of the skulls.

I think I spot at least two more. That means three more victims. This plus the four kids and the body in the ditch makes eight people we're sure of.

Eight people.

"Hey, guys?" says Kell.

"What is it?" I ask, still staring at the bones.

"I think I hooked another cage . . . and I'm pretty sure it bumped into another one. We might have a bunch of them down there."

CHAPTER THIRTY-TWO
SQUAD GOALS

Walter Denton, FBI special agent and director of the South Florida serial homicide task force, walks to the podium of the small auditorium in the FBI's Miami office and addresses the various law enforcement departments in the room. He's in his late forties and has a shaved head and a serious demeanor. His reputation, according to George, is that of a solid investigator. He's methodical but not particularly imaginative, which can be a good thing in many cases.

He sets his portfolio down. "Ladies and gentlemen, let me be very, very clear. There will be absolutely no leaks out of this investigation. Those of you who have to report to superiors, make this one hundred percent clear to them. If they have a problem, they can speak with me. If any of you have to report to a superior who you don't think possesses appropriate discretion, then speak to me privately and I will have a conversation with them." He looks around the room. "If you feel that I'm being insulting, or assuming that you lack professionalism, let me reaffirm that is not the case. I am speaking from experience. Just last year, we were on the verge of closing in on a suspect in Indiana wanted for the murders of three women. We had an eyewitness description and a suspect under surveillance. A local sheriff decided to get on the five o'clock news and essentially describe our suspect, out of what he said was a matter of public safety and nothing to do with his reelection campaign. That suspect fled, and it took us three months to catch up with him in Iowa, where he'd killed four more people. Four people because one man couldn't keep his mouth shut."

I think I like this guy. George is sitting to my left with no expression, while Hughes is on my right, already taking notes. Should I take notes? What am I supposed to take notes on? Should I look at Hughes's?

Relax, Sloan. This isn't high school.

Denton continues, "Now, I'm aware that there's been a little turf war regarding this case because of local politics."

Oh crap, he means us.

"But that's going to stop, right now." Denton stares directly at George.

George simply nods. Either he doesn't take that as an insult, or he's going to punch Denton in the parking lot. I put the odds at fifty-fifty. Personally, I'm no longer a fan.

"Okay, that's out of the way. We're all here because of the excellent work of the Underwater Investigation Unit, headed up by George Solar, who I believe you all know. George, we're glad you found a way out of retirement."

This gets some applause from the fifty or so people here. Huh, interesting. Denton seems to be a showman disguised as a cop.

"Yesterday, following a lead, they uncovered a dumping site in the Florida Everglades. A preliminary count puts the total number of remains at around thirty people. Forensics has only started, and we haven't made any identifications yet. Now, here are the two important takeaways. Please make note of this."

Hughes sits ready to do so.

"One, tomorrow, we're going to make a statement to the press. Currently there is a lid on that. If anyone leaks before then, I'll know it came from this room. We're going to tell the media that a tracker working for the park found the remains while doing an alligator count. The reason for this is that we do not, under any circumstances, want our suspect to know what led us to this crime scene." Denton stares directly at me. "This is all because of Detective Sloan McPherson's work on the Pond 65 case. We strongly believe there is a connection between these two sites, and we do not, I repeat, do not want our suspect knowing we know.

"Why? Because we believe he's an active serial killer with a routine. He wakes up every day in the same place. He drives the same car. He goes to work in the same place. If we're going to find him, that's how. But if he gets spooked and decides to leave South Florida, what could take a week may take years.

"Marybeth and Stanton Waldrop, Jepson Rivers, and Marcie Norris. Remember those names. They're dead because one asshole in Indiana couldn't keep his mouth shut. Am I clear?

"Whoever is behind this is in our midst. Catching him could be just days away if we do things right. His next victim could be saved if we proceed cautiously."

A hand goes up in front of me. Denton calls on the man. "Yes, Detective Upton?"

"I understand the need for discretion, but what are we going to tell the public? They're going to know something is up."

"Fair question," murmurs Hughes.

"We're going to tell them that we found human remains. We're going to tell them that the killer may still be active in South Florida."

"What about the description? I understand we have one," asks Upton.

Denton nods. "We have a person of interest. We'll circulate the image." He holds up a line drawing of an average face with sunglasses. "He looks like half the faces in front of me. I don't know how helpful this'll be."

Denton doesn't mention the image of Sleazy Steve from the concert photo. I'm sure he discussed this with George. But is not releasing it the right move?

"As far as strategy is concerned, we need every resource at our disposal. We'll be assigning different aspects of the case according to capabilities. Right now, our best evidence is probably in identifying the victims. We have our forensic teams from Atlanta and Washington flying in to assist. If we know who was killed, it might help us figure out who killed them." He checks his watch. "The clock's ticking. Let's get to work."

"So, what now?" I ask George.

"I figure we have about twelve hours before all hell breaks loose. The media storm is going to be big. Real big."

"I'm just glad they're keeping our names out of it for now," I reply.

George shakes his head. "That won't last."

CHAPTER THIRTY-THREE
STAINED

I'm standing in Lara Chadwick and Eric Timm's kitchen in a small, pill-box-shaped house just north of where Naval Air Station Fort Lauderdale was located. For the last eight years, this house has been the center of a local mystery, while the navy airbase, now gone, has been the center of an enduring mystery for over seventy years.

The air station was where the infamous Flight 19 took off, never to be seen again, except in movies and stories concerning the Bermuda Triangle. Dad has his theories on what happened, but, needless to say, the mystery has grown into folklore.

More recently, Lara and Eric's disappearance had neighbors wondering and police baffled. While it remained an open case, the local theory was that Eric murdered his pretty spouse and then fled with the body.

The fact that both their cars were still in the driveway required the assumption that Eric had an unregistered vehicle or an accomplice.

Another theory was that the two were involved in some drug deal and had to leave town.

Yet another was that they were the victims of a serial killer, a theory the police refused to validate.

After Kell pulled the crab cages full of human remains from the Everglades, the old theories vanished like Flight 19, and we now understand at least part of their fate.

The police were frustrated by the lack of forensic evidence. If Lara and Eric had been murdered in the home, there was no sign of it. No blood. No bullet holes. They had simply vanished.

If it had been a domestic dispute resulting in Lara's death, then there should have been some forensic evidence. Blood is almost impossible to completely get rid of. That's why I sold my old boat.

We now know that after vanishing from here, the young couple's bodies ended up underwater in the Everglades. How they got there is the question Hughes and I are trying to answer, along with every other cop in South Florida.

Lara's skeleton was largely intact. The animals that could make their way through the cage had devoured most of the flesh, but even the occasional battering from alligators was unable to break the trap open.

Eric's body, along with those of a dozen other men, had been dismembered into multiple pieces. Because the police were unable to find blood in his house or in the backyard, it suggests that he was cut up elsewhere, making the location of Steve's butchering operation yet another mystery.

"Swamp Killer," says Hughes as he flips on the light to the dining room and looks at the empty room.

That's the name the media has given Sleazy Steve.

"He didn't kill them in the swamp," I reply.

"True. But I think it's a better name. 'Sleazy Steve' sounded like we were looking for a flasher."

"Yeah, but that was his nickname. Assuming Steve is his name, our chances of finding him were better when that's what we were calling him," I explain. "If someone else knew him by that name, they're much more likely to come forward."

"Sure. But officially there's no connection between him and the Swamp Killer. Nobody has seriously suggested they're connected. The public doesn't even know that the kids in Pond 65 were murdered," he replies.

"I'm not sure how I feel about that. I'm worried that Denton's investigational advantage may be a hindrance."

"I see both sides," says Hughes. "Right now, I'd like to see a connection. Why did he select Lara?"

"Right. Why did he select *any* of the women?"

Hughes kneels and examines the lock to the back door. "No sign of forced entry."

"That's why police thought it might have been Eric or someone they knew," I tell him. "But I'm not sure I buy it."

"What makes you say that?"

"I think we put too much emphasis on signs of forced entry sometimes. Are all the doors in your house locked all the time?"

"I hope so. But I get your point."

I lean over and examine the lock. "How hard is it to pick a lock like that?"

"We check for that," replies Hughes.

"We check for amateur attempts to pick a lock. Plastic picks don't leave scratch marks. It's like when I yell at Jackie to clean up her room. If she doesn't look at the mess in her closet, it doesn't count."

"I'm not sure I track," replies Hughes.

"She likes things simple. If she can pretend her closet isn't her room, it doesn't count. If investigators can pretend the only way for a stranger to get inside is by breaking in, then you're going to rule out a stranger when you don't find forced entry," I explain.

He stands back up. "They're smarter than that."

"I'm sure they are. They're smarter than me. Jackie is smarter than me. But the thing about smart people is that they can be the most intellectually lazy of us all."

"Great to hear an anti-intellectual talking point from a woman holding down a full-time job and working on a PhD in archaeology. Did I mention I played *Fortnite* for five hours last night?"

"Jackie plays that game too. My point is that we like to shove things into convenient boxes, even when we know they won't fit. When all the leads dried up on Lara and Eric, the police should've thought of that. Same as the kids in the van. I don't mean the investigators had to spend their whole lives trying to track them down. I just mean they should have made a bigger noise and said something."

"Like what?" asks Hughes.

"I don't know. How about holding a press conference and saying, 'We really have no fucking idea what happened; if you have a theory, come on down and tell us'? You know?"

"I don't think that would instill confidence," says Hughes.

"How confident do you feel now? At least three dozen people went missing in the last decade, and nobody noticed. Do you think the neighbors feel confident? How about Lara's mother when she got that call?" I try to calm myself but fail. "What kills me, poor choice of words aside, but what really, really drives me up the wall is that the single most honest and credible person we've spoken to is a meth addict living in a bush."

"Rafferty?" says Hughes. "Yeah, I guess you're right."

"Nobody listened to him back then, and people like Aguilló are too afraid for their reputations to speak up. Maybe we're listening to the wrong people."

"Maybe we're not going to find anything here," says Hughes.

"I'm not looking for a bloody hammer or a confession on the ceiling in ultraviolet ink. I wanted to come here to understand it all." I point to his feet near the back door. "Sleazy Steve, aka the Swamp Killer, stood right where you are. Forget how he got in here or what he did. Why here? Why her?"

"Back to our main question. Okay. Why her?" Hughes replies.

"That's easy."

"How so?"

"She was pretty. All of them were. Did he see them in the super-market? How did he find them? He started before people put pictures online, so he had to have another way to see what the women looked like."

"Maybe he saw them at the mall."

I shake my head. "Let's go out to the car. I want to show you something."

I take a folder from my backpack and lay it on the hood of the SUV. It's full of aerial shots of the seven houses we've identified so far as belonging to Steve's victims.

"What are we looking at?" Hughes picks them up and scans them.

"What do all the houses have in common?"

"Middle-class? Nice neighborhoods?"

"Okay, that tells us something. No one ever reported a particularly suspicious person who stood out around the time of each murder. That means Sleazy Steve managed to blend in." A delivery truck rolls by. I point it out. "He could be in one of those, and you'd never notice."

"I think people would get suspicious if it was parked in front of a home all night."

"I'm not saying it was. Just that he managed to blend in. But that's not what I'm pointing out and why I don't think he found these women at the mall and followed them home. Look closely."

Hughes flips through the photographs. He seems confused, then his eyes narrow. "Huh."

"Yeah. See it now? The cops didn't know these cases were connected at the time; that's why they never thought about this feature that was common to all the victims' homes."

The first obvious feature on the satellite photos is that all the homes had pools, but that's not a rarity in South Florida. What sets them apart from their neighbors is that each house was at the end of a dead-end street or on a corner and thus enjoyed more privacy.

"So, Swamp Killer likes pretty women who live in secluded houses," says Hughes.

"Which means he's probably not just selecting random women and showing up," I reply.

"He finds out where they live before deciding to target them."

"Or, an alternative theory." I point to the delivery man dropping off a package and hopping back into his truck. "He finds the houses, then discovers who lives there."

"So now what?" asks Hughes.

"We need to tell Solar, then Denton. If we're right, the next dozen or so bodies they identify are going to follow the same pattern, and the theory will gain credibility."

"Makes sense," says Hughes. "Can I float a radical theory of my own?"

"What's that?"

"Maybe you're more of a killer hunter than you realize."

"Hey, I've only found bodies. I haven't found a killer yet."

Not counting when they've found me first.

CHAPTER THIRTY-FOUR
ROGUES' GALLERY

Craig Latrelle's unshaven face glances into the camera, then back to the interviewer. His shirt is wrinkled, and he has the look of a man who was rousted out of bed, which is pretty much what happened. FBI task force chief Denton pauses the video playback as Hughes and I take seats at the conference room table where he and the other agents are going over the videos of all the suspects that have been rounded up.

"What do you think, Hoyle?" Denton asks the agent sitting across from him.

She turns from the widescreen television and glances at us. "Nervous."

"They're all nervous," says Detective McCurdy, a senior detective from Broward County. "They're being questioned."

"Yes, but the way he looks at the camera. He's talking to us," she replies.

"That's because he knows the routine. Whenever there's a sex crime, he gets called in to explain his whereabouts."

The name Latrelle sounds familiar, but I don't know who he is. At the risk of embarrassing myself, I speak up. "What's his background?"

Another Broward detective, Anthony Wesley, gives me a surprised look. "Latrelle?" He shrugs. "You were probably in kindergarten. When he was sixteen, he pulled a girl off her bicycle, raped and killed her, then left her body in the woods at McFarland Park. The judge ruled it temporary insanity; he did three years in a mental institution and then did almost the same thing again when he was twenty. Same judge as before. She decided it was the mental institution and the state's fault for not properly treating him. He did five years more in a hospital and then was released to supervision. We haven't caught him doing anything since then—the operative word being *caught*."

I do the math in my head. Latrelle's too young to be the Swamp Killer, but I keep that to myself. I'm sure they already know that. The danger of pulling too tight of a net is that if you're wrong about something major, and you almost always are, you run the risk of missing the actual bad guy. The cops thought they were looking for an older white guy and a box truck with the Beltway sniper, not a black man and his teenage companion in a sedan. Ted Bundy slipped through several dragnets because people misidentified his hair color and his vehicle.

Maybe Sleazy Steve was an accomplice to the Swamp Killer . . . maybe my connection is an incredible coincidence. You have to take a look at all the weirdos. Sometimes they know something. Oddly enough, sometimes they talk.

Denton pushes a stack of folders toward Hughes and me. "These are some of the people we want interviewed. We don't have enough probable cause to ask them to come in and do taped interviews, and, frankly, we don't have the space. We're wall to wall with weirdos here. Could you guys take a look at those?"

Hughes and I exchange glances. This is basic work. The translation of what Denton just said is that he and his crew here are going to be talking to the *real* suspects while Hughes and I go interview every guy that got popped for taking a piss near an elementary school.

Hughes reaches over and flips through the stack of folders. There look to be a few dozen. That will mean days of driving all over South Florida and likely nowhere near the killer.

In a word, it's insulting. I'm not sure how to phrase it the right way.

"Background on misdemeanors?" asks Hughes, showing uncharacteristic disdain. "We were hoping to do something a little more . . . involved."

"It is involved," says Denton.

"You ever take the lead on a murder investigation?" Detective Wesley asks, directed at me.

"You ever find a murder scene that wasn't handed to you?" asks Hughes, interjecting on my behalf. "You're here because of what she found under your nose."

While I appreciate the chivalry, I can tell this is not going to have the desired effect. Hughes just gave Wesley's ego a smack to the nose, and the man doesn't seem like the type to back down.

"Okay, why don't you canal cops tell us what you'd like to do," Wesley gestures to the monitor. "Do you want to take the lead here? Want to talk to these perverts? Think you can get some confessions?"

I shake my head. "That's not what we're asking." I know I should play nice and figure out how to get what I want later.

"That's a good girl," says Wesley.

There's a loud banging sound. I realize it's my chair hitting the back wall as I leap to my feet and lean on the table with my knuckles down, my face in his face while I practically bare my teeth at the man.

Hughes covers his eyes. "Oh jeez."

"I'm sorry," I say as evenly as I can through gritted teeth. "I missed that. What did you say?"

"Lady, I got too much seniority and I'm too close to retirement to care what you say to Human Resources."

"Fuck Human Resources. Ever have your nose broken by a girl?" He blinks, unsure how serious I am—which makes two of us.

"Sit down, McPherson," Denton commands. "Wesley, don't be such a damn cliché."

Hughes slides my chair back under me, and I take a seat, doing my best to not act like I made such a big deal out of it and failing horribly.

There's condescension and then there's asshole-level condescension. I can handle the first—god knows I do my share of it. But the weaponized kind where he calls me a girl as a put-down just makes me want to go all prison yard—which is fine in the high school parking lot, but not in a multiagency task-force conference room.

Denton tries to defuse things by directing his attention to my partner. "Hughes, what would you and McPherson rather be doing for the task force?"

Hughes keeps his stare fixed on Wesley. "You mean us canal cops? Besides not dealing with bullshit put-downs? She can explain it better than me."

I use this opportunity to speak as calmly as I can. "We were at Chadwick and Timm's house and noticed something about *all* the murder scenes. Each house is situated in a somewhat isolated spot. In cul-de-sacs, at dead ends, or in large lots."

"We're aware of this," says an FBI agent named Bridget Jansen.

"Yes, well, we think the killer might be choosing his victims that way—finding the location and *then* the target. It makes more sense that way, rather than randomly targeting a pretty woman and hoping she lives in an isolated spot," I explain.

"This was also considered," says Denton. "What can you tell us that's actionable?"

"We'd like to go over all the reports and home security camera footage. We'd like to see if there's anything that may have been missed."

"Missed?" says Wesley. "Missed by the eight detectives we had on that case? We have hundreds of pages of logs and transcripts. We tracked every FedEx package, every cleaning lady, every stray dog in that area for several months back. What do you think we missed?"

While he's challenging me again, it's not out of bounds, although I can see him waiting for me to put on another demonstration.

"Probably nothing. But we'd like to have a look."

Denton shakes his head. "It's a waste of time and resources." He points to the pile of misdemeanor perverts. "That's where I need your attention. If that fails, then we can go back and revisit prior work. But right now is not the time for us to start second-guessing each other."

"I think that's a mistake."

"Noted. Is there anything else?"

"Everything we want is just sitting in boxes collecting dust," I plead.

"McPherson, I don't have people looking over your shoulder questioning you; maybe you should show the same respect if you want to be part of this task force."

I want to tell them that now is not the time to put our egos first. I want to remind him that the killer is still out there. But I'm facing a wall. It's almost like they're waiting for another murder so they can have fresh evidence to examine, but I can't say that aloud.

CHAPTER THIRTY-FIVE
NIGHT FISHING

I stare at the moon across the water beyond the pier and the ghostly halo that surrounds it. Behind me, George Solar's footsteps grow closer. My stomach is knotted in anxiety, not because I'm afraid of what might happen with the stolen-goods buyer we're here to talk to on Pompano Pier, but because I'm afraid of what George is going to say to me.

I turn away from the waves and see him walk past a row of benches and step around a fishing rod and a man half-asleep on the railing. His steady gaze meets mine, and I can already imagine the thoughts going on behind it. But in the months we've known each other, I've found it works best if I shut up and let him talk.

"So, I got a call from Denton," he says. "He gave me quite an earful."

"Yeah . . . I . . ."

He holds up a hand. "Then Wesley gave me a call. We go a ways back."

"Uh, yeah. Um . . ."

George shakes his head. "I'm not going to rub your nose in what you did. You know it. I know it. And now Denton's asked that I ask you to step off the task force."

Blood rushes to my head, and I'm tempted to shout an expletive. Instead, I count to ten . . . then to twenty. "What did you say?"

"I agreed."

"What?"

"What am I supposed to do? Keep you on and let them send you all the grunt work, while I could be using you for more important stuff, like the New River Bandits? If we want the UIU to be something, that something can't be done from the sidelines."

"Isn't that what you're doing? Putting me on the sidelines?"

"Well, to stretch the analogy, I'm taking us off the field. I'm pulling the UIU out of the Swamp Killer case completely. It's their investigation now. It was since the moment we found the bodies in the swamp. It's too big for us, and if they can't let us play at their level, then screw them."

I get his logic, but it's frustrating. This is my case. These victims . . . I'm the only one who knew where to look. I'm the only one who cared.

"This sucks," I reply.

"Correct. Let's be honest, we just don't have the resources to put together an investigation of this scale. It's not what we were built for. They're good at their thing—let them do it."

"Are they?" I ask.

"Are they what?" George replies.

"Are they good? You weren't there, but I gotta say, I have my doubts."

"It's not as if we have a choice but to leave them to it, Sloan. We don't have the people. We don't have connections with the district attorney."

"It wasn't like I asked them to treat us as equals, just with a little respect. One of us should have been in the meeting where the real decision making happened," I reply.

"We're not there yet."

"We? Or do you mean me?" I ask. "Would they have denied you a seat at that table?"

"I didn't want it. You don't want it. Trust me. Half their time is spent going over lunch menus."

"That's just it. That's my problem. They're nine-to-fivers. They clock in and clock out. If another murder happens while they're at their kid's Little League, whoop dee do."

"You just can't walk into a room and tell a bunch of experienced police that they're doing it wrong. Because chances are, they're the ones who know what they're doing and you aren't, and if you go running off at the mouth that they're doing things wrong, it could be a career ender . . . for all of us."

"So what are you saying?" I ask, feeling challenged.

"You gotta read a room, McPherson. There's a difference between getting what you want and having a tantrum."

"I didn't have a . . ." My words fade. Yeah, I kind of did.

The boards of the pier shake as someone else comes walking in our direction. It's a man with several days' worth of beard growth, a Hawaiian shirt, shorts, and a rod and tackle. From his reddish complexion, it looks like he's got more beer in that tackle box than lures.

He places the box near George's feet and casts his line into the surf. "Checking out the conditions?" the man asks George.

"Thought I might bring my own rod out here."

"She your daughter?" he asks, looking at me.

"Stepdaughter. Pain in the ass." George pulls a folded slip of paper from his pocket and hands it to the man.

He opens it and takes a look. "Huh. Just the dome?"

"Yeah. My friend lost his to a storm."

The paper contains the description of a ninety-thousand-dollar satellite system for a yacht that enables internet connectivity, a phone line, and that kind of thing. George is asking the man if he can find one on the black market.

"I can get you a Korean one, just as good, for half of what you're offering," says the man.

"It has to be that one. My client is very specific."

Very, very specific. The only satellite system matching the description that's in this hemisphere is mounted on a mast on a yacht sitting in a marina in Fort Lauderdale right now. It's also a boat we control and have under surveillance.

"Let me text a friend," says the man as he types into his phone. "How soon do you need it by?"

"We need to have it in the Bahamas in two days," says George.

The man looks up from his phone, skeptical. "Why not just ask the manufacturer?"

"My client isn't into paper trails."

"Yeah, well, that makes me suspicious."

"We can talk to someone else."

"Hold up. Let me see if my friend has one lying around the warehouse. Okay?" He taps into the phone. "Okay . . . he thinks he can do it. But it won't be at that price." He flashes his phone at George and shows the amount: $65,000.

George laughs. "That ain't going to happen. We're on a fixed budget. It's forty-five thousand dollars."

The man texts his friend back. "This comes out of my commission."

"Not my problem."

"He'll do it for fifty thousand," the man says.

"What part of 'I only have forty-five thousand dollars' isn't clear?" asks George.

"Damn it." The man dials his phone and walks away from us, covering the mouthpiece. I can't make out the words, but the emotions are clear enough. He comes stomping over to us. "Half up front."

George shakes his head. "All on delivery."

The man talks into his phone again, then relays the message. "No deal. Half up front."

"Nice talking to you. I'm sure someone else can find it in their warehouse." George starts to walk away, and I follow.

The man shouts into his phone behind us, afraid that we're going to take our business to some other crook. We just keep going.

We're fifty feet away when he comes running up to us, his hand over the phone like it's an old-school handset with no mute button. "What about Bitcoin? Can you pay in that?"

Bitcoin is safer for them if it's a sting. All they have to do is send a courier that has no idea what's going on and wait to see if the money is transferred.

"I'll pay you in Chuck E. Cheese tokens for all I care. Whatever," says George.

"Okay. We'll let you know if we can find one in stock," the man replies.

"Better make it soon before I check some other warehouse."

The man resumes fishing and takes a bottle of beer from his cooler and pops the cap. We start walking toward the parking lot.

"You sure our dome is the only one they can get?" I ask George once we're back in his truck. The plan is to catch them in the act of stealing ours, not trying to arrest whoever shows up to sell it. But if there's a comparable satellite dome anywhere else in Florida, we could be sending the bad guys somewhere we don't want to.

"I've asked Marine Patrol and coast guard. They tell me that's the case. But, yeah, maybe this wasn't such a good idea." He glances back at the pier, wondering if he should call it off, then thinks better of it. "We'll be fine. Probably."

CHAPTER THIRTY-SIX
Scum

Jeremy Shulme is fifty-six years old, with a paunchy build, black hair sticking to his forehead like a sweaty rag, and a Members Only jacket. He slouches across the parking lot of the West Broward cardboard packing plant toward his beat up Honda Civic, where Hughes and I are waiting. First he sees our shadows in the streetlight, then our faces and badges.

"Are you Jeremy?" asks Hughes, as if this poor SOB didn't match to a T the classic image of a child pornographer.

"Yeah?" he says, not too surprised. As a parolee, he's used to cops popping up at odd hours to check in on him.

Even though we're off the Swamp Killer task force, a friend of Solar's at the Broward Sheriff's Office asked if we could do a backgrounder on half a dozen people in exchange for lending us some guys to watch the *Pacific Miracle*, the boat whose radar dome we're using as Bandit bait.

Shulme was arrested eight years ago in a sting operation by BSO when he exchanged child pornography with a detective posing as an online perv. When they raided Shulme's home—actually his mother's house—they found hard drives with incriminating images and videos.

What popped him to the top of the list of pervs to talk to in the Swamp Killer case, though, were his folders full of violent stuff involving women and children.

Chances are he's just a guy with the inability to control his perverted curiosity and not a physical threat, but you never know.

"Is this about the bodies in the swamp?" he asks.

The fact that bodies were found, but not how many or in what condition, broke yesterday, but we've been tight-lipped about the connections with all the victims. We don't want the Swamp Killer to skip town without a trace.

"We're just checking up on you," says Hughes. "What have you heard?"

Shulme gives us a knowing look. "Right. Right. I heard you found a bunch of bodies in a crab cage inside an alligator pond. That right?"

"We don't know much about it," I reply.

"Right. Right. Crazy this happening after you found that van," he says, looking directly at me. "The cage yours too?"

Hughes and I have enough self-control to avoid looking at each other, but we don't offer up an answer. Shulme seems fascinated by this case. Of course, they did arrest him with a hard drive filled with snuff films.

"They didn't release any photos from the scene. Are they going to?" he asks.

"You into that kind of thing?" asks Hughes.

"Aren't you? Isn't it why you became a cop?"

"I became a cop so I could arrest assholes like you and put them behind bars so bigger assholes can have their way with them. Isn't that why you became a pervert? So you could have them do that to you?"

Shulme rolls his eyes. "My uncle started molesting me before I could talk. You think anything that happened to me behind bars was worse than that?"

Damn. There's this thing that's been happening to me lately when I talk to bad guys: I see two different men in front of me. One is the monster. The other is the victim.

The victim didn't make the monster. But it sure did nurture him. Shulme knew right from wrong and kept choosing wrong. But, still, assuming what he says is true, maybe we shouldn't be surprised, given the world he grew up in.

Shulme sees the reaction in my eyes. "That's right. Want me to tell you what he did?"

"Save it for your court-appointed therapist. We don't care how you got here, only what you did. And what you're doing now."

He sighs. "I know I screwed up. I let my curiosity get the better of me."

"You weren't just lurking on the dark web. You were running servers and helping men victimize children," I reply.

"Women too," he adds.

"Victimizing them too. Um, okay."

"No, I mean not all those people were men. Some were women who sold their own children or others. They helped their husbands. People always forget about the women."

"Well, thank you for pointing that out," replies Hughes.

Shulme shakes his head. "You're so tough. I've seen things you couldn't even imagine. Children being hurt in ways that would make you want to blow your brains out to get 'em out of your head."

"Too bad you didn't do us the favor," says Hughes.

"Ha. Want to know the really funny thing about my case? Want to know the part they left out? What never made it into the press? The reason I got a reduced sentence? Some of those videos, the worst ones? They didn't have too much trouble finding out who the victims were, because they already knew. They only had to look at the case number at the bottom of the videos. The worst footage I've seen? I got it from cops."

A question I've kind of always wondered about comes to mind. "How do you guys find each other?"

"A thing called the internet."

I ignore his sarcasm. "Yeah, but how do you trust someone enough to send them videos and vice versa?"

"You ever play 'I'll show you mine if you show me yours' as a little girl?"

"Watch it," says Hughes, maybe more to me than Shulme.

"You start with a little trade. Maybe something barely illegal. They trade back. You build trust as you share. Each of you is in it just as much as the other. Unless they're a cop using child pornography to entrap you."

I decide to not challenge him on his concept of *entrap*. "Mutually assured destruction, but with child porn. Each one of you is putting yourself into a vulnerable position."

"That's basically it," he says, but his voice fades.

"No, it's not," replies Hughes. "That's a big part of it for you, isn't it? That pervert signaling? That's a turn-on, isn't it?"

Shulme shrugs, not exactly denying what Hughes is saying.

"You have a boat?" I ask.

This catches him off guard. "A boat? No. You know how much I make? A damn boat?"

"We didn't ask if you rented the *QE2* for cocktail parties." Hughes nods to the car. "If you can afford a shitty car, you can afford a shitty boat."

"Hell, I can't even swim. I don't own a boat, and I don't think I've ever been in one."

"You like women?" I ask.

"Are you asking if I'm a homosexual?"

"No. I would have asked you if you liked guys. Do you like women? Have you ever had a healthy relationship with a woman?"

"Besides my mother?"

Hughes covers his eyes and tries to stifle a laugh. I keep my composure, but I'm sure my reaction shows on my face.

"That's something else to talk to your therapist about," I say.

Shulme gets agitated. "You said relationship. I don't think you asked me if I was screwing my mother. No. I was not. And no, I have not had much luck with women. But, yes, I like them. Why, do you like me?" He gives me a leer.

"Not the man you are. No. Unless Detective Hughes has any questions, I think we're done."

"I'm good," says Hughes.

"That's it?" asks Shulme. "Aren't you going to ask me if I'm the Swamp Killer?"

I look him up and down. "You're not."

Hughes and I walk back to my truck and get in. We watch as Shulme drives off.

Hughes speaks up. "Steve doesn't live with his mother and drive around in a busted-up Honda working the night shift at a box plant."

"He's more organized than that." I'm staring at the fading taillights of Shulme's car. Something he said, or rather some things he said, are running through my mind.

"What's up?" asks Hughes.

"If you saw Shulme at the supermarket, what would you think?"

"Hide my kid?"

"No. I mean just the image of the man. What would you assume?"

"There goes some loser who probably lives with his mother."

"A loner."

"Clearly. I'd hate to be at the party where he's the charismatic one."

"But he's not a loner," I say, thinking out loud. "I mean, maybe now. But not when they arrested him. He was the center of a large group of perverted men."

"And women," says Hughes. "He made it clear that it was an equal-opportunity pervert club."

"Right. Whatever. My point is that he's not a loner. He has people he talks to. People he shares his perversions with. Think about that level of trust. He shares the kinds of things you'd think he'd want to hide," I explain.

"He didn't exactly announce it to the world," says Hughes. "He shared it with other pervs."

"But not just to get more illicit material. Sharing was part of the thrill."

Hughes nods. "I see what you're saying. You're wondering if Sleazy Steve is the same way."

"Or maybe Sleazy Steve was, but that all stopped when he became the Swamp Killer. Who did he share his perversions with?"

"Would he? We both agreed that Shulme isn't the type because he's such a mess. I can't see that guy talking to a girl, let alone working his way into her home without her calling the cops."

"Maybe he doesn't look that way on the outside, but there are some awful men in benign-looking packages."

I check my phone and see an email I've been waiting for. "Oh great."

"What's that?" asks Hughes.

I almost tell him, but I don't. I can't drag him any further in. For the first time in my professional career as a police officer, I lie to a coworker. In my defense, it's to protect a friend who has access to inter-agency communications.

"It's nothing," I reply and immediately feel horrible about doing it.

CHAPTER THIRTY-SEVEN
ACCOUNTABILITY

The sun is rising as I pull into Darren Cope's driveway and block him from pulling out in his work truck. His house is in a blue-collar neighborhood in Sunrise, Florida. The lawn is a bit overgrown, and the fence on either side of the house has blue tarp blocking a view of the backyard. I can tell his vehicle's filled with junk because of the stack of air conditioners poking above the edge.

Cope gets out of his truck dressed in work overalls with his Cope AC & Electric logo stitched over his chest.

"Can I help you?" he says in a surly voice, striding up to me. He's got gray hair poking out from underneath his red cap and a weather-beaten face with a thick silver mustache. His build is large but wiry, as if he recently lost a lot of weight.

"I'm Detective McPherson with the UIU."

"The UI what? Never mind. Move your damn car, it's blocking my way," he says, turning back to his truck.

"I have some questions," I say, not budging.

He points to a camera aimed at the driveway. "See that camera? I put that there because of you guys. Now let me leave, or else."

"Or else what?" I open my jacket, revealing the butt of my gun.

"Or else you'll hear from my lawyer."

I call his bluff, fairly certain he doesn't want this to escalate. "Want to call him? Is he cheap? We can do this at the station."

"This is harassment," he complains.

"This is an investigation into the murders of Lara Chadwick and Eric Timm."

The email I didn't show Hughes was a list of persons of interest from the couple's murder: all service workers spotted in the area. Cope was at the top because he made six visits to the neighborhood, working on the AC unit of their neighbor. At least twice he was spotted walking into the couple's yard.

When originally interviewed, Cope said it was because they'd asked him to give them an estimate for AC repair. When he couldn't show a call log or email proving that, he claimed that he'd run into Eric Timm in a parking lot. This was probably after he realized that one of the neighbors had a surveillance camera that observed half of Chadwick's yard and there was no proof of either of them walking over to ask him to check their unit.

Cope folds his arms and leans against the tailgate of his truck. "You're making a huge mistake here."

"Am I?" I pull out my notepad but don't take my eyes off the man. "It says here in the notes that on the night of the disappearance your alibi checked out, but it seemed kind of sloppy to me. I was wondering if you could tell me where you were?"

"Not there," he replies.

I shake my head. "That's not how it works."

"Enlighten me. How does it work?"

"Six visits to the neighborhood? That's a lot. I figure either you're really bad at your job or maybe you had a thing for Lara Chadwick."

"Never saw her," says Cope.

"That's not what you said when you told detectives that you ran into Eric Timm."

"I don't remember what I said. Maybe she was in the car. Maybe she wasn't."

"What restaurant was it again?" I ask. "They say they couldn't find a credit-card charge for either of them."

"Maybe they used a magical thing called cash. I don't know where they ate. I ran into him in the parking lot. You really need to let me go now."

"Where were you that night?" I ask.

He shakes his head. "You really are a dumb bitch."

"Say that to my face."

He steps right up to me, glances at his camera and then back to me. "Dumb. Bitch."

I make a tiny lunge at him, and he flinches, covering his face.

"You're so done," he growls as he recovers. "I'm getting into my truck and backing up. If you're still there, then I'm going to hit your car. It's my property. It's my right."

He gets into his truck and puts it into gear and revs the engine. Is he serious?

He guns it at my truck and skids to a stop in front of my bumper.

"Ten seconds," he calls out through his open window.

There's something seriously off about this guy. I'm thinking he might go ahead and do it. Technically speaking, he's right about this being his property. I glance at the large dent on the right side of his rear bumper and realize he truly doesn't care.

I grit my teeth and get into my car and back up. He drives past me in the street and stops, a cocky grin on his face.

"Thought so," he says.

I lose my temper and say something I shouldn't. I regret it before it even leaves my lips. But I want to see what he does.

"See you later, Sleazy Steve."

His face doesn't freeze in horror. He doesn't appear shocked. He doesn't react at all. He also doesn't seem confused. He simply processes the information without telling me what he makes of it. Then his attention snaps back to the road and he flips me the finger and peels out, racing down the street.

After he's gone, I get out of my truck and catch my breath. What was I thinking? What was *he* thinking?

I glance at his house and walk over to the sidewalk. Do I take a closer look? The camera is right there. He'll know, but what will he do?

I decide to step onto his property and take a peek over the fence. The path between the side of the house and the fence is crowded with AC unit covers and plastic sheds. It takes every effort I can muster to not hop the fence and start poking around. I have to know my limits, and I'm afraid I may have already pushed them too far.

CHAPTER THIRTY-EIGHT
THE FOG

The rain is coming down hard on our boat's canopy and draining from either side in waterfalls at the creases. The *Pacific Miracle* is directly across the waterway from us, its satellite dome still firmly attached to the spotting tower. George and I are watching from his boat while Hughes and two BSO deputies do the same from another boat nearby. Since we're assuming the Bandits make a careful surveillance of their target before they strike, we couldn't have a Marine Patrol or coast guard boat stand by. It'd be too easy to spot from the water.

The owner of the two-hundred-foot yacht, Tariq El Momet, is currently under house arrest in Saudi Arabia, and his boat's in arrears for dockage fees and coast guard violations. When George heard the State Department had taken possession, he leaped at the chance to use it for this purpose. After some horse trading, we were able to get use of it for three days.

Today is the last day. After that it gets sent to Miami and eventually government auction if Mr. El Momet doesn't step up and pay his fines.

A small cabin cruiser makes its way up the canal, a lone man standing at the helm.

George watches him with his night-vision goggles until he passes out of sight.

A cigarette boat comes next, its massive outboards sending waves all the way to us, rocking our boat.

I glance back at the *Miracle*. Something is odd. "Solar. Check out our boat."

He swivels his scope toward the yacht. "What am I looking at?"

"I don't know. Something doesn't feel right."

"Feel right?"

I call into the radio. "Locomotive, this is Sidecar. Do you notice anything?"

"Could you be more specific? Over," says Hughes.

"Something weird? Odd?"

"We only saw the two boats pass, over."

I glance back at the yacht's satellite dome.

It's gone.

"Look!" I tell George, pointing.

"What the fudge? Hold on . . ."

I squint, trying to see through the rain. It's simply not possible for them to have taken it so fast.

"Hold up," says George. He calls into the radio, "Locomotive, be advised, the suspects are on the boat. I repeat, they are *on the boat*. They appear to have thrown a black cloth over the dome. I think that's so they can work under it."

But how the hell did they get on the boat?

"What do you advise?" asks Hughes.

Hughes and the deputies can reach the yacht first, but if they spook the suspects, then we risk them vanishing the same way they appeared. If we rush the yacht at the wrong time, that might make the bad guys open fire, and things could get nasty.

"How much does that dome weigh?" asks George.

"Forty pounds?" I say.

"How did they get aboard? More importantly, how are they going to get it off?"

I glance down the waterway and realize the cigarette boat has stopped and is poking out beyond the corner of a seawall about a half mile away. "Look there. They probably dived off a docked boat while that one was making itself seen."

"Two boats? Clever. You're the resident pirate—what do we do?"

"Taking the dome is at least a two-man job. We can try to grab them."

"But then the boat gets away. I have a feeling the guys on the yacht are hired help. The moment we move on them, the cigarette boat's out of here."

"We can tell the coast guard, give them the description," I say hopefully.

"Any other solutions?"

"Yeah, but you're not going to like it."

"Any solutions that don't involve you going into the water?"

"Um."

"Yeah. Thought so. We need to decide now. It looks like they've got the dome. Any second now that boat is going to come racing down here to do a pickup, and there's no way we can outrun them," says George.

"Don't," I reply.

"What?"

"They're not drug runners out in the open ocean. The guys on the yacht are going to take the dome to the edge of the pier and climb aboard. The cigarette boat will then leave slowly. Racing out of here would attract too much attention," I explain.

"And then what?"

"We follow them. Get Hughes and his team ready to follow by road while we follow from a safe distance."

"I don't like that. We could lose them."

"We can get the BSO helicopter here in fifteen minutes, and Marine Patrol can block them at the other end."

In the distance, the cigarette boat's engines roar to life, and it starts cruising back down the canal. George watches it approach, weighing his options.

"Is there a plan C?" he asks.

"Yeah," I reply. "Let me drive."

"We can't go faster."

"No. I just have to drive smarter."

George considers this. "I'm not sure if I prefer the cautious McPherson or the impulsive one." But he backs away from the console, letting me take the wheel. "Now what?"

"Lower the canopy. It's gonna get windy. And grab the anchor. Get ready to throw it when I say so."

"Jesus Christ. I hate this plan already."

"Relax." I nod at the cigarette boat heading down the waterway. It's beginning to make a curving arc that will take it to the edge of the pier, exactly as I predicted.

It's my pirate blood.

"Okay," says George as he takes the top down. "What's next?"

"Tell Hughes to get ready and . . . hold on!"

I gun the engine and head straight for the cigarette boat as it nears the closest point to the pier. The sound of the rain covers the rev of our engine initially, but soon enough the man on the cigarette boat jerks his head around, trying to see what's coming at him.

Two men carrying a black bundle race across the dock and prepare to leap into the cigarette boat once it gets closer. But it's still not there yet. The cigarette boat captain isn't sure what to do. Should he let them jump aboard? Or should he cut and run?

He decides not to take a chance. He guns his engine and turns away from the pier and flies across the waves and into the waterway.

"McPherson! He's getting . . ." CRASH!

George's words are drowned by the sound of the cigarette boat smashing bow first into the black dredging barge anchored at the far end of the pier, plainly visible to anyone making a getaway in broad daylight . . . not so much at night, in the rain, at full speed.

As Hughes and his team run across the pier with their guns drawn, George and I motor to the site of the crash to pull the unconscious pilot from the wreck of his boat.

"I hope we got the right guy," says George over the roar of the engines.

Me too . . . Me too.

CHAPTER THIRTY-NINE
Low Tide

I walk into our warehouse office, holding my morning cup of coffee, and find George Solar sitting across from a man I don't recognize at the conference room table. Hughes has joined them at the far end.

"Oh, hey," I say, setting my coffee and case down on my desk. I check my watch. "Did I miss an email?"

"Have a seat, McPherson," says George, his voice devoid of emotion.

"This about the bust last night? Everything get processed?"

We pulled out the driver of the cigarette boat, Armand Alejo, and sent him to the hospital with an armed escort, then spent the next several hours interrogating his accomplices, two men from Venezuela with arrest records for narcotics and armed robbery.

Alejo served in the Venezuelan Navy before fleeing the country. He showed up in the US a few years ago, working on luxury yachts, but he kept getting fired. Presumably because he was ripping them off. At some point he paired up with the other two and decided to grow his budding business.

Why did he choose boats instead of banks? It's what he knew. He also had contacts in the marine-electronics market and the ability to move stolen goods.

But the interesting part was when we pulled up his Facebook profile and recognized the watermark on certain photos of his girlfriend. It belonged to Greg Hesher, the boat photographer we'd tenuously linked to most of the other robberies. We're still not sure if Hesher was a willing accomplice or if Alejo's girlfriend simply had access to his photos.

Either way, she was taken into custody and will now have the opportunity to explain her side of things. Or, more wisely, lawyer up and figure out how to pin the blame solely on her boyfriend.

"This is Ty Russel," George says as I take a seat opposite Hughes. "He's with the Broward district attorney's office."

Russel is in his midforties and has a shaved head on a skinny neck. He's wearing a suit that seems too warm for our office.

"Oh great," I reply.

"No. Not great," says George. "Mr. Russel is here because Darren Cope's attorney says he's filing another lawsuit against the state. Did you speak to the man?"

"Wait? What?" I'm so confused. "What do you mean, *another* lawsuit?"

"Right now, we're involved in a ten-million-dollar lawsuit with Cope that looks like it's going to go to trial. He's suing us over perceived improprieties in the investigation into the deaths of Chadwick and Timm."

"I just spoke to him," I say. "What's he claiming?"

"Mr. Cope says you held him captive, threatened him physically, and trespassed on his property," replies Russel. "Can you address any of these allegations?"

"I . . ."

"Shut it, Sloan," says George. Then, to Russel: "If this is off the record, she'll answer. If this is in a legal capacity, she'll want her attorney present."

I feel like I'm drowning. I ask George, "What exactly was the original lawsuit about?"

"That's not relevant to this discussion," says Russel.

"Like hell," says George. "It seems some investigators on the Chadwick-Timm case got a little too aggressive and pulled Cope's medical file without a warrant to check up on his alibi for the night of the disappearance. He'd claimed that he'd had complications from outpatient chemotherapy for his lymphoma and had to spend the night at the hospital. They didn't believe him. Turns out he was telling the truth. Now you've stepped into that shit storm."

"His attorney notified us yesterday that he intends to add your visit to the suit," says Russel.

"I didn't know any of this," I tell the prosecutor.

Russel looks down at a sheet of paper. "That's not what I've been told. I'm to understand that, in a meeting with investigators, they told you specifically to leave the matter alone."

"We asked for case files," says Hughes. "That's all. They declined. There was no mention of any pending litigation or that they'd already screwed up the investigation."

"We're an independent investigative agency," replies George. "We don't answer to BSO, the FBI, or any other organization that fouled this up. We have the right to ask any questions we see fit, regardless of whether your investigators bungled things."

"Well, you may be independent, but he's going to name you in the suit," says Russel. "Do you even have counsel?"

"That's what the state attorney is for," replies George.

"Were you the one that authorized Detective McPherson to interview Mr. Cope?" asks Russel.

George hesitates for a moment, trying to figure out how to answer the question without throwing me under the bus. "She doesn't need my permission."

"Detective Hughes? Were you aware that she was going to speak to Mr. Cope?"

Hughes looks even more uneasy. "We often divide up the workload."

"That doesn't answer the question."

I interrupt. "He didn't know. Solar didn't know. I was following a lead."

"Which lead?" asks Russel.

"That's none of your business," snaps George. "It's what we do. We chase down leads."

"Well, this lead says his rights were violated. He also says he has it on video with audio. He claims that he has you making threats."

"Verbally?" asks George.

"Yes. Generally, that's how it works," Russel says snidely.

"Then, generally speaking, isn't it your job as a lawyer to know that in the State of Florida recordings require two-party consent?"

"I'm very familiar with the law, Mr. Solar," Russel shoots back. "I don't need a lect—"

George slaps his hand on the table. "Hold up. You mean that Mr. Cope's attorney flat-out told you that he'd recorded Detective McPherson without her permission, and you didn't point out that this was both illegal, inadmissible, and grounds for *her* to sue *him*?"

"We're weighing all the options . . ."

"You're so full of shit. You're going to use this as leverage against him in your lawsuit, aren't you?"

Russel is quiet.

I'm still processing what George is suggesting. I think he means that since Cope illegally recorded our conversation and admitted as much through his attorney, the state is looking at this as a bargaining chip to get Cope's original civil suit thrown out.

George glances down at the table in front of Russel and notices something. "What's that?"

Russel puts his hand over the document for a moment, then pushes it toward him. "It's an agreement to let us handle the litigation of the claim."

"So you can bundle them together and get out of your lawsuit?" George picks it up, reads it, then slides it over to me.

I scan the document. Basically, it would allow the county attorney, Russel and company, to represent me. Exactly what George suspected.

"Has Mr. Cope filed the new suit yet?" I ask.

"No. But his attorney has filed a motion with the judge."

"The judge of *your* civil suit," I add.

"But he's trying to name you in it."

"You mean add her name to the list of investigators. But he's still suing the county, correct?" asks George.

"Correct," Russel replies, his eyes on the table in front of him. "But his attorney specifically mentioned a separate lawsuit concerning you, Detective McPherson."

"Thankfully, qualified immunity is still a thing, and that would be the state's problem if he was serious," says George. "But we both know he's not. Although that wasn't your intention here, clearly. You wanted to scare us into having you represent us so that you could bargain."

I rip up the agreement. "I think I'll wait until Mr. Cope serves me papers. Until then, I'm not going to worry about this."

"Or you could hire your own attorney and sue him for illegally recording you," suggests Hughes.

"We all want the same thing here," says Russel. "Doing that wouldn't be very productive."

"We want the same thing?" George points to the door. "Get the hell out of here."

"We still have to discuss things," says Russel.

George stands. "Tell your boss Woolsack that she'd better tell me face-to-face what those things are. We're done dealing with you."

"You're making a mistake," says Russel, still seated.

"GET THE HELL OUT!" George glares at the man with murder in his eyes.

Realizing he's gone too far, Russel gathers his documents, jams them into his briefcase, and makes a hasty exit.

After the door shuts, George's fury is directed at me. "Goddamn it, McPherson! Just when we're looking good with the New River bust, you go pull this dumb bullshit. What were you thinking, talking to a person of interest after they specifically told you to stay clear? And threatening the man? On camera? You're damned lucky his attorney fucked things up."

"I'm sorry," I say quietly. Blood is flushing my face. I can't even look at him.

"Bullshit like that could close us down! That asshole who just left here? We're going to need a favor from him one day. Guess what? We're not getting it. He's a petty, vindictive little man that will leave you out to dry just to get back at you. And when BSO finds out that we just snatched their golden ticket, they're gonna be pissed too." He collapses in his chair. "I'm too old to manage this kindergarten crap."

"I don't think—" begins Hughes.

George cuts him off. "Don't even start. Your job is to babysit her."

I'd be offended by the remark, but I'm too devastated to care. George is right. I crossed the line. I was careless.

"One-week administrative leave," says George.

"What?"

"Go home. Think about things," he growls.

"With a paid vacation?"

He glances at me, locking eyes. "Will it feel like a vacation to you?"

"Please don't do this."

He points to the door. "Golden Boy and I have to clean things up from last night. You're a distraction."

I'd protest, but that would only make things worse. I grab my case, toss my lukewarm coffee in the trash, and head for the door.

As I'm about to leave, he calls out, "And stay the hell away from Cope."

CHAPTER FORTY
TIDE POOL

Under a setting sun, Hughes sits on the gunwale of my boat, gently bouncing his baby in his lap, while Jackie shows his wife how to cast off the bow. I was sent home two days ago. I've heard nothing from George since, but Hughes has been keeping me up to date. Today, he practically insisted that his wife and he drop by for a visit. I wanted to turn him down, but it was my day with Jackie, and I figured they'd make for better company than her brooding mother.

The plates from our dinner of swordfish are sitting in the galley along with mostly still-full glasses of wine. Hughes and his wife like the taste, but not the aftereffect. As for me, I'm trying to break a McPherson habit for Jackie's benefit.

"It killed Solar to have to do that to you," says Hughes, broaching the topic of my forced leave.

"Not half as much as it kills me to have put him in that situation."

"I'm sure. After you left, he had Denton and the DA yelling at him. It was not a pretty scene."

"What did George do?"

"He just took it, at first. He told them you'd been put on official leave. One of them called bullshit, and then Solar unloaded on 'em. I wish you could have seen that."

"I messed up," I reply.

"It happens," says Hughes.

"I crossed the line. I was harassing Cope. I was dumb," I admit. "I was bad police."

Hughes shakes his head. "Know why I came to the UIU?"

"I think we had this conversation."

"We had the ideological one. Let me tell you the practical one. I had a reputation in the department . . . one that followed me all the way from the service."

"For punctuality?" I joke.

Hughes stares down at his baby. "No. I let some guys down in my navy unit. The short version is a guy did something he wasn't supposed to. I mean really crossing the line, resulting in a local getting killed. He was a sadistic asshole. We all had to give testimony. There was a ton of pressure. Other guys were telling me we have to stand up for each other. Protect one another. Only . . . I couldn't protect this. I didn't see the guy as a brother; I saw him as an evil person in a uniform."

Tiny fingers wrap around his.

"What happened?"

"I told the truth. Life got difficult. I was called a traitor. I would have taken a bullet for any of them, but they didn't see it that way. I'd betrayed one of our own." Hughes shakes his head as he gazes at his child. "But I know I did the right thing. There's always a gray area. We live in them every day. But this was evil. Once you can't tell them apart, there's not much difference between us and the guys we were sent there to kill."

Oh jeez. This poor man. I can see the hurt in his eyes. I don't know what to say.

"I came back. Got into the police force, except a couple other guys I'd served with joined the department too. Word got around that I wouldn't have their back. It didn't matter about the details. I wasn't going to be one of them."

"And that's when George found you?" I ask.

Hughes nods. "Pretty much. He knew my story."

"It's a lot like his. He did prison time as part of a long-term case. First they called him a crook, then a snitch. He loves the gray area, but he can clearly see what's black-and-white."

"Yeah. He's solid. He admires you, McPherson."

"Me?" I reply. "I feel like I'm a nuisance."

"You're kidding, right? You're his legacy. That's why he came down so hard."

"Because I let him down." I sigh.

"No. Or rather, in his words, 'That Sloan is so damned stubborn this is the only way she's going to learn to get smart.' Or something to that effect. He's trying to teach you. In his own way."

"I wish I was a better student."

"You'll get another chance," says Hughes. He looks over his shoulder and speaks almost in a whisper. "I'm not supposed to say this . . ."

"Then don't," I tell him. "I don't want you getting into trouble."

"Okay. Um . . . let me put it this way: there's been a development today with the Swamp Killer. Don't be surprised if your suspension is suspended."

"What kind of development? Wait, don't tell me. But why me?"

"Not you in particular. Just about every cop in South Florida. Since you're one-third of the UIU, Solar's going to need all hands on deck."

"George told you this?" I ask.

"What? No. But I'm going to suggest it to him tomorrow."

"Oh," I say, deflated.

"Look, you're on the bench, but you haven't been sent home. Solar will want to keep you as far away from Denton as possible, but he's not going to keep you out of the largest manhunt in South Florida history."

My curiosity is killing me. "So, there's a lead?"

"Let's just say my friends at BSO are very, very excited. They're hinting that Steve screwed up big-time."

"Anything to do with what we found?"

"I don't know. I think it's something else. But if they're right—a big assumption—we could actually nail this guy."

For the first time since George sent me home, a ray of light breaks through my gloom.

CHAPTER FORTY-ONE
MANIFOLD

FBI special agent Denton is standing at the podium of the small auditorium in the Broward Sheriff's Office next to two detectives from the BSO. Curiously, there are armed deputies standing at all the doors. In addition to submitting to a security check at the front desk, we all had to show ID to get into the room, including George and Hughes.

While George is up front with the other chiefs, Hughes and I are sitting toward the back to put as much physical distance as possible between Denton and me. I'm not afraid of the man. I just don't want to be a distraction.

I haven't learned anything else since Hughes and I talked yesterday. The FBI and local police departments have done an extremely good job of keeping whatever they know under wraps. What I can't figure is why all the police are at this briefing. For something so secret, it seems like the fewer ears and mouths, the better. My best guess is that they're going to need a lot of manpower.

"Thank you for coming at such short notice," says Denton. "We believe we've made an important break in the hunt for the Swamp Killer. Yesterday afternoon, the editors of the *Sun Herald* received an anonymous email from someone calling themselves Manifold." Denton nods to the side, and an image appears over his head, showing a redacted printout of an email message. "In this message, this individual identified himself or herself as the Swamp Killer and made a series of demands, including a deposit of ten million dollars in Bitcoin in order to stop the killing."

Denton pauses. "I know what you're all thinking—this is just another nut that crawled out of the woodwork. However, in this case, Manifold provided details about the murders that haven't made it into any news reports. Some were only known separately by different agencies. In fact, we spent all day yesterday corroborating details, including some we hadn't been aware of, such as items missing from the homes, et cetera."

Holy cow. That's a break, all right. But I'm not sure how much it helps us. And, frankly, I'm surprised that Sleazy Steve would poke his head up.

"Now, despite these details, that does not mean Manifold is our killer. There could be leaks in the different agencies we're unaware of. He could have had contact with the actual killer and been given this information. We consider the latter more likely than the former."

I mentally remind myself which one is "the last one," then quietly nod in agreement. Still, if what Denton is saying is true, then Manifold really is a big break.

"At this time, we have no plans to publish the full email, but we've agreed to let the *Sun Herald* publish a partial version," says Denton. "And now, as to the reason you're all here: we think this is a big mistake on Manifold's part. I can't get into the specifics, but we've developed a plan to locate him. We're going to need your help with surveillance. We're requesting you use personal vehicles and plain clothes. We'll be giving each of you assignments, but we request that you do not share them with anyone other than your immediate supervisors. If word of our approach gets out, we may miss our only opportunity to catch him. Now, I'd like to turn it over to Detective Rowland to go over the specifics."

During the break, Hughes and I go through a packet that was handed to us. It's a list of stores that sell newspapers that they want us to collect surveillance tapes from, plus nearby bus stops we're supposed to watch.

Hughes glances around the room at the other packets that have been handed to people. "That must cover every 7-Eleven and supermarket in South Florida. I'm not sure how watching half the state counts as effective surveillance." He looks to me. "We're supposed to photograph anyone buying a newspaper."

"Well, that does narrow it down a bit." I pull out a copy of Manifold's email and scan through the nonredacted parts, which doesn't leave much—only the names of the *Sun Herald* editors and some details.

"How do they know he even buys the paper?" asks Hughes.

"I'm sure there's an online aspect to the surveillance too. They're probably covering all their bases. But, yeah, it does seem broad. Maybe it's some kind of honeypot? They're going to try to trick him to go to a certain web address?"

"Him and every other crazy that reads the article. That's still too broad. What's the point of having us photograph every person who buys a paper?" asks Hughes, echoing my own thoughts.

"What if it's more than that?" I go back and look at the list of places we're supposed to get security video from and check them against a map on my phone.

"Like they already have a description of him?"

I direct Hughes to the list. All the addresses are in the same zip code, although some of them are separated by a highway. "See that? They didn't get this list from looking at a map."

Hughes shrugs. "What, then?"

"I read somewhere that newspapers can target specific neighborhoods with advertising. What if they're doing that with the print version?"

"You mean publish different versions in different parts of town? Like, change some details?"

"Maybe have slightly different email addresses for the reporter? It's like one of Jackie's logic puzzles. Send out two different versions based on location. If Mr. Manifold sends an email to John J. Doe at the *Sun Herald* instead of John M. Doe, then they know he's in the area that got that specific edition of the newspaper."

"That only reduces the pool by a few million people," says Hughes.

"No. You could break South Florida down into as many smaller sections as you want—twenty-six for each possible middle initial, or whatever. And if they do another article with some other detail that he repeats in emailing to them, that breaks it down further. If a hundred thousand people buy a newspaper each day, then . . ." I do the math on my phone. "With twenty variations, you'd narrow it down to two hundred fifty people in two days if he responds each day."

"*If* he responds," says Hughes.

"I'm sure he will," I reply. "I'd bet on it."

"Then that's good news."

"I guess. Assuming Manifold is the Swamp Killer."

"Looks like the chief wants to talk to us," says Hughes, noticing George motioning us to join a huddle with Denton and some others.

"Uh, is this a good thing?" I ask.

"Let's find out."

CHAPTER FORTY-TWO
NET

Denton nods to me, which isn't the worst possible reaction, though not the friendliest. He's standing with the BSO and Palm Beach Sheriff's Office detectives near a side table as George explains something to them.

"McPherson," George says, waving me into the huddle.

Denton gives me another glance. "It's been suggested that having you on disciplinary action may not be best for the case."

"What does that mean?" I ask.

"It means that they don't want a defense attorney to use a documented disciplinary action as proof before a jury that we screwed up," says George. "As far as we're concerned, there was no administrative leave."

Great, but that doesn't take the sting away. I feel as much like a pawn as I did before. More so, actually. The idea that they can wave their wand and the Ministry of Magic can undo it all is a joke. But I don't argue.

"Okay. What can we do to help?"

Denton points to the packet in my hands. "Same as the rest of us. Keep your eyes open. Take photos."

"Will it work?" I ask. "Narrowing it down by using different versions of the response?"

His ears rear back like a cat's, and his eyes dart to the other detectives. "Who told you about that?" he demands, clearly afraid there's already been a leak.

"Nobody. It seemed like the logical thing," I reply.

"We have reason to believe an approach like that could work," he says, deciding not to deny it.

"So, you've used it before? And it worked?" I ask.

"McPherson," says George. "Do you really not know when to shut up?"

"Clearly I do not." I try to clean things up. "I'm happy . . . *we're* happy to do whatever we can. I think it's a fine plan."

"I'm so glad you think so," says Denton, not hiding his sarcasm.

Well, I had it coming. He's thirty years senior to me and doesn't need my input.

Feeling dismissed, Hughes and I leave Denton and George with the other bosses and step to the side.

A tall young man with a bow tie walks over to us. He's got an ID tag that says *FBI analyst.* "You're McPherson and you're Hughes, right?" he says, offering his hand.

"Yes. And you?"

"I'm Brian Merton. I'm with the CBL at the FBI—the computational behavior lab," he explains.

"Is that like profiling?" asks Hughes.

"Sort of. But we let the computers do the profiling. I'm actually a computer scientist. We try to build a predictive model based on behavior."

"How does that work?" I ask.

"It's a prediction model. We start with ones that have been successful in the past, find one that matches this, and then add new details," he explains.

"Sounds sketchy," says Hughes.

Merton nods. "It is. Our models are wildly inaccurate right now. Barely better than human profilers."

"Barely better?" I reply.

"Yes," he says with a small grin. "That's the important detail. They're better and improving all the time. The goal here is to make them better faster. I overheard you talking to Denton about locational fingerprinting. Clever to figure it out on your own."

Ah, so that's what it's called. "Let's just hope the killer doesn't."

"Oh, he won't," says Merton.

"That seems pretty confident," says Hughes.

He shakes his head. "I put the entire Manifold email through the system. It's remarkably good at IQ estimation, social awareness, and a number of other factors. Manifold has average intelligence but thinks he's much smarter than he actually is. Just sending that email was a sign that he's unaware of how we can track people."

"Or he knows he can't be tracked," adds Hughes.

"Fair point. But he matches up with the type that uses public computers, the kind you find in libraries, to send emails, because he thinks that's safer than doing it from home—which is the exact opposite. We'll get him."

"Unless," I reply.

"Unless what?"

I try to put my finger on what I've been thinking. "Your experience with him comes through that email. Mine comes from his crime scenes going back three decades. The man I'm looking for has been very, very careful. So much so, nobody even knew he was out there."

"Like the Grizzly Killer," says Hughes.

"That was a fluke," says Merton.

"They said that about the Toy Man too."

Merton shakes his head. "I respect Dr. Cray, but those were outlier cases. Manifold is a classic attention seeker."

"But he wasn't until now. Maybe he's doing this to throw us all off." I gesture at Denton and his group. "Have they thought about that? Like . . . why now?"

"It's all thanks to you. Because you found the bodies," says Merton. "He knows time is running out. So, what does he do? He asks for a ransom so he can get away. That's what changed. You threw him off his game."

I appreciate the flattery, but I'm not sold. "He's smarter than this."

Merton sighs. "With all due respect, you need to rid yourself of the Hannibal Lecter mythos. These guys aren't geniuses."

"Theodore Kaczynski was," says Hughes. "And that weapon scientist Cray caught qualifies too."

"Outliers," insists Merton.

"I'm not saying this guy is Lex Luthor," I reply. "I'm just saying that the longer one person stays in an area and doesn't get caught, the smarter he has to be."

"The data says otherwise. Lonnie Franklin, Dennis Rader, and Dahmer . . . none of them were geniuses. Not by a long shot."

"They all preyed upon prostitutes or marginalized people," I reply. "The Swamp Killer's victims don't fit that profile."

Merton's about to say something, but he hesitates. Clearly this is a variable he hasn't considered. "So, you think he's smarter than us?"

"I'm not making any assumptions," I reply. "I just don't want to underestimate him."

"Fair point. You're working on your PhD, right? Anthropology?"

"Archaeology," I reply.

"I can see it in the way you think. We should all talk later." He nods to Hughes, then steps away.

"That was weird," Hughes says. "I like the whole let-the-computer-figure-things-out-and-remove-human-bias concept, but it reminds me of a saying: garbage in, garbage out."

I laugh. "Maybe. Let's just hope Merton learns as fast as his computers. Us too."

"Do you think he's right? That this is Sleazy Steve's exit plan?"

"Maybe. But whatever the intention, I'm worried we're spending too much time trying to figure out where he's going and not enough on where he came from." I look across the auditorium at all the cops. "Imagine if we had these people talking to former classmates and poring through yearbooks. I bet we could figure out Sleazy Steve's identity in no time."

"True. I think the task force is too obsessed with the mature, cautious serial killer who left the bodies in the swamp," says Hughes, "not where he came from."

CHAPTER FORTY-THREE
Rip Curl

You reflect a lot on life while staking out a 7-Eleven. Both on your own life and that of those you see. I'm not a judgy kind of person—okay, I hate judgy people and dislike it in myself—but it's hard not to be judgmental while watching the humans coming in and out of a convenience store.

There's the mom balancing one child on her hip while holding the hand of another in school clothes as she walks out somehow toting a jug of milk. Then there's the middle-aged man in the dirty shirt with a case of beer and lottery tickets sticking out of his pocket. Clearly, she's a kidnapper and he's on his way to a senior citizens' home to hand out beer and lottery tickets to lonely people. At least that's how it works when I play the opposites game in my mind, trying to assume the opposite of everyone I see.

I imagine sketchy-looking people as benevolent and the upstanding as shady. It would be more fun if I could share my mean observations with someone else, but Hughes is five blocks away, watching a supermarket. So I'm stuck inside my head.

I get a photo of the lottery-ticket man, the fifth in the last hour, and make a note of which direction he walks off in. I have a mean thought about cockroaches disappearing into crevices and then feel a rush of guilt over my assumption. He could be a good guy, looking after his mother, and maybe he's hit hard times. At least he's not standing there looking back at me, judging me.

I glance in the mirror at my own face. What do I see? Thirty is approaching soon. I have my mom's laugh lines. The skin still has its freckles. Eyes like my father's stare back.

Who am I? What *am I?*

Ever since high school, I've wanted to be an archaeologist. It was my science teacher, Mr. Friedman, who pulled me aside one day and pointed out that my experience in the water, diving shipwrecks, and my penchant for history could be put to use as something besides being a treasure hunter's daughter.

"Have you ever thought about becoming an archaeologist?" he asked.

To be honest, no. That sounded about as likely as becoming a space captain for the Jupiter Navy. Not that my family was averse to college. Dad attended the University of Miami—and dropped out. Mom got her degree at Kansas State. But nobody else went that far.

The police officer part came later, when I started working as a contractor for smaller departments that didn't have dive teams or larger departments that couldn't handle the more technical dives. Then came the offer to work part-time with Lauderdale Shores. Somewhere along the way, I realized I liked policing. Or at least parts of it. I liked hearing the name *McPherson* in a positive light when associated with law enforcement.

But now what? Do I want to spend the rest of my life sipping lukewarm coffee, watching weirdos come in and out of a convenience store, hoping one of them is a serial killer?

It's certainly more exciting, at least in the moment, than spending months on an archaeological dig, hoping to find a manatee bone with human bite marks. But in the long run, those manatee bones are more fulfilling. I mean metaphorically, not literally. I'd never eat a manatee. I think.

What's next for me? Assuming Denton and company find Manifold, aka the Swamp Killer, aka Sleazy Steve, then where do I go from here? Catching the New River Bandits was a good thing but in no way deeply fulfilling.

I like being underwater. Not sitting in a parking lot on a muggy day with the nearest body of water a stagnant canal three blocks away.

My first archaeological dig was exciting. As a high school sophomore, I got to tag along on an excavation near Loop Road, out in the Everglades, where mobsters made booze and ran whorehouses. Digging through old trash piles and finding glassware and newspapers thrilled me. Which is weird, because I'd explored wrecks and made treasure dives hundreds of times. But this was different. It wasn't about what we could find—it was about the stories the objects told us.

A yellowed newspaper with cutout articles held far more interest than a corroded silver ingot. Who cut the articles out? What were they, and what was the person looking for?

I went to the library the next week and pulled up that same *Sun Herald* paper from 1926.

The "articles" that had been cut out were actually ads for bridal arrangements.

Who was planning a wedding? A prostitute? A lover? Was it a real wedding? Or just something in their head?

As a cop, you don't get the same kinds of mysteries. Sure, I can't say for sure whether the twitchy man by the dumpster is a meth head or on crack, but I'm fairly certain I know the rough outline of his story. The details are just that . . . details.

Even Sleazy Steve doesn't hold too many mysteries beyond his identity. He's got something wrong with his head. He kills. The end. There's no way to romanticize that.

"How's it going?" asks Hughes over the phone speaker. I'd forgotten that we left it open.

"Thrill a minute," I reply.

"I just watched a woman pee into a coffee cup," says Hughes.

"You might want to reconsider the internet sites you visit," I reply.

"No, she . . . oh, ha-ha."

"Is this our life?" I ask. "Is this the job?"

"Would you rather be back in the cave with the alligator?"

It takes me a long moment to come up with an answer. "Uh, no?"

"When I was on patrol in Afghanistan, I was happy when nothing happened. But the boring days were never the best days. Even when people got hurt. I mean . . ."

"I know what you mean," I reply. "It's like how zookeepers hide food from gorillas."

"They what?"

"Zookeepers move the food around each day so the gorillas don't get bored. They turn it into an Easter-egg hunt. The gorillas need challenges. The lack of one makes 'em go nuts. We need someone to hide our food," I explain.

"But not shoot at us."

"Ideally. You think—" I stop as I see a text message arrive.

"You getting this?" asks Hughes.

"Yeah."

We're being pulled off surveillance.

I text a friend at the Fort Lauderdale Police Department and get a response. Same thing.

"It's everyone. We're all being pulled off. I guess that can only mean one thing . . ."

We caught him.

CHAPTER FORTY-FOUR
ANCHOR

We're gathered back in the BSO auditorium only three days after the manhunt was put together. This time there's only about a third of us here, forcing me to sit closer to the front so I don't stand out.

Denton and his task force are chatting, grins on their faces, relaxed postures. Clearly, they feel good about this.

"Think there'll be a cake too?" asks Hughes, mocking their excitement. "They didn't have to smell the bodies we pulled out of the swamp."

"It's easy to get lost in the moment," I say, defending them for some reason.

"It's easy to forget that there were real victims. Real people. They look like they just won the office football pool."

Man, Hughes takes this stuff harder than I realized. Underneath that cool-as-ice exterior beats a tender heart. The real Hughes is the dad I saw on my boat cradling his baby. The tough, analytical one is the machine he built to protect the good in the world from the bad.

George breaks away from a group of other silver-haired men and women and takes a seat next to me. "Well, that's interesting."

"What's going on?" I ask.

So far, we've had no details, only the notion that the snare apparently worked. Someone responded to the articles and unwittingly revealed where he was getting his paper—apparently the only person who even bothered to buy a paper all day in whatever zone he was picked up in.

"They're being tight-lipped. We've also been asked to send them all our interviews," says George.

"We already sent them," I reply.

"We're being asked again. Might be a clerical thing."

"Anything else?"

"We'll find out." George nods to the podium, where Denton is gathering his notes.

"Good evening. We wanted to provide you a briefing before this hits the press. We also need more help in tying up loose ends. But to get right to the point, we think we may have caught the Swamp Killer. Right now, he's in holding downstairs. He's waived his right to an attorney but hasn't said anything. However, we were able to get a search warrant for his residence and found evidence that connects him to several of the murders. We're still filling in the details, so I must ask that you coordinate all press inquiries through us. We don't want to jeopardize our case through careless commentary. Most important, I want to thank all of you for your hard work. It's amazing what teamwork can do. Questions?"

Denton is barraged by requests for more details, but he waves them all off. "We'll tell you when we can."

"This feels like a press conference, not a briefing with peers," I whisper.

"No kidding," says George.

After Denton finishes, one of the agents he works with comes over to George and us. "Agent Denton would like to speak with you in the conference room."

"What about?" asks George.

The agent shrugs. "He didn't say."

We follow him out of the auditorium and over to a small conference room and take a seat. Merton, the computer guy, is there along with Chandler Balstrada, a detective with BSO, who's going through piles of paperwork. Merton acknowledges us with a nod, then returns to his computer.

A minute later, Denton enters and sits at the head of the table. "What a couple of days. Chandler, you have that file?"

The detective slides a folder over to him. Denton picks up a sheet and reads through some text, then says, "This job can be hard. The details are the killers."

"I thought the killers were the killers," I reply.

Hughes smirks, but George's face remains its usual granite. He's reading something in the room that I can't. Now I'm worried.

"McPherson. I think you're going to make a good cop. You, too, Hughes." Denton nods to George. "The key is your boss here. Or rather, what he has and you don't. Experience. All the seminars and textbooks in the world can't prepare you for the real world. You have to go out there and live it."

Remind me to ask him for the YouTube link to his TED talk, I tell myself, dying over the fact I can't share my joke with Hughes.

"Who did you catch?" asks George, getting to the point.

Merton speaks up. "He fit our profile to a T. I mean, almost textbook."

"More important," says Denton, "is the evidence we found at his home." His phone buzzes. Denton reads the message. "He just gave us some more unknown details. No confession, but he's revealing things."

"That's great," I say. "And you really can tie him to everything?"

"Yes. This doesn't leave this room, okay?" He reaches into another folder, plucks out a photocopy of something, and slides it over to us. "We found this in a shed belonging to a neighbor—an elderly woman he mowed the lawn for."

The photocopy is of a Polaroid of a naked young woman with her hands tied over her head to a doorknob. She's unconscious or dead. A gloved hand is touching her face, with the thumb in her mouth. Underneath the image someone wrote, "What the eyes do not see, lips reveal."

"Bad poetry too? Wait, is this Olivia de Bauch?" I say, recognizing the face.

"Yes. She went missing in 2002. We found a partial photo of another victim we think is Karen Rose."

"He just named another victim," says Merton. "One we never released."

I can't take my eyes off Olivia, but this sounds good. Really, really good. I feel the right kind of butterflies in my stomach.

I slide the photo to George. "We got him?"

"This started with you, McPherson," Denton offers magnanimously. "All of you. Your perseverance is amazing."

"Thank you—" I start to say, but he continues.

"Which is why we're going to throw this away." Denton picks up a folder. "I suggest you do the same with any records you have."

"I'm sorry?" I reply. "What?"

"Your interview with the suspect. It's for the best if there's no record. It doesn't reflect well on you, and it won't help our investigation if we look bumbling."

"Bumbling?" I blurt out. "Help me out. What the hell are you talking about?"

"The Swamp Killer. You spoke to him."

My pulse pounds in my head. "Cope? You mean that motherfu— SOB was the killer all along? And you raked me over the coals?" My fingernails bite into my palms. George puts a firm hand on my forearm to calm me, with questionable results.

Denton is shaking his head. Why is he shaking his head?

He raises his voice. "It wasn't Cope." He throws a folder across to me.

I flip it open and recognize the face after a moment's hesitation, then slide it over to Hughes.

It's Jeremy Shulme.

"*Him?* The sad-sack pervert at the box plant?"

"Yes," says Denton. "He's lived in South Florida since he was a teenager. In fact, when he was fifteen, he molested a neighbor, but the records were sealed. The photos, the information he just gave us. You pray for a case this open-and-shut."

"He didn't seem like the type," says Hughes.

"I wish we could tell just by talking to people. But we can't. I don't think I would have known had I only spoken to him. But the problem is, you didn't even get to the rest of the questions on the questionnaire. To be honest, it was sloppy work."

I'd argue with him, but he's not wrong. I measured Shulme up and decided he couldn't be the man I'd been imagining. I let my own biases guide me. To begin with, he doesn't look like the guy in the photo at the concert . . . but that was just one unreliable witness claiming that was Sleazy Steve. There's also the chance that the Swamp Killer and Sleazy Steve are two different people after all, and I messed up somewhere.

I was convinced of Cope's guilty nature, yet his alibi checks out. He was just an asshole. I didn't want to believe it, but I can't refute the fact that he wasn't there on the night of the couple's murder.

"Could there be others involved?" asks Hughes.

It's a good question. He doesn't want to let it go either. He was misled by Shulme too.

"We've only found one set of consistent footprints across the crime scenes—which we haven't been able to match to anyone con-clusively. The size is close to Shulme's." Denton points to his folder. "The part about his uncle molesting him? Never happened. Living with his mother? She died ten years ago. He wanted you to think he was

243

pathetic. He wanted you to think he was a loser who couldn't have done all this. He didn't just play you—he played us all."

Shulme, you lying piece of crap.

Denton picks up the copy of our interview and holds it over a wastebasket. "We don't have to mention this ever again." He looks to George. "Fair enough?"

"It's your call."

Denton drops the folder into the garbage. "Now that we've done that," he says, "we need to fill in all the blanks and make sure it sticks. Can I have your help on this? I want to make sure he doesn't get away a third time on some technicality."

"We're in, one hundred percent," I say. "Let's nail the prick."

CHAPTER FORTY-FIVE
PIRATE CODE

Danielle Ross, an attorney from the State of Florida working on the Swamp Killer case, is assessing me as she sits across the table. Shawn Baym, an FBI agent and liaison with local law enforcement agencies, and Broward detective Eddie Cantata watch me as well.

They're preparing me for an interview with the *Sun Herald*, going over what I can and cannot say to the press. Although I'll have these minders in the room, and the editor of the *Sun Herald* has promised a friendly interview, they want to make sure I don't blurt out anything that could blow the case.

It's still early in the investigation, but part of the agreement with the *Sun Herald* was that they'd get exclusive coverage. To the chagrin of Denton and others, I was the first interview they wanted.

"How would you describe your involvement in the Swamp Killer case?" asks Assistant State Attorney Ross.

"It started with the discovery of the bodies of the kids in Pond 65," I reply.

Baym shakes his head. "No. Say it started with the discovery of Alyssa Rennie's body near the Everglades."

"Excuse me?"

"We need to simplify the narrative," says Ross. "Drawing the dots from too many places complicates things. Just explain how that body led you and Hughes to look into suspicious activities in the Everglades."

"That's not what happened," I reply.

"It's a confusing case," Ross explains. "We need to focus the narrative."

"Focus the narrative? Is this a TV show?"

"In the mind of the public, yes. What you have to consider is how many of our potential jurors will have read coverage. We don't want to confuse them."

"Aren't we, like, screening jurors? We still do that."

"People lie to get on juries for cases like this," says Ross. "Especially now. It's like reality television. We need you to stick to the basic points."

"But the van is one of them. It ties them all together," I reply.

"No. The cages full of bones in the alligator swamp are what unites them all."

"Are we even going to charge him with their murders?" I ask.

"We're handling it on a case-by-case basis. We don't want to go to trial unless we can prove it. His style changed over the years, and he's only offered up evidence about a select number of victims."

"Why is that?" I ask.

"He was playing games with us, giving us details from selected cases. His lawyer told him to shut up."

"Okay. So, what do I say?"

"Talk about diving for the bodies in the Everglades," says Baym. "That's a great detail."

"I didn't dive for them. Kell dragged them out with alligator hooks."

"Kell . . . what department is he with?" asks Cantata.

"He's a civilian. He was our guide."

Ross shakes her head. "Just say, 'We pulled the cages out.' Don't get into specifics."

"We?"

"Yes. It's better if Kell doesn't get called to the witness stand. We don't want to run the risk of a defense attorney tripping him up."

"Like how?"

She shrugs. "Maybe making him seem like the killer."

"What?"

"I've seen it happen. Jurors think it's an Agatha Christie novel. Every person is a character in the story, and any of them could be the bad guy. Even you."

"Oh brother."

"On that topic. Let's also avoid any mention of your uncle," says Ross.

"What? I mean, what if the reporter asks?"

"I'll talk to them," says Cantata.

I feel like I'm running for political office. Nobody has told me to lie, but this "narrative shaping" seems a lot like manipulation. Does this always happen with cases like this? What don't I know about what goes on behind the scenes?

Based on the press staging at crime scenes and the sheer number of off-the-record comments I've seen other investigators make and reporters respect, it all feels like a movie set where there's the reality of what's going on and the agreed-upon story that's decided by a tug-of-war between the media and the authorities.

"I'm not sure I want to do this interview," I say.

"It would look bad if you don't," says Ross. "With the rumors of infighting and the alleged story that you spoke to Shulme and let him go, we can't hide."

"I did speak to Shulme. I didn't let him go because I didn't have him."

"That's not how people will see it. You didn't take him in for questioning. You didn't request a search warrant. It'll look bad," Ross insists.

"I had no cause. He was one of thousands of weirdos that were interviewed."

"Exactly. Don't comment on him or any other specific person. The point of those interviews was to find the Swamp Killer. You didn't. That looks bad," says Cantata, "even if it's not your fault. Don't address what we don't need to."

"Do you want Shulme to have his attorney get you on the stand and ask you point-blank if you thought he did it at the time?" asks Ross. "If you say yes, he'll ask what you did, which is nothing. If you say no, he'll use that to discredit the investigation and you personally. Do you understand the situation this puts us in?"

"He can still ask, regardless of what I say to the reporter," I reply.

"It diminishes the likelihood of that. His attorney will go by what evidence we present and what he sees in the paper. If there's no mention of you talking to him, then chances are it won't come up."

"And if it does?" I ask.

"Let's not worry about that now. If this goes to trial, we'll have plenty of conversations about testimony beforehand."

"You mean I have to go through this again?"

"This?" says Ross. "This is nothing."

"I worked with a speech coach to help me on the stand," says Baym. "I'll give you her name. She also teaches improv. Um, not the comedy type, just how not to seem flustered—like you seem right now."

"Flustered looks like guilt," adds Ross.

"But I'm not on trial!"

"In a way, we all are, once we step into the courtroom," Baym says.

What kind of madness is this?

CHAPTER FORTY-SIX
SHORELINE

Jackie and her two friends run along the crashing waves, playing in the surf. She's already a head taller than they are, with no sign of stopping. Fortunately, she moves with grace and isn't tripping over her feet, like I did when I was her age. My problem wasn't being tall—I wasn't—it was that I hated shoes, which I considered prisons for my feet.

"Want to try?" Tilda, mother of Stacey, hands me a Mason jar from the cooler filled with a fruity liquid and ice.

I hold up my water bottle. "I'll stick to this for now."

"Narc," she jokes before returning to her book.

I managed to make my way through the newspaper interview without divulging too much or getting cornered, which is to say that I handled it robotically and made for a boring interview—which George told me afterward is something every cop should aspire to.

Jackie's beach day with her friends was planned ages ago. Even though it's a Saturday and the loose ends on the Swamp Killer case are being tied up, I feel a little guilty for being here. I'm grateful to spend time with my daughter. I only wish I had more frolic in me than angst.

I know I'd feel worse if we hadn't caught the suspects in the New River thefts, but that's small consolation given the enormity of guilt I felt for letting George down.

He's not your damned father.

"Who?" asks Tilda.

I try to cover, not realizing I said that out loud. "Oh, uh. My father . . . I see a lot of him in Jackie. The good parts. The kind heart."

"Ah. I thought you were talking about her father," says Tilda, trying to pry where there's not much to pry into. "Uh, how is that?"

"Good. Great. Run's a wonderful dad."

"That's great," says Tilda.

I've never had a problem with small talk. I'm just more direct. Tilda is trying to dance around the details, curious about our relationship. Which makes sense.

I keep my eyes on Jackie and her friends, also watching the two smaller children playing in a tide pool while their mom sleeps under an umbrella. Farther out, three teenagers are splashing around on an inflatable pool toy, maybe a little too roughly for the ocean, but nowhere near as brutally as my brothers and I played together.

Will all those kids be okay? Probably. I've wrestled with this my whole life—how far should we go in order to do the right thing?

Here I am, subconsciously counting all the kids on the beach and deciding which ones I need to keep a watch out for . . . That's the job of the lifeguard sitting two hundred feet away, but I've watched him pull out his phone five times in the last ten minutes.

These kids are his responsibility, but can I really leave their fate in the hands of a hormonal nineteen-year-old making plans to get laid tonight? I ask this as a former teenage lifeguard who made said plans and managed to get pregnant.

The first time I was presented with one of these ethical situations was my freshman year at a fancy private school that I had to leave a year later when the family money dried up. But during that year, when

I first started flirting with Run and hanging out with the most popular of the popular kids, I became a kind of friend to a girl named Pauline.

I say *kind of friend* because it didn't take me too long to realize her friendship had ulterior motives. Pauline was a dark-haired beauty who looked several years older than the rest of us. Her mother had been some kind of beauty queen in Argentina. Her father was a lawyer from New York. She had this exotic look about her that could have come from a fashion magazine.

I'd talked to her at school a little, and she was a fixture at the different house parties. She seemed to know everybody, even the outcasts. One day between classes, she came up to me and asked if I wanted to get lunch at the mall on Saturday.

Lunch at the mall? That sounded so much more sophisticated than "shopping," even though it was essentially the same thing.

Being asked to hang out with a girl as popular as she was felt like a form of acceptance. I'd always felt out of place among the other kids at the school. I was popular enough, probably because I was sufficiently pretty and had a sense of humor. Run pulled me into his circle because I could bust his balls and those of his friends. I could compliment one buddy for a great basketball game, then ask his teammate if he'd thought about switching to the theater department instead. A lot of my jokes were put-downs, a family skill, but I could make myself the butt of a joke too. I had no trouble telling my own embarrassing stories, like trying to hold in gas during silent reading. All this made Run laugh hysterically, which was really the point. Watching his sly mouth break out into a broad grin sent shivers through me. Run was well liked . . . no, Run was loved by everyone. I wanted to be as close to that as possible.

The day Pauline, the prettiest of the pretty girls in that orbit, asked me to be her friend, it felt like a graduation of sorts.

As we sat there in the food court, my salad half-eaten in front of me, she showed me a little packet of pink ecstasy pills and asked me if I wanted to make some money.

I was confused at first. Was my new friend bringing me into her confidence? Or was I merely a recruit for her mini drug-dealing empire?

Until that moment I'd had no idea why Pauline was so popular with everyone. Now I understood. She was a drug dealer. Pauline was always close to the center, but not in the center precisely. The way she moved around a party, whispering to people, made sense now. She talked to everyone because everyone was a potential client.

I glanced at the packet in her hand. "I'm okay."

"Don't be worried," she said, looking around. "Nobody cares. It's not like it's crack. Everybody does this."

"I don't," I replied nervously.

"I'm not asking if you want to *do* it, but you can have some if you want. I'm asking if you want to make some money."

"I'm okay," I said again, terrified someone would see me in the middle of what looked like a drug deal.

She leaned in closer to me. "Look, I know money is tight. I wanted to do you a favor. You could get some nice clothes. These other kids we go to school with—it's not fair. They have everything."

At this point my family wasn't struggling, but we certainly weren't financially secure. Some of the kids I went to school with had their own drivers. "I'm good," I insisted, trying to figure a way out of this.

"Run does it," she said, trying to manipulate me through my obvious attraction to him.

"I'm okay. I gotta go." I stood up.

"All right. Just think about it." She stood too, grabbed me by the shoulders, and kissed me on the cheek.

From that moment forward, she was as cold as ice to me. I barely existed. She didn't go out of her way to avoid me, but she never so much as acknowledged me.

It took me a while to understand what had happened. Eventually, I realized that she thought of me as the poor kid. For that reason, she assumed I'd be an easy mark. By rejecting her, I was putting her on a level below myself, and she'd apparently considered me extremely low to begin with.

But that's not where the ethical challenge came into play. Not becoming a dealer was as simple as an ABC *After School Special* moral dilemma. The real challenge was putting together the pieces of what I saw while leaving the mall and what happened a few weeks later.

I circled around the shops, trying to decide what to do next, since my afternoon with Pauline was over. I was inside Macy's when I saw her again. She was sitting by an older man on a bench, having a heated discussion. Her mother came over to the bench and sat with them. Pauline argued with her as well. I couldn't make out the words, just the emotions, which were intense.

When the police came to school and pulled Pauline out of class, it never made the newspapers. But word got around. The story on campus was that she'd met some older boy whose family was into drugs and she'd started selling for him.

She was back in school a week later and behaved like it was all a misunderstanding. Life moved on. Or rather, it moved on around her.

One day I found her crying in a corner of the locker room. I wanted to ignore her and treat her the same way she'd treated me, but I couldn't. I sat next to her and said nothing.

"I'm sorry for being such a bitch to you," she said between sobs.

"It's okay."

"Everyone here is so fake." Her arms wrapped around my waist, and her head fell on my shoulder.

"People are stupid." This was the best explanation my fifteen-year-old brain could come up with.

"You're real. That's what I like about you."

O-kay . . . I hadn't realized she'd ever noticed anything about me to like. I didn't know what to say.

Her arms squeezed tighter around me. She wasn't putting the moves on me. She was clinging to me.

"I'm sorry for what you're going through," I told her.

"It's okay. Ottavio says once it blows over, he and I are going to go somewhere far away."

"Ottavio?" I asked. Was he a new kid?

Pauline whispered, "My mom's boyfriend. Don't tell anyone? Okay? He could get into a lot of trouble."

He could get into trouble? This girl was facing drug charges, and she's worrying about the pervert that's been abusing her?

"Promise you won't say anything?" she asked.

"Uh, sure."

She wiped away a tear and kissed me on the cheek. "You're the best, Sloan. We should hang out more often. You make me laugh."

Now I was facing an ethical dilemma that none of my mother's VHS tapes of *After School Specials* had prepared me for.

Pauline's mom was cheating on her husband with a drug dealer who was sleeping with Pauline and using her to deal. And the poor girl was willing to take a fall for him.

Walking away from the food court had been easy. What was I supposed to do now?

I knew I couldn't ask any family or friends, because I didn't want to risk them telling me the wrong answer—to do nothing.

I spent all night and day trying to figure out who I should tell. My teachers? The police? The news?

Then I remembered someone saying that Pauline was being tried in juvenile drug court. The name of the judge was in the newspaper. I found his address and knocked on his door the next evening.

He was confused at first, thinking I was trying to lie to get a friend out of trouble, but I told him everything, including the food-court attempt to recruit me, the argument afterward, and the truth about Pauline's situation.

A week later, all charges were dropped. A few days after that, Pauline and her mother vanished, and an Ottavio Spencer was arrested for running an MDMA ring in South Florida.

The competing rumors around school were that Pauline and her mom had fled to Argentina or that Pauline's mob-connected lawyer dad had them killed.

I was the only one who knew the truth.

A few weeks after they vanished, I received a text message from an unknown number along with a photo: it was Pauline standing in front of a mirror, flipping me off. Arizona sucks. I know it was you, bitch.

Did I lose sleep? A little. The older I get, less and less. The more important question is, What did I learn? How far should I take things?

If I saw one of the little children wade out into the ocean, I'd run after them. But what if I saw their mother smoking near them? What if I thought they had an abusive home life? How far do I take it? Do I really want to police the world around me? I start to get up.

"Where are you going?" asks Tilda.

"That little girl over there needs more sunscreen. I'm going to tell her mom."

CHAPTER FORTY-SEVEN
BARNACLES

Jackie is leading her friends on an offshore snorkeling trip toward a small reef. She turns back from time to time to check on the other two girls, making sure that nobody is getting too far behind. She's also making slow, measured strokes, careful to not outpace them. Moments like this make me proud.

I stay at the rear, on the lookout for boats and fish, like a mama orca protecting her pod. I've got my speed fins on. That way I can catch up to a girl in seconds if a problem arises, although on dives like this the problems are usually lost fins and leaking masks.

Jackie spots a school of fish and dives down like a torpedo to inspect them. One of the girls tries to follow but stops as water rushes into her snorkel. I kick hard, and I'm next to her a moment later. I guide Tabitha to the surface, putting her arm over my shoulder. When we breach, I take her mask off and let her cough out the salt water while I keep an eye on Clare and the blur of my daughter below.

"You okay?"

"Yeah," she coughs. "Forgot to not breathe through the snorkel. Where'd you come from?" she asks, looking around.

"Behind you. Are you okay?"

She nods. I hand her mask back to her. She manages to get it back on and goes back to snorkeling.

Jackie pops her head above the surface. "What happened?"

"She tried to follow you."

"Oops," she says, embarrassed. "I saw the fish."

"Just be more careful around the girls. They're not your cousins."

"Okay." And just like that, she does an elegant flip in the water and sidles up to her friends.

I'm still thinking about Pauline from high school and the boundaries of my ethical responsibility. Something's nagging me. Unfinished business. A question at the back of my mind.

What is it?

Well, I could start with the fact that nothing about the Swamp Killer case sits right with me.

Yes, they have some solid evidence. Yes, Shulme made something of a confession. Yes, but . . . what?

It doesn't *feel* right. It feels like . . . we're not trying hard enough to prove he's *not* the Swamp Killer.

Why is that? It would be embarrassing to get the wrong guy, not to mention bad for the poor slob who gets wrongfully convicted. So why are we pushing so hard?

Jackie and her friends point toward a large cobia gliding along the sand. Its prehistoric features give it a menacing look, but Jackie shows no sign of concern. She's been close to bigger and meaner fish. Her friends hang back behind her.

Okay, the girls are fine, and there appear to be no apex predators in the vicinity. So . . . back to the case. Why aren't we afraid of embarrassing ourselves? Who would want to be wrong about the Swamp Killer? He's one of South Florida's most prolific and organized killers ever. He's elusive . . .

If Shulme isn't the Swamp Killer, then catching the real one may be impossible. Shulme probably is Manifold, but that's not the same thing. And that's the problem. We've convinced ourselves that Manifold is the Swamp Killer. Get Manifold, you get the killer. Only I'm not so sure that math adds up.

Tabitha is starting to slow down and is having trouble keeping up. I swim over to the girls and motion for them to surface.

Jackie gives me a look, wanting to stay out longer, but her brain intercedes and she says nothing, realizing this is about her friends, not her stamina.

We swim back to shore, take off our fins, and stretch out on our towels to dry. I make sure they all reapply their sunscreen so they don't go home looking like tween lobsters.

I apply my own sunscreen and listen to the girls' chatter. It bounces between which K-pop star they have a crush on and how much is too much YouTube versus Netflix.

They're oblivious to my eavesdropping, and Tilda's snoring under her sun hat, empty Mason jar at her side.

"Should I send a picture to Caden?" asks Clare.

"No," says Jackie. "He's a perv. He'll just send it to his weirdo friends."

"I can use Pixy. That way he can't save it," she replies.

"He'll just screen grab it. Boys are pervy. They always figure out ways around that."

Damn right, daughter. Boys aren't to be trusted.

My stomach does a flip. For a moment, I feel suddenly nauseated. That thing at the back of my mind just stepped forward.

"Do the boys in your school trade photos around?" I ask.

"Oh, not *those* kinds of photos," says Jackie. "I mean, not that I know of."

"The older boys do," replies Clare.

I'm not terribly surprised by that, or by teen and tween behavior generally; it's something else that has me alarmed. "Stay here, guys. I'm going to make a call."

I walk over to a picnic table with a clear view of them, take a seat, and dial my phone.

"Wesley," says the Broward Sheriff's Office detective.

Let's hope this interaction goes better than the last one we had. "It's McPherson."

"Ah, to what do I owe this pleasure?"

"The evidence for Shulme. How familiar are you with it?"

"Is that a joke? I'm sorting through file boxes right now with the district attorney's office. Is there a problem?"

"I have a question. The Polaroids Shulme took of the victim . . . how many are there?"

"Three," he replies. "Can I help you with anything else?"

"Did they track down the film? When the prints were made?"

"The film? There's no way to tell."

"What did the lab say? Can't they tell from a serial number?"

"That would be on the back," he explains.

I'm confused. "Okay. Why don't you flip it over?"

He laughs. "That's not how photocopies work, kid. They only copied one side."

"Wait. How many actual Polaroids do you have from Shulme?"

"Actual Polaroids? None. He destroyed them all," Wesley replies.

"Then what was I looking at before?"

"A photocopy."

"Right. You mean *that's* the original? A *photocopy* of a Polaroid?"

"Yes, McPherson. This conversation is getting boring. Anything else I can help you with? Maybe explain how email works?"

Ass. "So, the physical evidence for Shulme is literally a photocopy of a Polaroid?"

"That and the fact that he knew details nobody else could know. Things we had to go back to the crime scenes to find out."

"Things only the killer knew."

"Exactly."

"Or that the killer told him."

"Oh, don't get started with that horseshit. You had Shulme and you didn't know it. Don't start trying to cover your ass now."

"I don't care about that. I just want—"

"Goodbye." He hangs up on me.

Oh jeez. This is worse than I thought.

Shulme isn't the Swamp Killer. At least that's what my gut is telling me. He's still out there.

My eyes fall on Jackie and her friends giggling in the sun, no cares beyond those of a sheltered child. A cool breeze rolls in from the ocean, and I start to shiver.

This is worse than going back to square one. Nobody wants to believe the real Swamp Killer's still out there. They all want to swim straight ahead, ignoring what's lurking just out of sight.

The Swamp Killer must be loving the fact that we're so far off his trail. He must feel invulnerable now. Uncatchable. And ready to kill again.

CHAPTER FORTY-EIGHT
Bottom Feeder

Shady Tree Villas is even creepier at night. TVs flicker from inside trailers while the occasional group of men sits on steps or in lawn chairs, cigarettes glowing, waiting for . . . what? Redemption? Some time traveler to burst out of the stars and help them undo the horrible acts that put them on the fringes of society?

Once upon a time, you could outrun your sins by going off to the frontier. There are still some places left like that. I've met a few people with criminal pasts in remote ports and fishing towns. But for most, the only choice is to sit in one place, diving deeper into your own psyche, numbing your mind with whatever pop culture or pharmacology has to offer.

I wonder about Uncle Karl. His crimes aren't nearly as morally reprehensible as those of these men, but what does he look forward to after he's out of his halfway house and back among society? If I had to bet, I'd say he'll leave South Florida for a while. I don't blame him.

The part of me that demands justice and wants the wicked to be punished deeply understands the lock-'em-up-and-throw-away-the-key mentality. But that can't be the solution for all crimes. I still don't have an answer for what you do with the truly unredeemable, and I surely won't find it here.

What I *do* hope to find lies in Smokey Joe Ray's trailer and mind.

I contemplated bringing Hughes as backup but decided to keep him away from this until I have something more than a bad feeling. If I make another mistake like I did with Cope and Shulme, Hughes would share the blame.

I knock on the screen door. Joe's coughing answers back. The door slides open, and he's wearing a tattered bathrobe over a stained shirt and shorts. He waves me inside and drops down into his easy chair.

"So, you caught him?" he asks.

"Did we?"

Joe shrugs. "How would I know?"

I have a theory, and I need him to confirm it for me. But I know I have to approach this delicately. Smokey Joe Ray could be my only chance at learning the real identity of the Swamp Killer.

The first part of my theory is that Sleazy Steve has gone through a few phases. "Early Steve," the one who murdered my van kids, was trying to figure out and understand who he was. What he knew was that he got off on violating people, maybe not directly through sex, but by taking control of them. He also liked to memorialize those moments. That's why he had the instant camera. With photos he could relive those moments over and over, and Polaroid film meant he didn't have to get the pictures developed by an outside service.

At some point, maybe in the late 1990s, Steve craved a new thrill and tried something different. He told people. Maybe not explicitly, but he shared his crimes with others. I don't think it was the photos, at least not at first, but rather written accounts of his exploits. Steve started describing what he did for other people.

Somewhere along the way, Shulme came across these . . . confessions?

What I can't connect is how. From what I've been able to gather from Shulme's selective confessions and the evidence left behind, Steve carefully left out anything that could link back to him. The forensic details Shulme offered up—such as where to find the knife marks in Lara Chadwick's kitchen—were the kind of clues the police could have found.

Steve wasn't trying to reveal himself. He was bragging. But to whom? And through what means?

This is what brings me to Smokey Joe Ray's dirty living room. The man is at the center of a lot of shady stuff. I originally came here for information about the missing kids; now I'm here to find out about the dark, interconnected webs of South Florida.

I'd rather be talking to Shulme, but Denton won't let me anywhere near him. So I'm stuck talking to this pervert. I need a strategy, and the one I've decided on is honesty. The one thing I think is true of most of the men in this godforsaken place is that they all want to see themselves as better versions of what society sees them as. They don't want to be monsters.

But what about Smokey Joe Ray? I suspect a man who loved the limelight so much might still want to be loved, or at least liked. While he's smart enough to know that's probably not in the cards, he might not have given up all hope.

"He's going to kill again," I say flatly.

"Shulme? You think so?"

"It's not Shulme," I tell him. "Sure, he knew a lot of details about the murders. But I don't think that means he did it. I know a lot of details too." I pause. "I think others do as well."

"Really? How so?" asks Joe.

"Shulme told me how perverts like him trade photographs and videos. That got me to thinking, what else do they trade?"

"Like snuff films?"

"Ever watched one?" I ask.

"Watch CNN much? That's all that cable news is, one never-ending snuff film. We watch it to say, 'Thank god I'm not one of those people in that shopping mall' or whatever."

"I'm talking about the other kind. You know what I mean."

"Nope. Not my thing," he says flatly.

"You were never curious? Maybe you wanted to reassure yourself that there were worse people out there than you?"

"Worse people than me? Lady, pick up a history book or a rock and roll biography. What I did wasn't even really a crime twenty years ago. When I was in the navy in the Philippines, care to guess what the average age of the hookers in the brothels across from the base was? Think my commanders didn't know? Think the Pentagon didn't know? We were *encouraged* to go there. Now, here I sit, and what's the difference? Those girls weren't Americans. These were. So don't even start trying to play on my self-doubts. Despite what I told the judge, I regret shit. Once I can get out of here, I'll head off to Thailand or wherever, where I can do whatever the fuck I want."

Classy guy.

Okay, Sloan, try a different approach.

"Violent stuff?"

"What? No. I'm not *that* kind of prick."

"Okay. But maybe you could tell me how Shulme knew so much? How would he know about the murders?"

"I think you were on to something before. Somebody told him."

"Did anyone ever tell you?"

He stares at me. "Don't be stupid."

I take my copy of the photocopy from my folder and hand it to him. "Ever see this?"

It's the Polaroid of the victim with the gloved hand touching her face. Below it is the text description that makes so much more sense now that I know the killer wrote it: "What the eyes do not see, lips reveal."

"This reads like bad poetry," says Joe.

"I'm sure there's more of it. Does it look familiar?"

"Have I ever read snuff literature? No, Officer. Any more questions?"

He's being evasive, so I tell him, "Remember this conversation when you see a murder in the news. It'll be another young woman. Ask yourself if what you knew could have made a difference. Was that tiny little detail really worth holding on to? Will you be so sure you're not a bad guy then?"

Joe is about to say something. Instead he leans back and laces his fingers behind his head and thinks. "You're different. You take all this personally."

"I try to make myself care, even when I want to let it go. But, yeah, I do take it personally."

He sighs. "I know I'm a creepy guy. I prefer the term *transgressive* or *free thinker*, but I know I'm a little beyond that. I also know my limits. There are people that freak me the hell out." He shakes his head. "I should keep my mouth shut. But, the hell with it. After the second time I got in trouble—when the papers were all over my ass—a guy comes up to me at the Wolf Lounge."

"Wolf Lounge?"

"The sex club in the warehouse by the airport? You never heard of it?"

"Uh, no."

"It's not what you think it is."

"I literally have no image in my head," I reply.

"I mean there's leather stuff and rooms and all that. Anyway, I was at the bar, and this tall, skinny guy starts talking to me. He recognizes me and says he's a fan."

I'm super curious to know what the protocols are like for local celebrity-fan interactions at a sex club, but I keep my mouth shut.

"He says his name's Lexi, and then the conversation gets a little weird. He asks if he can show me something. I tell him I'm probably not into whatever it is, but he insists. He takes out this little booklet, the kind of thing you make on a photocopier, and he shows it to me. It's page after page of photos of women being violated. I'm like, whatever, and then he starts showing me women with stab wounds. Each shot includes a caption like the one you just showed me. My guess is that Shulme met up with Lexi too. Maybe took a copy of the booklet."

"What did Lexi look like?" I ask.

"Younger guy. Tall. Accent. Maybe Australian or New Zealand. They're all pervs."

"Did he say how he got the booklet?"

"Yeah. He said he stole it. Said he met up with some guy who got drunk and started talking and showing him this shit. Lexi said he stole it to make copies. Said he wanted to sell 'em."

"Did you buy one?"

"*No.* Jesus. I told you, that's not my thing," he replies a little too forcefully.

"What about Lexi? What happened to him?"

"That's the funny part. The little prick hung himself a few weeks later, trying to do some autoerotic thing. Maybe he was killed. I don't know. Anyway . . ." He shrugs. "End of story."

"Do you know anyone who might have had a copy of that booklet?"

"Zine," he corrects me. "He called it a zine. You know, short for magazine. And no. I don't. I'd go back to jail if I was caught with something like that."

His last comment sounds like an admission. "If you were caught?"

Joe's visibly uneasy now. "That was a long time ago." He waves a hand at his trailer. "They search my place for all that kind of stuff."

"What are you telling me, Joe?"

"I'm going to go outside and grab a cigarette. And, FYI, you're not my parole officer, so you need a warrant to search my place. Anything you find without one isn't admissible." He gets up and goes outside.

What the hell? Does Joe *want* me to search his place? Confused, I get up and walk around the small space. There's a folder sitting on his kitchen table, out in the open. Written across the front is *For my lawyer.*

Is this a trick? I glance around, afraid I'll be caught on another camera. Is he trying to set me up for something?

I stare at the folder. What am I supposed to do? What would George do?

If I take this, it's not admissible evidence in any case unless I explain how I acquired it.

Joe's afraid to hand it to me because of his parole status. Or at least that's how he's acting.

I walk back outside. He glances up from the steps and sees my empty hands. "Seriously? Could I have been more obvious?"

"No, you couldn't have."

He goes inside and comes out with the folder. "Don't tell anyone you don't have to. And understand, the only reason I kept it was because it was . . . so damn weird."

"We're going to need you to make a formal statement."

"No way in hell." He pulls the folder back. "You want this?"

"I can get a warrant," I reply.

"I can light a fire."

"Destroy evidence?"

"What evidence? You don't even know what's in here."

"Can we skip the games? I'll tell your parole officer you volunteered it. You can tell them whatever you want about how you found it." I gesture to the other trailers. "Tell them one of these other perverts left it in your mailbox, for all I care."

"Fine." He thrusts the folder at me. "Take it. You're the reason I hate women." He goes back into his trailer and shuts the door.

"Glad to be of service," I murmur as I return to my truck, then stare down at the folder in my lap. Am I ready to open this? Am I ready for what I'm going to see?

To be honest, I half expect it's going to be some perverted photo of Joe, just to irritate me. I decide that if that's the case, I'm going to knock on his door and have my Mace accidentally go off in his face.

I put on my gloves and open the folder.

It's not Smokey Joe Ray committing a lewd act. It's something much, much worse.

Below the words *Murder Manifesto* is a photograph of a young woman with her throat laid open so wide you can see her spinal column.

I want to throw up. Instead, I turn the page.

CHAPTER FORTY-NINE
ZINE

Denton stares at the manuscript in the plastic bag as if it's radioactive. I guess in a way it is. George called this meeting after I got off the phone with him while driving away from Smokey Joe Ray's trailer park. George didn't have to see it to understand the importance.

"What is this?" asks Denton, pretending that George hadn't already explained.

"It's a zine," I tell him.

"A what?"

"A mini magazine thingy made with a photocopier and staples. The pictures you found at Shulme's place? They're in there. So are a number of others. Details, times of death, other things." I try to take my mind off the images.

"This is Shulme's?"

"No. This belongs to another man. A convicted child molester. He turned it over to us. He says someone stole this copy from the real Swamp Killer." I'm not sure how much I believe the Lexi story, but one thing at a time. "Shulme must've gotten ahold of a copy. He pretended he was the killer and made up the whole Manifold thing."

"Why?" asks Denton.

"Because he honestly thought there was a chance we'd pay his ransom. He saw an opportunity and jumped in. He never saw your newspaper dragnet coming, is my guess."

I also suspect it's because I humiliated him.

Denton takes the pair of gloves I placed next to the manuscript and slides it out of the plastic wrapper. George and I sit quietly as he leafs through the images and text, letting it wash over him.

Finally, he finishes, closes the booklet, and pushes it away. "We have a confession out of Shulme. And other evidence."

"Bullshit," says George. "This throws everything out the window. You got a con man is what you have. And if you're not careful, you're going to have an even bigger mess."

Denton looks like a man on a sinking ship. He's smart and he's ethical, but right now he's contemplating all the hard work he put into the case—and the stapled stack of photocopies that just destroyed it all.

Shulme looked like a sure thing when it seemed there was no way anyone else could know the details of the crimes like he did. Now, that's not the case.

"Think about it. Shulme told us nothing about crimes after 2005. That's also where the zine stops."

"It doesn't have anything about the van or some of the other earlier murders," Denton replies.

"Exactly. The kids in the van tell us something about Steve's identity. So do some of the other murders. He left those out because he didn't want to incriminate himself," I explain.

"And yet he saw fit to self-publish this . . . this garbage?"

"I can't tell you his motives. I only know that this exists along with the evidence Shulme had. Plus what the person who gave me this told me—which is suspect."

"How so?" asks Denton.

"He's a manipulator."

"Do you think he could be the killer?"

270

I shake my head. "He doesn't match anything we know about Steve, plus he was in jail during a few of the killings."

"What about working with the killer? What if all of them are in on it?"

"I don't know. I think the Swamp Killer may have been reaching out, but when the manuscript was stolen, that's when he decided it was too dangerous. My source said the guy who gave him this zine hanged himself. It's possible Steve killed him."

"Did that guy have a name?"

"Lexi. That's all I have."

"Damn it," says Denton. "We were this close. Shulme's been fighting with his attorney. We think he might be ready to plead guilty if he doesn't get the death penalty."

"Why would he do something like that?"

"Notoriety," says George. "They don't make movies about child pornographers. Serial killers, yes. He may not have meant to be caught, but now he wants the world to think he's the Swamp Killer. The whole Manifold extortion scheme would likely put him in jail for the rest of his life alone. Why not go for broke?"

"If he makes a public statement, it gets worse for us," says Denton. "Christ." He glances at George. "What a mess."

"We didn't make this one."

"I know. I know." Denton stares at me. "You're a pain in the ass. We're going to have to change him to a person of interest and let the press know we're looking elsewhere."

"Do we?" asks George.

"Of course we do. You of all people, George. We can't go on letting people think we caught him."

"What if it helps us catch the real Swamp Killer? Maybe we sit on this for a few days and quietly reopen the investigation?"

"My task force's dispersed. We're in the wrapping-up stage, moving on. We don't have anywhere near the resources we had before."

"We can do it," I blurt out. "Just let us have access to all the files."

"It's not going to work."

"Give us three days," I reply. "It's Thursday. Shulme won't drop a statement on a Friday. He'll want a whole week of media coverage."

"Three days?" asks George. "Care to explain how that's going to work?"

"Three days to make a dent and find a new lead."

"Fine," says Denton. "You guys can have it. But what if the real Swamp Killer decides to murder again while we're letting the public think he's behind bars?"

I don't have an answer to that question. Neither does George.

CHAPTER FIFTY
MOVIE CLUB

Hughes and I have our laptops set up on the conference room table playing security camera footage from the three houses near Lara Chadwick and Eric Timm's home. None of the cameras is aimed directly at the home, but they show a pretty good sample of who came and went from that neighborhood. It was this footage that originally made the AC repairman, Cope, a person of interest. While on the night of their disappearances there was no suspicious activity in front of the victims' home, it would've been easy to access it from the yard behind.

Along with the footage, we're going through the logs the Broward Sheriff's Office made of every vehicle and person on the tapes.

"Another Domino's delivery," says Hughes.

"Same guy with red hair?" I ask.

"Hard to tell from the blur, but, yeah, looks like Clifford Spivey."

Clifford is a regular in that neighborhood, with five appearances in two weeks' worth of security cam footage. He's one of two dozen other people who made frequent visits there in the course of their day-to-day work. BSO already ran thorough background checks. Cope wasn't even the most suspicious of the lot, but he did raise flags. False ones, apparently.

"Check the license on the Kloofs' camera?" I ask.

"Their car was in the way," Hughes says. "Same make and model, though."

Byron and Renata Kloof had a security camera that faced the street and had sufficient resolution to record license plates as cars drove by—provided Byron didn't park his car in the way. Something he did often, to our frustration.

Watching the various suspects come and go has become a mini reality television show for Hughes and me. We see the paper-delivery couple drive by in the morning. We watch early-morning people shamble out to their cars with cups of coffee and sleepy expressions. We see moms and dads chase their kids out the door for school. During the day, we see package-delivery people knock on doors, throw boxes, and scratch themselves. Then comes a procession of kids returning home, playing in the street, and being called to dinner.

Of all that, the most interesting character is Mr. White. We watch him sneak out and pay visits to several of the other houses. He's a cat—a highly promiscuous cat, from what we observe. After he returns home at night, a parade of raccoons roams the neighborhood, looking for trash and sometimes succeeding.

All aspects of human and animal life are represented on these videos, except the one we've been looking for: a creep in a murder van rolling through and leering in the direction of Lara Chadwick's home. It's simply not there.

What's even more frustrating is that the night they went missing is like any other night.

We see Lara and then Eric drive past the Kloofs' camera, and that's the end of it. There are no other cars that night except for the neighbors'.

I press fast-forward and watch a video I've seen twice already, this time with the speed increased. "He's here," I murmur.

"I know. But who?" Hughes drops the binder full of suspects on the table. "They checked everyone. They even tracked down the people they couldn't get license plates for. They were thorough."

I grab the binder and flip through the pages. It contains times, names, and plate numbers for hundreds of people. The entries number in the thousands.

I wave to my screen. "We've seen him. He came in through the back door to kill them, but he's been by the house."

"Maybe not within the time period of the camera footage?"

"Nah, he's careful. He'd check the place out close to the date." I keep flipping through the pages. "Any word on George?"

"He's still digging under rocks. Shaking trees."

While Hughes and I are here, George has been interviewing some of the persons of interest, including Smokey Joe Ray. If anyone could get him to talk, it would be George. The fact that he hasn't texted us tells me that nothing has come of that.

Cope's truck speeds past on the screen, and I mentally flip him off. He'd be the perfect suspect if it weren't for the fact that we have him on hospital security camera footage at the time of the murders. He's an asshole, but he can't be in two places at once.

I even watched *that* footage to make sure the same guy checking in was the jerk I encountered.

Yep. Same douche.

I also checked to see if he had a twin brother. Nope. He's a one-of-a-kind asshole. Man, that would have made it so much easier.

"Why did they like Cope for this?" I ask Hughes.

"Because he's an asshole?"

"Besides that."

"Because he lurks a lot. He takes three days to fix an AC unit? They should charge him with fraud."

I scroll back the video of his truck driving by. The windows are too tinted to see inside. The truck passes. Same dumb sign affixed to

Andrew Mayne

the door. Same dent in the bumper I saw in the driveway at his house. You can barely make it out here, but it's there. The guy's been driving around with it for years.

"That window tint has to be illegal," says Hughes.

"You're looking at him too?" I get up and stretch my legs as I walk over to his side of the table.

Hughes has a freeze frame of the truck as it's driving away from the camera. The tailgate is down, so you can't see the license plate from this angle, but the sign on the door is the same. Everything is there . . .

Except . . .

"Go back a couple frames," I tell Hughes.

"What?"

"Just go back."

He scrubs the footage a second back. "Okay?"

"The bumper."

"What?"

"The damn bumper! There's no dent! Scroll all the way back and let's see it." The truck rolls by, giving us multiple views.

No dent.

"That's not Cope's truck! It's a different truck!"

"It has his sign," replies Hughes. "He never denied it was him."

"But it's not. Not this time. Check the other clips. Look for other times he drove by. I bet the last time we see the truck, there's no dent."

Hughes pulls up the other footage, and we spend several minutes confirming it. Cope makes two visits to the neighborhood. Mystery Man with the undented truck makes four. *Four trips.*

"What does this mean?" Hughes asks, trying to piece it all together. "Is this other dude pretending to be Cope? That seems like a lot of work."

"Yes. No. There are a million Ford pickup trucks in South Florida like that one. We only think it's Cope's because of the magnetic sign. They can make those for you in an hour down the street."

"Okay. But he's shadowing Cope? Pretending to be him?"

I shake my head. "No. I don't think that's it. I think they're working together."

"Killing together?"

"I don't think so." I grab a binder and flip through Cope's hospital visitation times. "I think he had someone cover his jobs while he was out of commission."

"But why didn't he tell us? Assuming they're not partners in crime?"

"Because Mystery Man doesn't have a license. Damn. What if Cope was using several unlicensed electricians?"

Hughes's eyes go wide.

"Yeah," I say. "Multiple license violations are a third-degree felony. If Cope admitted he was having an unlicensed guy handle his jobs, it could mean five years in jail *per incident.* He may not have known that his guy was the killer, but that doesn't mean he wants the truth to get out now."

"He had to suspect."

I shrug. "Maybe. Certainly, after the murders. But Cope doesn't strike me as the guilt-ridden type."

"Okay, how do we catch this guy? Bring Cope in?" asks Hughes.

"I don't know if that'll work. He's lawyered up and has no reason to talk to us at the moment. We need to run it by George. Maybe there's a better way."

Hughes bursts from his seat, scaring the hell out of me, and rushes over to a box filled with folders. He starts digging them out like a madman until he finds what he's looking for and drops it on the table in front of me.

A small label marks the contents: *Darren Cope Cell Phone Records.*

"They got a warrant for his phone bill," says Hughes. "How they got a judge to do that is beyond me. But they did it."

I flip through the folder. "It's just a list of numbers. No names."

"Yeah, but one of these is Sleazy Steve's." He digs into the box and pulls out a thumb drive. "Let's check 'em out."

Hughes accesses the USB drive and pulls up a spreadsheet of phone numbers and call times. One by one, he plugs the phone numbers into Google and searches for them. After about twenty numbers, I start to get bored and decide that we need George to put the thumbscrews on Cope.

"McPherson!" shouts the usually unexcitable Hughes. He's pointing to an old web listing for general handyman repair: *Stephen Dunn Handyman & Boat Repair.*

"It's a Stephen," he says expectantly. He types the name into a police search engine. No results. "Huh."

"The Dunn part is probably an alias," I explain. "The real question is whether he still answers that number." I pick up my phone.

"Wait," says Hughes.

CHAPTER FIFTY-ONE
THE SCENT

My body's a ball of nervous energy. Three hours ago, Hughes called the number for Stephen Dunn Handyman & Boat Repair and left a message asking him to fix the pool pump at the house next door to the one I'm in right now.

The houses are at a dead end of a street and used by the FBI and DEA to conduct sting operations. They're isolated in case of gunfire—which makes the one I'm in the ideal target for Sleazy Steve.

What helps me relax somewhat is that Hughes and George will be watching security camera feeds of me. George is watching from a panic room hidden in my house; Hughes is watching from next door. Both stand ready in case there's a problem.

There shouldn't be. All we're hoping to do is get the man behind the phone number to show up, then track him back to where he lives and find out his actual identity. In the event that he seems like our suspect and takes an unusual interest in me, we plan to use the house for a few more days to see if he drives by or tries to stalk me.

I consider this unlikely. I suspect that even with Shulme in jail and the news out that the Swamp Killer has been apprehended, Steve will be cautious. That said, catching him driving by the house a little too often might be enough to convince a judge to issue a search warrant for his home and a collection of forensic evidence.

Hughes called him for a pool repair at the other house so that Dunn would assume that anything he does in my house will be harder to connect to his work next door. It's flimsy but feels less like an obvious sting operation. Steve is smart. He has to know an obvious trap when he sees one.

"His truck is driving past my driveway," Hughes says over the phone.

I'm listening via my AirPods, pretending it's music.

I'm stretched out on a deck chair by the pool behind my house, pretending to get some sun. It feels a little obvious, but this is also the best way to watch Hughes's backyard.

"Okay, it's pulling in."

I hear the sound of the pool repairman and Hughes talking as they make their way between the houses. Hughes sounds convincing as he explains the problem he's been having.

I casually glance at them as they walk to the back wall of the house, where the pump is located by a hedge. The plan is for Hughes not to acknowledge me and vice versa. If Dunn asks, Hughes will explain that I'm watching the house for my mother while she's in the hospital, but that he doesn't know me personally.

Dunn is tall. He's got a strong build with a bit of middle-aged weight, but he's no slob. Gray hair sticks out from behind his hat. His face is tanned and slightly rugged. He looks like a movie cowboy villain. I use the word *villain* because even from here, his eyes are penetrating but cold.

I hear Hughes tell him that he's got to go run an errand. We figure that if Dunn thinks his interactions with me won't be observed, he'll be more likely to strike up a conversation.

Hughes walks away, leaving Dunn to his work. At the moment he's kneeling by the pump, using a hose to spray off all the dirt. I go back to pretending to listen to music, waiting for the right moment.

"Hughes is down the street," says George in my ear.

George is watching footage from tiny cameras we have hidden around the houses. We made a point of not having any visible security cameras and no dogs. If we want to see Dunn act naturally, we can't have him feel observed.

"He's got the cover off the pool," says George.

My foot starts to shake. In a minute I have to get up and walk over to a potential serial killer, wearing only a bikini and a forced smile.

George and Hughes argued that we didn't need to do it that way, but I insisted. I'm in good shape. I clean up well, and I definitely don't look like a cop and nothing like any photo or video of me in the news that I can find. And most importantly, I know that Dunn will only let his guard down if he sees my vulnerability.

"You ready?" asks George. "I can be out there in five seconds if there's a problem."

"I'm good," I whisper nervously. I get up, grab my towel, throw it over my shoulder, and walk over to Hughes's house.

The moment the door to my house's pool enclosure shuts behind me, Dunn's eyes dart toward the sound, and he sees me. Or at least visibly acknowledges me.

I sensed that he was watching me the moment he entered the backyard with Hughes. It could all be in my mind, but I had the same feeling a mouse must have after she realizes the owl has spotted her.

Dunn is using a wrench to take apart the pump. I could tell him it's a fried motor because I watched George short it out with 220 current earlier that morning, but better to let him find that out himself.

When I get within conversation distance near the small fence that separates the yards, I take the AirPods out and, trying not to sound nervous, speak. "Hey, sorry to bother you. But do you fix things?"

Dunn sets down his wrench. I notice the other tools in his toolbox: box cutters, a small saw, a rusty hammer, and other implements that could have been used to kill the victims we found in the swamp.

His eyes linger over my body before stopping on my face. Lots of guys do that, but there's something about how slowly he does it that sends a chill down my spine.

"Yeah. Most things," he replies. "What's broken?"

Oh jeez. This already sounds like the dialogue to a bad porno movie. The realization makes me grin inwardly. *Keep it together, Sloan.*

I suck at undercover.

I gesture back to the house. "My mom's air-conditioning. I want to get it fixed before she gets back next week. I'd like to get it fixed today, if I can. It's murder in there."

Why did I use that word? God, I'm bad at this!

Dunn stands up, and I almost jump back but manage to not freak out visibly.

He's tall, all right. Taller than I realized.

He wipes his hands on a red rag. "Let's take a look."

I wasn't expecting that quick of a response. I glance down at the dissected pool pump.

"What about that?"

"It'll be here when I get back."

The phrase *I get back* creeps me out, because it sounds like only one person will be returning . . . which should be obvious, because I don't need to come back and fix the pump. But still, it weirds me out.

As I walk toward my house's AC unit, he's a few steps behind. I get the sense that he's looking at my butt, visible just below the towel over my shoulders.

This is the special bikini, Run's favorite. It's not skimpy—it simply accentuates the curves I like to have accentuated. It also has what my friends call "ass magic," as in it makes your butt look magical.

We come to a stop by the large metal box containing the AC unit. Dunn stands there and makes a small nod. "Okay. I can see you have an air handler, but I need to check out the control panel and see what happens when I turn it on."

I smack my forehead. Maybe a little too cutesy. "Oh, of course."

This means I have to take him inside the house. George is in the panic room, but since I took the AirPods out, I haven't heard his voice. Knowing but not having proof that he's watching me makes me nervous.

Dunn follows me onto the patio and through the open glass doors. I glance back and see that he's no longer checking me out—he's looking all around the house. Not in an obvious way, but his eyes are probing.

I've seen this behavior before with sharks.

When you're in the water with a big shark like a tiger or a bull, they'll circle around you, assessing you, observing what you're doing. They can quickly decide you're not food, but that doesn't mean there isn't food near you. Some sharks can pick up the sound of a spear gun and will swim toward it, not away, because they know that means the awkwardly swimming fish that's not worth eating—that's you or me—just caught something that is worth eating. They'll try to take it from you on the spot.

I lead Dunn over to the thermostat in the living room. He goes up to the controls and starts to make adjustments.

"How long has it been broken?" Dunn asks.

"A few days. It only blows warm air now."

He nods, then takes the cover off. As he scrutinizes the circuitry, looking at absolutely nothing that has anything to do with the problem, he asks, "Did your husband take a look?"

"No husband," I reply. Oops. I'm afraid that sounded too vulnerable. He's used to women being on guard when they're alone in their homes with him. I quickly add, "My boyfriend's no good at these things."

Andrew Mayne

"Oh, what's he do?" Dunn asks, pretending to make small talk while probing me for information about my imaginary boyfriend.

I'm about to answer the way I'd expect a single girl to answer in this situation—by describing her last boyfriend—but I stop, because if I described Run, it would be pretty clear that he's capable of fixing this. Instead, I draw upon Hughes. "He was in the military. Now he's looking for a job."

"I see," says Dunn.

What do you see?

"Mind if I use your bathroom?" he asks.

I point him toward the guest bathroom down the hall. It's right next to the room where my stuff is. Under the pretext of me watching my mother's house, we decided that we'd leave the master bedroom as is, full of an older woman's belongings, with me staying in a guest room.

Dunn walks away, his eyes gliding over the picture frames on the walls—photos of me and my mother—then disappears down the hallway.

I take a deep breath, put an AirPod back in my ear, and go into the kitchen and grab two water bottles.

"You're doing good, kid," says George, whispering because his safe room is only a few feet away from where Dunn is right now. "Just stay relaxed. When you're not looking, he's really checking you out. I'd punch him if I weren't stuck in here."

I nod, afraid to speak. I have to maintain my act even when Dunn's not around. Otherwise I may slip up and ruin everything.

"Just keep calm," says George. "Most guys would do that. To be honest, it's probably not him. I'm not getting the vibe."

Really? I'm creeped out like I've never been in my life. Of course, I'm expecting to meet a serial killer. As desperately as I want to catch Sleazy Steve, George's hunch relaxes me. George is rarely wrong.

Footsteps echo from the hallway, and Dunn emerges. "Water?" I offer him a bottle.

He takes it from me and unscrews the cap. "We need to check the outside unit."

We return to the AC unit. Dunn stands there for a moment, staring at it. "I think you're going to need an electrician," he tells me.

"Isn't that what you do?"

"I can do it. But I'm not licensed for that."

I gesture toward Hughes's pool pump. "What about that?"

"It's different. I'm just replacing a unit, not working on the electric. This is more complicated."

"Oh," I reply. Inwardly it feels like a weird form of rejection.

"However, I can get the parts for you. Your boyfriend might be able to put it together. Or I can recommend an electrician. It'll be expensive."

"How expensive?"

"Those licensed guys tend to overcharge. That's why people ask guys like me to fix it. Like I said, I can get you the parts. I don't need a license for that. If you catch my drift."

"Ah, so if I buy the parts from you, do you think you could help me put it together?" I ask.

"If your boyfriend doesn't want to. It would have to be in cash," he adds.

He knows the boyfriend is bullshit, but I don't get the sense that he's hitting on me. If George hadn't told me the guy didn't give off a vibe, I'd think he's testing to see how vulnerable I am.

"Okay," I reply. "How much?"

"Normally it's about a nine-hundred-dollar job. Probably cost two hundred for me to do it. If it's more, I'll let you know. And I won't take any money from you up front. In case you're worried that I'm gonna try to scam you."

"Sounds good."

He holds out a calloused hand. "What's your name?"

"Pauline," I say, pulling that name from memory. "Pauline Cameron."

"Okay, Pauline. Let me fix Scott's pool pump, then I'll go get some parts and fix your AC unit later this afternoon. And just as a favor, don't tell him I'm doing this for you. It would be better for the both of us."

❧

I go back to the pool and sit in the sun until Dunn finishes the pool pump. He walks over to the screen door and tells me he's going to get parts. I thank him, then go inside the house.

After a few minutes, George emerges from his hiding place. "Hughes is going to follow him."

"Is it worth it?" I reply. "You said you didn't get the vibe."

"Oh, I got the vibe. I was trying to help you relax. I didn't want to make you any more tense than you already were."

"Wait, you think it's him?"

George nods. "I watched him on the bathroom cameras. He went through your entire toiletry kit, the cabinets, and even the trash can."

I can feel every square inch of my exposed skin turn to goose bumps. "Do you think he's onto us?"

"No, McPherson. He's onto you. Like, fixated."

CHAPTER FIFTY-TWO
Bait

I'm sitting at the kitchen counter with my iPad, my back facing the living room, when I catch the reflection of the silhouette of someone standing in the sliding glass doorway.

I'm being watched.

I watch the watcher reflected in the glass of my tablet's screen. I'm pretending to be absorbed by the clickbait article I'm reading. George is in the panic room, radio silent. I have to trust that he has my back and is paying attention.

He already lied to me once. It was an understandable lie, but I still feel manipulated. I also get the feeling that there's more to what he's not telling me.

I can feel Dunn's eyes roam over my body. What's he thinking right now? What if he just decides to go for the kill?

Our plan was to find out who he is, not necessarily lure him into a trap where I'm the bait waiting for him to kill me. But to that end, although I don't have a gun on me—it would obviously show—I've hidden one just over the counter and another under a couch cushion. I've also made a mental note of every object in the house I can throw at him. Every table I can overturn. I can go from docile to full rage machine in a second if I have to. At least I keep telling myself that.

I lean back and make a yawning-sigh sound, a vulnerable noise. It says I'm tired and not paying attention.

"Excuse me, Pauline?" says Dunn's deep voice from the doorway.

"Oh?" I turn around, pretending to be startled. "You're back?"

"Yes. Actually, I've been working on your AC unit." He looks at the threshold. "May I come in?"

Vampires ask to come inside. "Yes. Of course."

"I got it apart and realized I'm going to need a different part."

"Ah, I see." I narrow my eyes. "Will this end up costing more?"

"No. No. Actually, it'll be cheaper. It just means I have to come back tomorrow and do the rest. I hope that's okay."

"That's fine, Stephen," I reply, suddenly panicking: *Did he ever tell me his name?*

"Thank you for being so understanding."

If he didn't tell me, he's excellent at not showing it.

Dunn turns around and walks back to the sliding glass door, then stops. "Quick question: Do you have any kind of laundry detergent I could use to clean one of the parts?"

"Liquid?" I ask.

"Yeah, that would work."

"One second." I go to the laundry room in the garage and look, finding an almost-empty jug on top of a shelf. When I return, he's still standing by the doorway.

"Thanks," he says, taking it from me.

"You can keep it," I reply with a smile.

Half an hour later, George and I are sitting in the living room while he watches a small monitor showing the street in front of the house. Hughes is on the road, following Dunn. We have him on speaker.

"He's heading to North Broward," says Hughes as he tails Dunn.

"Where did he go when he went to get parts?" asks George.

"That's the weirdest part. He actually just drove his truck down the street and sat there for twenty minutes. I couldn't get a clear look, but it didn't seem like he was on the phone."

"Just sitting there?" I ask.

"Yeah. My guess is that he was looking you up. Or rather, Pauline Cameron."

We used a service for law enforcement departments that helps you create fake social media profiles. They take an existing account they control and substitute photos for your undercover operative. Pauline Cameron's Instagram is full of nature shots and a handful of me at the beach, looking like a wannabe Instagram model. The account's thinner than I would have preferred, but hopefully it makes me a real-enough person.

"After that, he drove to an industrial park and went to a medical supply company."

"Drugs?" asks George.

"No. Equipment. Parts maybe? It might be another service call."

"Okay," says George. "Keep shadowing him until you find out where he lives. After that, head home for a few hours, check in with the family."

"I sent Cathy to her friend's house. She knows I'm on a detail. I'll come back to you guys."

"You don't have to do that," I reply.

"Are you kidding? This is a six-man job, at least. Unless we can get backup, I'll be there."

"Probably a good idea," says George. "While McPherson was getting soap for Dunn, he was inspecting the lock on the sliding glass door."

"Interesting. We should check the old cases. I wonder if he just pops the lock out and replaces it with another one," says Hughes.

"Could be. But you can pick one in a second with a skeleton key. That's why people use stoppers to keep them from being opened."

I walk over to the sliding glass door and look at the frame. "We don't have one."

"Nope," says George. "There was a wooden closet rod that sat in the track, but I pulled it out."

"To make me more vulnerable," I reply.

"I'll be here too."

"In your panic room," adds Hughes. "I don't like this. I really don't like this."

"Hey, you'll be here too," I explain.

"Well, keep in mind it didn't turn out too well for the guys either." Hughes is only pretending to be afraid, but it does worry me.

"We still don't know how he approached his victims," I point out.

"Probably differently based on each case," says George. "If he was going to come here, he'd wait until late and come through the back. Either way, if he comes by, it'll probably be just to check on the house at night and make sure everything is as it seems. Hughes and I will be in the panic room, ready to come out."

"Okay, I feel more relaxed now," I reply.

"I didn't say you should be relaxed. This man's a killer. I just want you to know the facts."

"Great. All I have to do now is wait for a serial killer to stalk me. Wonderful."

CHAPTER FIFTY-THREE
BREATHING ROOM

I pretend to go about my nightly routine as if I were a childless woman living alone in her mother's house and not a cop who happens to be in a complicated relationship. We don't know if Dunn is watching me. The sliding glass door that opens to the patio faces a canal and the tree-lined shore on the other side. He could be watching me from there with night-vision goggles or an off-the-shelf thermal imager. Maybe that's extreme, but we don't know how he's gone so long without being caught . . . assuming that he is Sleazy Steve.

I'm convinced, and so are the others. The challenge is catching him doing something that we can arrest him for, then using that opportunity to investigate him more closely.

The apartment Hughes followed him back to is paid for with cash. Same for the storage unit where he keeps his tools. Cash everywhere. Even the phone he uses is prepaid and refilled with credits paid for in cash.

Stephen Dunn doesn't exist. Yet as far as we can tell, he's never left South Florida. He's been around for decades, lurking in the shadows. If he has any roots, they're not attached to that name. If he has another life, it's clearly separate from this one.

Is there a Mrs. Dunn somewhere? Are there little Dunns? We don't know, because there is no Stephen Dunn, only a figure that we conjured up with a phone call. Until that moment, he was hidden from the rest of the world.

Like the rhythmic sound of a fish in distress or an infant whale's cry, my seeming vulnerability has drawn him in. Now as I glance at my reflection in the sliding glass door and into the night beyond, I sense that he's circling. Waiting.

I go to the master bathroom, the one without the cameras, and take a shower while George and Hughes sit in the panic room, watching the video feeds, waiting to see if Dunn does a drive-by or peeks inside.

So far, it's been a no-show out front. But that doesn't mean his presence isn't felt.

I sit in the living room and read my iPad, then watch a documentary for an hour.

Visible to anyone looking through the windows.

I pour myself glasses of colored water from a bottle of wine on the coffee table. I need to look vulnerable while not *being* vulnerable.

It's almost midnight. I yawn, get up and walk to the guest room, change into shorts and a T-shirt, then climb into bed with my gun.

"How you doing, McPherson?" asks George through the speaker under my pillow.

"Fine. How are you guys doing? Anyone need a bathroom break?"

"No, but I'd recommend you not drink from the Gatorade bottles in here."

"Gross."

"How do you do it on the boat?" he asks.

"In the ocean, like all the other dirty mammals. See anything?"

They have their eyes on the monitors, watching for Dunn's truck. I trust them, but it only makes me feel slightly less terrified.

"Don't worry, kiddo, we'll let you know when he's coming," says Hughes.

"Did *you* just call me 'kiddo'?"

"Yeah, sorry."

"We're the same age," I reply, "son."

I stare at the ceiling and wait, making occasional conversation with Hughes and George, but not too loudly in case Dunn has managed to sneak past our cameras and lurks below my window.

Sometime after midnight, the AC kicks on, and the breeze, even though it's warm, cools me. It's probably in the mideighties in here. I can't imagine how George and Hughes are standing it in the sweatbox.

I yawn and wipe my eyes. Maybe I am getting tired. I hear a yawn from Hughes too.

"We should have done a coffee run," I say.

My body wants to sleep, my battery plummeting toward red. I try to resist, but it doesn't work. Even with Hughes and George watching, I have to be on my guard. Dunn could try anything. We don't know a thing about his tactics. In none of the murders did we see much sign of a struggle. This is the part that confuses me the most. Did he charm his way in late at night? That seems unlikely.

I stifle another yawn. The urge to sleep is overwhelming. Am I coming down from an adrenaline high?

"I think I need coffee," I say quietly. No response.

"Guys?"

Nothing.

I lift my head up from my pillow. It feels like it weighs a million pounds. All I want to do is go to sleep.

I feel funny . . .

I've felt this way before.

It happens when testing deep-sea-diving air mixes and getting the ratio wrong.

I struggle to sit upright.

I know how Dunn does it.

"Guys?" I whisper and hear my own slurred speech.

Dunn put something in the air-conditioning unit. It's why he went to the medical supply store.

He's using some kind of sleeping agent . . .

If I'm barely conscious, George and Hughes are definitely passed out in the panic room. The AC vent is their main air supply.

I try to get to my feet. And fall to the floor.

There's a sound . . .

The sound of a sliding glass door being slid open.

CHAPTER FIFTY-FOUR
GASP

I'm on the floor. I hear footsteps. Careful, slow footsteps. The corner of my vision is growing darker. Everything is slowing down.

I want to gasp for air, but I don't. My body is already metabolizing the gas I've inhaled. Taking a deep breath could render me unconscious.

More footsteps.

I try to crawl toward the door, to at least try to block it. My muscles refuse to cooperate.

I'm slipping into a dream.

Don't slip away, Sloan! Don't let go.

The door handle is turning. *Stop!*

The door is opening.

Leave me alone.

And then suddenly I don't care.

I don't care about anything. Everything's okay.

That's the gas talking, Sloan. You're not okay!

I'll be fine.

The face looking down at me is wearing a ninja mask and night-vision goggles.

And booties on his shoes.

Booties.

"You're not supposed to be here," I mumble.

He squats down and flips up his goggles. A gloved hand gently grabs the back of my head.

"Just take a breath. You'll be okay. I'm a cop. I'm here to help." I see the badge on what looks like some kind of uniform.

"Everything's okay. You're going to be fine."

I relax. I prepare my lungs to take a breath.

A tiny voice . . . Jackie's? . . . calls to me. She's telling me something. *What is it, baby? I'll be home soon.*

I see her face. I want to let her know it's okay. I'm safe now. The police are here. I fall back, my head too heavy to support any longer. He gently cradles it. Something my dad told me when I worked on dive mixes comes to mind.

Stop breathing.

Stop moving for a moment. Think about the problem.

If you have a spare tank, get to that.

If you don't . . . plan out your next action and don't think. Reach for the valve. Let your muscle memory guide you. Just let your body solve the problem—not the panicked part, but the part that you've practiced with a thousand times. Let the muscles do the work.

Why, Dad? I'm safe now. The police are here.

The man's other hand brushes away my hair. The glove then slides down to my neck. "Just breathe," he tells me. "Breathe deep."

His voice is muffled. That's odd . . . Is there a tube under his mask?

I hear a metallic sound as a cylinder by his side bumps the door frame.

To me, the clank of an air tank is like the sound of a dog bowl hitting the floor. My hand reaches up. I touch his face and feel something hard. A breathing mask.

"Just relax," he says, grabbing my wrist and pulling it away.

My other hand finds the air hose. It jerks it away from his body. The hissing sound startles him. He jumps back and hits the wall, and his oxygen cylinder clatters to the ground.

I grab the twisting tube, shove the end to my lips, and breathe deep. It's pure oxygen.

He's moving back at me.

I breathe again.

My brain is on fire. It's a good fire.

I suck another deep breath, roll to my feet, and shove him back into the wall.

I don't have all my energy yet, but between the pure oxygen and the adrenaline, I might have enough.

Seizing his loose tank, I swing it up and strike him in the jaw. He goes sideways, lands on the floor, and springs back to his feet.

He has a knife.

"Fucking bitch," he growls as he lunges and misses.

As I slip past him out of the bedroom, I throw the tank at his head and make for the living room couch. I reach it, roll over the top, and land next to the coffee table.

The couch is pulled away as he slides it aside to get at me. I sit there, cowering, as he readies to stab me.

I'm fading again because I haven't taken a breath since I let go of his hose. As he moves forward with his knife in front of him, he stumbles. Clearly, he's not used to breathing the sleeping gas. Granted, there's less of it in the air now after dispersing, but it's still there. He lurches forward.

I fire my gun . . . the one from under the couch cushion.

He spins to the side, his shoulder spraying blood.

I was aiming for his head, but I'm still groggy.

He throws the knife at me and rushes past me, almost over me, heading for the back of the house.

I'm forced to raise my arms to stop the blade from hitting my face. Instead it slices into my arm. Deep.

I fire a wild shot after him and shatter the sliding glass door, which he runs through. As I follow, the night air rushes in, reviving me. I fire into the dark at his retreating figure.

"Sloan?" Hughes calls out as he emerges from the panic room, hauling George over his shoulder in a fireman's carry.

"Get him outside!" I yell back as I chase after Dunn, who turns into the space between my house and Hughes's and runs for the street. I keep pace but feel weak, blood pouring down my arm now. I would take a shot, but I'm afraid at this distance it would go wild and hit someone in their home.

At the street, he turns again and runs for a pickup truck. He gets inside, and the lights go on. The keys were probably already in the ignition.

The truck's moving, straight at me.

I drop to my knee, aim, and fire. First I hit the engine block; then I hit the front tires.

The second tire blows out as I jump to the side. The truck hurtles past me, out of control on its suddenly flat tire, and crashes into an electrical utility box.

There's a popping sound and a blue flash. All the lights in the neighborhood blink out.

I fire at a shadow in the flash of light, then collapse in a pool of my own blood.

Footsteps come from behind. I don't shoot.

It's Hughes, looking down at me.

The darkness finally takes me under.

CHAPTER FIFTY-FIVE
HIDEAWAY

The paramedics want to take me to the hospital, but I insist they use the skin stapler here instead. I'm not going anywhere until the killer's found.

Stephen Dunn is on the run. His truck is smashed and fried, and the blood splatter from the shoulder wound tells us that he fled on foot. But the blood trail ends almost immediately, so we can't tell which direction he went.

George is talking to the Broward sheriff's detectives about the search while Hughes keeps an eye on me.

Overhead, a helicopter sends its powerful searchlights into backyards while K-9 units prowl the neighborhood, seeking his scent.

It's still dark. The only lights are the helicopter's beams and the blue-and-red wash of the police cars' lights. People step out from their homes, only to be told to go back inside by deputies on megaphones.

Is it better for them to be huddled inside in the dark? Or outdoors? Dunn could easily be in one of their homes.

"We really should stitch that up," says the woman treating my arm. "It's going to scar."

"Think I give a fuck?" I growl. "Sorry. I'm sorry."

Her brown eyes look back at me with kindness. "Not needed. Us tough bitches have to stick together." She tilts her head back toward the smoking truck. "I hope you shot his balls off."

I look to Hughes, who's shaking his head, red in the face. "Sloan . . . I'm so—"

"If you say the word *sorry*, I'm gonna punch you in the dick. Understand? You said we needed more people. You were right. George didn't want me to act as bait. He was right. Want to blame someone, blame me. But let's find this asshole first."

"Maybe you should sit down a little while longer," says the EMT.

I glare at her.

"Okay. I'll be here."

"Where's my gun?" I ask Hughes.

"Forensics has it."

"Already? Do they realize that we're in the middle of something?"

"Here." He hands me my sneakers, jeans, and socks. "Put these on first, then I'll give you my backup."

I throw the socks aside and slide the jeans over my shorts and put the shoes on. Hughes hands me the snub-nosed service revolver he keeps strapped to his ankle. "This okay?"

"Thanks." I check the gun, then tuck it into my waistband. "Let's talk to George."

He's in a huddle with a major as they look down at a map of the area. Two captains are also standing by, listening.

"You said you got him in the left shoulder?" asks Major Dane, a tall woman with dark hair pulled back in a ponytail.

"Yeah. I think I may have hit him coming out of the vehicle too. But he could've been wearing body armor."

"He has to be," she says. "We pulled black overalls from the canal down the street. He stripped them off to throw the dogs off his scent." She points to her sternum. "There was a bullet hole right here. Good shot."

"Should have aimed higher," I reply.

"Yeah, well, you're alive, they're alive," she says, nodding to George and Hughes. "It could have turned out worse."

"The night is young," I say.

"Sunrise is in thirty minutes," she fires back. "You should go home." She glances at my arm. "Or to the hospital."

"I'll stay until we get him."

"McPherson," says George. "Maybe—"

"Maybe we should all focus on catching this asshole."

"Okay . . ."

I raise a hand. "If you say *sorry* about anything, I'll punch you in the dick too."

"Your unit is, um, interesting," says Major Dane. She returns her attention to the map. "We've gone house to house to every place on this block. The dogs lost the scent up here." She puts a finger on the map to show me. "We're extending the search area out to here and blocking all traffic. People will complain because they'll be heading to work, but we plan to search their cars and let them through one by one."

I check my watch. He bailed out of his vehicle forty minutes ago. The critical time to catch him has already passed. If he grabbed someone and had them drive, he could be anywhere now.

Sensing what I'm thinking, she adds, "We're already handing out the photo you guys gave us. That plus the security camera footage. It'll be all over the morning news. We'll get him."

Probably, but I don't want him killing anyone between now and then. Unfortunately, that happens a lot on manhunts. When cornered, murderers tend not to care who they hurt. If they ever did.

"Okay," I say and start walking down the street.

"Where is she going?" asks Major Dane.

Hughes catches up with me. "What's the plan?"

"Checking the houses again."

"They have it covered."

I death stare him. "Does it feel like anybody has anything fucking covered right now?"

"Okay. We'll check 'em again."

I go up to the house closest to where Dunn ditched the overalls and knock. A man comes to the door, rocking a baby in his arms.

"Is it safe yet?" he asks.

"Not yet. Mind if we have a look around while you step outside?" I ask.

"Sure. Want me to get my wife up?"

"No, that's okay." I stick my head inside and glance around. "We're good. Thank you."

"That was helpful," says Hughes.

"Did he seem distressed or afraid?"

He shakes his head.

"It'll have to do. We don't have time to search every house."

I knock on the next door. An older woman in a bathrobe answers. Her husband is standing next to her. She has her phone in her hand.

"What's going on? Did they catch him? Are they going to turn the lights on?"

"Not yet. Are you okay?" I ask.

"Yes. When can we let our dog out?"

"Just wait. And let the police know if you see anything."

I knock on six more doors, and the interactions are the same. I'm not sure what I'm looking for, but no one seems afraid to leave their house in my presence or to let me have a look inside.

Hughes and I reach the intersection at the end of the block. The helicopter is in the distance, and the K-9 units have moved farther out by now. I stare down the street in both directions, deciding which way to go.

"He could have stolen a car," says Hughes. "Or kidnapped someone."

"I know. But nobody's reported anything." I stop and think. "They found the overalls in the water?"

"Marine Patrol's already on the water, looking."

"Okay." *Which way?* I clutch my hand to my left shoulder. "This way," I say, turning to my right.

"Why's that?"

"Animals move away from the site of an injury. I shot him back there. When he reached here, going left or straight would have felt more vulnerable."

"Is that a real thing?" asks Hughes, hurrying to keep up with me.

We walk up the steps to a house. An older man answers the door, holding a cup of coffee. "Is it safe to come out?" he asks.

"Not yet. Is everything okay here?"

"Yes. My wife is sleeping. We're fine."

"Mind if we look around?"

"Sure." He opens the door wide.

"That's okay," I reply. "We might come back in a couple minutes for a witness statement."

"All right," he says and shuts the door.

Hughes and I walk to the next house. I reach my hand to the door and pretend to knock. "Did he seem odd?" I ask.

"A little."

"Notice the coffee cup?"

"Yeah?"

"The power's been off for an hour. He's not drinking a fresh cup. Also, no barking from the dog."

"What dog? Maybe they don't have a dog."

"The hair on his pants says otherwise. Stay here. Keep an eye on the front. I'm going around."

"Sloan," he says under his breath.

But it's too late. I go all the way around this house, then backtrack through the yard and over to a small fence that borders the old man's backyard. The moment I lean over the fence, I can tell something's wrong. The whole backyard smells like dog. There's even a big dog door on the back door.

I carefully climb over the fence, hoping that Steve's attention is on the front windows. I should tell Hughes to call for backup, but I'm worried about the man and his wife. The only thing worse than a hostage situation is one where the suspect knows the cops are outside. Right now, I have the edge.

I think.

I step through the grass, placing my feet on the garden stones, trying to keep from making a sound. When I get to the patio, I have to step over palm fronds to avoid crunching the dry leaves.

A phone rings from in front of the next house, and I cringe. It's Hughes's ringtone. *Damn it.* Why did he leave it on?

Wait . . . he didn't. He probably turned it on and texted someone to call him back. He wants Dunn's attention on him out in front . . .

Clever boy.

I keep my body low and squat down by the dog door. Using a finger, I slowly push it open to peek inside.

My heart sinks when I see a large mutt in the middle of the floor. He's bleeding out onto the tile. When I look back on the patio behind me, I see splashes of blood. Dunn stabbed him here. Although some of the blood might be his too.

I try the door handle. It's locked.

Okay, next step. I stick my head through the dog door. I almost jerk back when I see a woman sitting in a wheelchair near the sink. Her eyes are wide with fear, and she's staring at me.

Please don't scream.

She remains silent, but I can see tears running down her face. A withered hand points elsewhere in the house, then makes the shape of a gun.

Dunn has a firearm.

I hear footsteps coming from the living room and the sound of blinds being pushed apart.

He's watching the street.

I start squeezing myself through the dog door, using my hands to keep my weight off the floor. My palms make a slapping sound as I move them, sounding like an explosion in the quiet house.

Footsteps . . .

I watch the woman's eyes to know when Dunn is near. I'm almost through the dog door.

Clack.

The pistol in my waistband catches on the top of the door.

Louder footsteps move in our direction. The woman's eyes grow wider, and she leans back in her chair. Dunn enters. He stares at her, then catches sight of me.

I drop flat on my belly and pull my gun from my waist. Before he can raise his own, I have the barrel pointed at his head.

His arms are at his sides and we're both frozen, waiting for what happens next.

I could shoot him. End him right now. But that's not the job I signed up for. Although if he moves even an inch . . .

He lets his gun fall to the floor and raises his hands in the air.

"Turn around and face the wall. Put your hands behind your head."

He complies.

Carefully, I hop to my feet, move to his back, and push Hughes's pistol against the back of his skull.

"Tell my partner to come in here," I yell to the old man in the front room.

He opens the door and calls into the street.

Dunn doesn't move.

The only noise in the kitchen is the sound of crying.

His.

EPILOGUE

Jackie casts her line with a kind of grace that makes a mom think her daughter could do anything. The lure drops into the water by the edge of the mangroves, and little ripples of moonlight reflect back at us. The only sound is the waves lapping against the shore of the canal and a distant radio on another boat broadcasting a baseball game.

I take a sip of my Corona and cast my own line, not caring if the snook are biting tonight. This is mother-daughter time. No texting. No Netflix.

Her eyes fixed on her line but attention on me, Jackie finally asks me the question I know she's been waiting to ask ever since I saw her reading an article about serial killer Stephen Dunn and how I apprehended him.

"Why did he kill those people?"

It's a child's question without a grown-up's answer. "Some people just don't think like you and me."

"But the things they found in his house."

Oh jeez, I didn't realize Jackie had read that deeply. She's smart enough not to talk to weirdos online, at least not knowingly, but I have no way of knowing where her Google searches might lead her. I tell myself it's not that different from my childhood trips to the downtown library, where a journey up the atrium staircase could take me a thousand miles away or a thousand years into the past—or deep inside some twisted mind.

"He was a weirdo, honey. Something didn't work right in his head." I'm about to explain to her that people like Dunn are exceedingly rare, but she cuts me off.

"Yeah, but they say he shared those things with other people. Other people knew about what he did," she replies. "My teacher could be someone like that."

"Which teacher?" I ask.

"I don't know. I'm just saying . . ." She lowers her rod and turns to me. "You just can't trust people. You never know."

What do I tell my daughter, who already has older boys looking at her in ways that make me uncomfortable? How can I tell her she's safe when I've put her in harm's way in the past?

How do I tell her that Dunn's a rarity when we've had hundreds of men with the potential to commit crimes like his sitting in our inter-rogation rooms? Do I tell her about the trailer park filled with sex offenders? Do I tell her that not all the murder photos we found were attributable to Dunn?

Do I tell her about the remains we just found in the Everglades of a girl only a year older than she is?

"There are a lot of bad people out there." It's all I can say. Then I ask, "Does it bother you that I'm a cop?"

She shakes her head adamantly. "No. According to Grandma, you're safer the more time you spend out of the water."

I have to laugh at that. "What about you? Do you feel safe?"

"Dad's been teaching me how to use a gun."

My face starts to burn, and I have to stop myself from pulling out my phone and calling Run to scream at him. This should have been a two-parent conversation . . . and maybe it would have been if I'd been home more often.

Perhaps it was the right choice, but Run will hear from me about this. I'd say she's too young, but she's smarter than her older cousins. Still, gun lessons for a twelve-year-old aren't the right way to teach her how to stay safe—especially when the most dangerous aspect of her life is her connection to me.

"I'd like to learn from you," she says.

"The goal is to never have to use a gun," I say firmly.

"It'd still be useful."

"For what?" I'm afraid to ask.

"I think I know what I want to do when I grow up."

"What's that?" *Please don't say cop. Please don't say cop.*

"I'm not sure exactly. Maybe a doctor of some kind. Maybe a scientist. But I want to figure out a way to keep people like him from ever happening."

"Like a psychologist?"

"Maybe, but a good one. Is it wrong for me to think that when Dunn was my age, if he had someone to talk to, he would have turned out differently?"

I think whatever made Dunn started earlier than that, but I don't want to crush her hopes. Maybe she's right, after all. Maybe some monsters can be guided into being lesser monsters . . .

"It's not wrong at all."

I think back to the moment when I had my gun drawn on Stephen Dunn, possibly one of America's worst serial killers in decades, and he cried.

Later, when he confessed, he told them that he wasn't crying because he got caught.

He was crying because it took us so long.

I don't know if he was simply trying to manipulate us, but I do believe that even monsters hate monsters.

It takes an innocent like my daughter to think that there could have been some help for him if only someone had paid attention early on.

Maybe Jackie's right. Maybe Run is. Either way, I'm glad she's learning how to defend herself.

ABOUT THE AUTHOR

Andrew Mayne is the *Wall Street Journal* bestselling author of *The Naturalist, Looking Glass, Murder Theory, Dark Pattern,* and *Angel Killer,* as well as an Edgar Award nominee for *Black Fall* in his Jessica Blackwood series. *Black Coral* is the second book in his Underwater Investigation Unit series. The star of Discovery Channel's Shark Week special *Andrew Mayne: Ghost Diver* and A&E's *Don't Trust Andrew Mayne,* he is also a magician who started his first world tour as an illusionist when he was a teenager and went on to work behind the scenes for Penn & Teller, David Blaine, and David Copperfield. Ranked as the fifth bestselling independent author of the year by Amazon UK, Andrew currently hosts the *Weird Things* podcast. For more on him and his work, visit www.AndrewMayne.com.